A Love Story for Witches

A Novel By

Jaysen Headley

A Love Story for Witches

A Novel By Jaysen Headley

Cover Art by L.W. Marks

Senior Editor: Carl Ka-Ho Li

Assistant Editor: Amy Chang, Carina Jollie

ISBN 978-0-9908283-0-3

ASIN B00O1BDU6K

This book is printed in the United States of America

For Carl,

Who supported me at my best, my worst and everywhere in between

You made me believe.

"Let it be known that I have seen love and it is a vile, contemptuous thing. It has left me forsaken and powerless. Beware, my sisters, for she whomsoever loves, will surely perish."

Joan D'Arc, 1431

Prologue

You might call this a bad day, Adam thought, as he ran down the tracks of the L subway line in nothing but a white silk blanket. Above, the steady beat of cars racing home towards the Brooklyn Bridge thrummed, sending a tinny echo through the tunnels surrounding him.

Adam Smith had never seen himself as a risk taker or a rule breaker. Or, for example, the type of guy who would run down subway tracks, let alone be on them in the first place. He followed the script of life. He woke up at 7 AM every morning and went to bed promptly at 11 PM. He was always ten minutes early. He actually separated his whites from his colors, and his socks from his underwear, and his weekday clothes from his weekend clothes. He was rigorous in his cleanliness, sweeping after the smallest dust bunny, and wiping at a spot on the counter until it was rendered lifeless and non-existent.

This was all well and good until *she* showed up.

1

Adam screamed at the top of his lungs, hoping that someone might hear his fear and come to his rescue. Who? He had no idea. Who did you call in a moment like this? Did the Ghostbusters handle psychotic, blood-hungry witches on their weekend shifts?

Adam was an average 26-year-old. He was thin with fair, peach-colored skin, dotted only by a few freckles. He had brown hair that, luckily, fell in a good spot on his head and wore a pair of black rimmed glasses. He had an air about him that said, 'I tried, but not too hard.' He had a good smile but nothing that would make you look if you saw him on the street. In fact, chances are, you *have* seen him, and you didn't give him a second thought. That was just how run-of-the-mill he was.

He threw the blanket off himself, choosing the ease of running over propriety, leaving him running in only his tight white underwear. Of all the days to not wear the Calvin Klein's. *Maybe a bad week,* he contemplated. *A bad month?* If Adam really thought about it, he might conclude that it had been one bad night, followed by a string of bad choices, culminating in this one truly sucktastic day.

On the ground behind him, purple tendrils slithered towards him, like snakes. They darted along the ground, silently hunting their prey. They were jagged and fierce bands of color, with little arrows at their tips pointing towards him. They slithered with a mind of their own. Somewhere in the tunnels behind him, the low note of a guitar string echoed in 4/4 time. She was like a bat waiting to read the sound waves before making her next move.

And then there were lights.

In front of him, Adam could just make out headlights. Two beady little spots, signaling that the L train was, for once, of all days, on time to its stop at Bedford Avenue.

Adam whispered a curse under his breath, directed harshly at the L train. The train approached even more certainly, as if offended. Adam stopped in his tracks, looking in front of and then behind himself, contemplating which death was the lesser of two evils.

There was always the moment he could have walked, and she could have just been the girl who got away. Always the moment he could have avoided all of this. As the train barreled towards him and the jagged serpents of color raced up from behind him, he remembered every moment of it, every bad choice that had led him here.

She had said witches didn't get love stories and now, he realized, she was right.

Chapter One

One month Earlier

In the darkest Lower East Side alley of Manhattan, on the darkest night of April, Zelerot, or Zot as he was called, stood taking in the landscape of the world around him. Though since he was a small pug dog, all this amounted to was him panting heavily and scooting his irritated bottom along the ground neurotically. He had a pinched-up nose and rough tan hair and around his neck was a large metallic chain, which culminated in an ornate padlock, which dangled in front of his chest. The lock had no keyhole and seemed to be heavier than any pug or canine for that matter would be willing to tolerate. He sneezed and scratched behind his ear with his back foot, which of course made his rear end even more uncomfortable, resulting in yet another butt scoot.

Fog rolled through the alleyway, as if coming from nowhere and a cat ran along the roof above, hissing at Zot, and then continuing on its way. The sounds of sirens and car alarms came and went, and an older woman could be heard yelling at her children in Portuguese. Every so often, the loud clang of a dump-truck or cellar door closing would cut through the air, like the percussion in the symphony of night music.

From down the alleyway, a distinct *thud* caused Zot to perk up his ears. As a faithful watchdog, he was trained to listen for thuds, clunks, slurps, murmured incantations, whispered curses and cats. A backlog of instincts shot into effect.

"Yip!" His bark was loud enough that his tiny legs hopped off the ground. "Yip Yip Yip!" A small pair of wings suddenly sprouted from his head and on his last hop, he took off into the air, floating away half on purpose and half because he wasn't quite sure how to land once he'd gotten excited. "Yipyipyipyipyip!" He floated up into the sky like a balloon that has just been set loose by a small child on the street.

In the shadows behind him, she stood like a statue looming in the mist. Eva Grey was 25 years old but carried herself like one who had lived through too many lives to count. Eva's skin was a light brown, a trait of her parents: one Dominican, the other Mexican. Black hair hung in a ponytail behind her. A full necklace of little skulls and beads hung from her neck, standing out against her cream-colored hoodie. Her black skirt had maroon lines down its sides, giving it extra flair. To her side, she held a long birchwood staff. It twisted and curled in on itself all the way to one end where the wood grasped a large purple orb. Mist swirled slowly in the orb, so slowly in fact that you would have to watch it for some time to even realize it was moving; an exercise in patience. Her whole appearance summed up to one of a beautiful young woman who seemed capable of kicking your ass if given the chance. And that was exactly what she was going for.

At the other end of the alley, another girl appeared, shorter and less patient. Miyako had all the attitude and urgency of a nineteen-year-old. She didn't like to wait. She didn't like to lose. She didn't like anyone telling her what to do. She was Japanese, with a flat nose and round face. She had several ear piercings and a streak of purple in the tips of her black hair, which hung to the side of her face. She wore an oversized red sweater and a black pair of shorts. She walked down the alley, sure footed in her black sneakers. She carried a can of spray paint, the white nozzle removed to reveal the small metal tube that allowed the paint to be sprayed straight up from the tip. The word "BREW" was written on the can, slanted up along its curves. She shook it slowly, glaring down the alley at Eva.

Eva took her first step forward, the orb end of her staff dragging along the ground behind her. As she walked, sparks shot up from the ground, sending a harsh crackling sound reverberating along the alley walls. It played along with the sounds of the city's sirens, horns and garbage truck thumps.

Miyako aimed the can at the brick wall beside her, never taking her eyes off of Eva. It spewed paint forth onto the wall. The red of the paint resembled blood in its harsh clarity. As she pushed forward, the spray created a long red line on the wall, strands of paint dripping down the bricks.

Eva's staff shot up from the ground, circling her as a white rune appeared beneath her, shooting light into the alleyway. Around her, the ground began to rumble. Little bits of cement broke as three skeletal creatures pushed up from the ground. They were short in stature, coming up just to Eva's knees. They wore large sombreros and had intricate inked designs covering their faces like the most fanciful Day of the Dead decorations. Each of them wielded its own pair of silver revolvers. Their teeth chattered threateningly. The first of them lunged forward, pistol slinging as the guns shot off their rounds.

Miyako's hand pulled away from the wall with a jolt, and with it came the red paint. It erupted from the wall, curling through the air like a stream of liquid electricity. It cracked like a whip repelling the oncoming bullets.

Eva and Miyako had come into contact only a year ago when Miyako had first shown up in the city. Eva knew every witch in town and had fought with all of them at some point or another. Every witch had their life at stake at all times, but Miyako was different. She fought like she had something more to lose. Where other witches searched for new territory or went out exploring for spell-books or potion ingredients, Miyako stayed hidden and only played the defensive. She was careful, cautious even, yet if you found yourself in her neighborhood, she was ruthless. Her attacks were random and backed by pure instinct, like a mother bird protecting her nest. It was rumored that Miyako had killed her own mother in order to become stronger. Eva, who many witches considered the top dog in the city, barely came out with her head after their first encounter. Miyako didn't care for survivors, and so the rivalry had begun.

Eva's staff cut through the air, sending two skulls, engulfed in white flame, hurdling towards Miyako. *Shwoom!* Miyako flicked her wrist, sending the red stream of paint to wrap around the skulls and flung them into the nearby wall. Miyako's body twisted and with the force of a hellish wind, the streamer snapped across Eva's face, leaving a thin line of blood behind.

Eva turned back to Miyako, rage now in her eyes as she began to swing her staff around her. A white light burst from it, streaking through the air. Miyako lunged towards Eva, the red line circling her like a vortex. As the

8

two converged on each other, the sounds of their battle echoed through the streets of Manhattan, blending in with the hum of the city. Even if you were standing right outside that very alleyway, you would never imagine that a magical battle of the ages was taking place.

*　　　　*　　　　*

Beers poured, glasses clinked, and men and women laughed, guffawed and shouted as they went on about their week, or their job, or the new man in their life. The girl they couldn't get out of their head or the exam that was taxing on their nerves. It was Friday night in the Village, a happening neighborhood with a Bohemian flair on the Lower West Side, and the bar was alive with people glad for a much-needed break and a well-deserved drink.

"CHEERS!" Shot glasses slammed together at a long table. The suited band of brothers took the whiskey in stride, swallowing it like a sugar-coated pill. At the center of them, sat Adam, looking giddy in his drunken state. He seemed much less together than normal, his hair messy, his shirt untucked and wrinkled. He leaned on the table, his body absorbing the alcohol of his third drink. Or was it his fourth? It was starting to get hazy. Seated next to him was his best friend, Diego. Diego had perfectly placed black hair and a well-maintained goatee.

He was fit and had a natural athleticism that other men envied, and women adored. He slapped Adam on the back as they laughed loudly.

Adam and Diego had met in school. Diego had been a year ahead of Adam and had taken the younger man under his wing early on. At first, Diego had been attracted to Adam, and had sought a relationship with the boy fresh off the plane from a little town in Colorado. One drunken night, when it had become painfully clear that Adam was not gay, the two men had moved forward as friends, caring for each other in a way that neither of them had ever known before. They applauded victories together and cried when things went horribly wrong, usually over a bottle of wine. In truth, they had become like brothers over the years, barely ever seen apart from one another. Tonight was no different.

The shot glasses slammed down on the table, and anything that remained in the glasses spilled out haphazardly. Diego stood, flashing a grin that was sly and playful at the same time.

"To my best friend, Adam!" He raised a nearly-full beer glass to the sky proudly. "And his fancy new Masters of Fine Arts."

Adam had graduated from Pratt only hours earlier. He'd toiled away at school for years through his Bachelors in Colorado, and more recently, his Masters in New York. It had been painful and stressful, and at

10

times he didn't think he would make it. But now that it was all over, he was surprised that he did not feel relief. Instead, he felt a permanent knot under his lungs where he assumed that he might be getting an ulcer. An ulcer wouldn't be so bad. If he died he wouldn't have to find a job. Adam often thought of things in terms of his death and how that was the only way out of the impending stress that followed him day in and day out. *If I fell down these stairs, I wouldn't have to take that exam. If that taxi hit me, I wouldn't have to meet my adviser. If I jumped down onto the tracks at just the right moment, that train would hit me, and I wouldn't need to answer this phone call from my mother.* A therapist might comment that this behavior was neither productive nor healthy. Adam didn't care for therapy.

"Adam, give us your scholarly words of advice." Diego swirled his stein in Adam's direction.

Adam stood, teetering a bit as he worked to catch his balance. He moved his beer cautiously into the air. He became all too aware of the fact that he might spill it on someone in the immediate area. Knowing his luck, it would be the waitress, whom he found to be hot. She would come over at just the right moment and end up with his beer squarely spilled down her front. "To graduation," he exclaimed, less than sure that was a good thing. "Yesterday a Senior Honors thesis winner. Tomorrow: jobless!"

11

"HERE HERE!" The men at the table cheered, all drinking again.

Adam promptly lost his balance. He fell just as the waitress approached to ask who needed another round. She left with a full beer down her front and Diego laughing hysterically on the ground. Adam contemplated what horrible accident could have prevented this shameful moment.

* * *

One hour and a generous tip to the waitress later, Adam had sunk himself into a large couch in the lounge of the bar. Most of the men had either gone home or had found themselves someone at the bar to distract themselves with. Diego sat down next to Adam, handing him another beer.

"You really think that's the best idea?" Adam said, not refusing the drink.

"It's your night," replied Diego. "Get shit-faced or go home."

"My mother's right. You're a bad influence." Adam took a sip from the beer as Diego poured half a rum and coke down his throat with one swallow.

"So, what's next?" asked Diego, gingerly wiping a bit of liquid from the corner of his lip, with a cocktail napkin. "You got the degree and the rent control apartment. Time to get a fancy design job and meet a nice girl?" Diego chuckled at the thought. "I'm thinking a second home in the Hamptons? Two, maybe three kids? Possibly a dog? Don't get a cat though. Cats are crap. And not one of those small dogs either. My people can get away with it. You'd just look queer."

"Can we say that?" Adam's finger rotated anxiously around the lip of the bottle.

"I can, you can't."

"Double standard."

"World we live in."

They clinked their drinks together in a mock cheer.

Adam ran a hand through his hair. "Is it wrong that I'm less worried about the job part?"

"You'll meet someone." Diego gave Adam's shoulder a tight squeeze.

It was true that Adam had not had much luck with the ladies. He was bad at first impressions, and really didn't have a firm grasp on the second or third either. "I haven't been in a relationship since high school." He grimaced at the thought. "I wouldn't even know where to begin."

His high school girlfriend had been controlling and overbearing. She was exactly the kind of girl Adam needed then, and maybe still needed. The kind of girl who could make a decision for him. The kind of girl who could get him to let go a little bit. The kind of girl who set a fire in his locker when she thought he was seeing someone else. So, what if she was a little unstable? She loved him and put up with all his teenage emotional bullshit.

Now here he was, eight years later, with just as much bullshit and even less of an excuse. If he couldn't make it work back home with a wreck like her, what shot did he have with classy, world-traveled women like those he met here in the city? *If a meteor hits Earth tomorrow and we all die, I won't have to deal with this.*

Diego grinned again. Ever the rock. Ever the pillar of strength. Adam was one of those straight guys who was under the impression that it was easier for gay men, and that that was why Diego was so much luckier with love than he. Or at the very least, he got around. Even a little making out would have softened the coldness that Adam felt towards women, yet even that seemed out of his grasp.

"I even joined one of those online dating sites," said Adam, waving his cell phone through the air, as if it was the phone's fault that he was alone.

"You did not!" Diego was giddy at the thought.

"Heart Heart Hug," said Adam, "Dot com."

"I can't even deal with how pitiful that sounds."

"I want the classic love story." Adam pondered what this meant for a moment. "Take my parents. My dad was out squirrel hunting."

"Of course he was."

"Went to check his gun after a kill, boom, shot off his ear." Adam clapped to give the 'Boom' an added effect.

"And why wouldn't he?"

"Went to the hospital. My mom was his nurse. Poof, happily ever after." Adam looked off as if he was counting the stars.

"That's so magical, I might puke. Please, tell me *more* about squirrel hunting." Diego laughed to himself. "Can you do that upstate?"

"Probably have it on one of those 'More to New York than 'NY' ads.' Adam took another drink from the bottle. The state of New York had recently started advertising the scenic views and adventures one could find within the state borders as a means of boosting tourist activity to areas other than the city. Sadly, most of them seemed like mock versions of things people actually cared to do on a vacation.

"Still, online dating is a far cry from squirrel hunting with the safety off," chuckled Diego. "Any takers?"

Adam cyed his phone, biting his bottom lip. "Well..."

Diego's eyes brightened, slapping Adam across the shoulder. "Tell me EVERYTHING! What's her name? What's she look like? She have a hot brother?"

"I don't really know." Adam's trepidation was clear on his face.

"But you've met in person, right?"

Adam winced at the questions, taken aback. "Not yet."

"Adam's playing it safe, shocker of the century." Diego leaned forward, finishing his drink in a single swallow. "My advice? Stop waiting for perfect. Make a bad decision for once in your miserable little life."

The waitress appeared, another rum and coke in her hand. Adam sank into the couch, as if this would hide him from her. Rolling her eyes at him, she handed the drink to Diego, replacing his empty one. Diego made a weak attempt to refuse. "I didn't order another."

"It's from him." She motioned to a man across the lounge. He had blond hair and a tight shirt, Diego's type. The man raised his glass and smiled at Diego. Diego's face filled with excitement at the prospect.

"Or you could always give my team a shot," said Diego, turning back to Adam slightly. "We're always looking for new members."

Adam shook his head. "I'm not gay."

"Your loss." Diego stood up, taking a sip from his newly acquired drink and preparing to head into his newly acquired night. "Later." He took off towards the man, leaving Adam to contemplate it all. How easily Diego jumped headfirst into something without thinking about the consequences or weighing the costs and benefits. Only minutes had passed, and already Diego and the man were touching. Sure, Diego was a bit of a man whore. But even so, if he could do that, why couldn't Adam? Adam glared at his phone, willing it to make a decision. He gripped it so firmly that his knuckles turned white. With alcohol still coursing through his system, he requested another drink and swiped his finger across his phone screen, unlocking all the possibilities that came with drinking too much with a cell phone in hand.

*   *   *

The battle had ended abruptly. One second, Eva and Miyako were attacking each other in full force, throwing curse after hex and paint after skeleton warrior. The next, a cop car pulled up to the alley, and the two women ran in opposite directions. As Eva limped through another alleyway across town, nursing her wounds and feeling the sore spots where the bruises would surely be the next morning, she could only hope that Miyako had taken a worse beating. Zelerot, or Zot as she affectionately called him, floated listlessly behind her, panting and snorting as pugs do, the little lock around his neck, jangling like a small wind chime.

From her pocket, a low buzzing sound rumbled. *Zzt*

zzt. She stopped, reaching for the cell, cringing from the pain in her arm. The screen of the phone lit up.

NEW MESSAGE FROM ADAM ON
"*HEARTHEARTHUG.COM*"

Eva selected the message and read to herself.

ADAM: Hey. How r u?

Eva began typing, disregarding the alley around her. Adam had messaged her months ago, mentioning her love of horror movies in his message. It was always nice when a guy had something to say other than "Hi" or "Cute." The message that could be sent to any girl got old fast. They had hit it off quickly, discussing books, movies and the like. Eva was always careful to avoid anything that might lead to her family or any of her witch-related secrets. She took comfort in the fact that the men she chatted with on Heart Heart Hug could never get too close, allowing her to be herself without the dreaded part of possibly falling in love. She usually would talk with a guy online for a while to pass the time, and, inevitably find something out that would give her a reason to stop talking to them and move on to the next. It was mostly a way for her to escape the overbearing loneliness of being a witch. She never intended to actually meet one of these losers.

Adam was different. He'd lasted longer than most and had been unintentionally charming, without trying. She hated when a guy tried too hard. She had yet to uncover a secret fetish, or weird hobby of his that raised an eyebrow. In fact, she was beginning to think that Adam was a genuinely good guy amongst the sea of hyper-sexualized basement dwellers. It was because of this that Adam's contact info had stayed in her phone for far longer than any other. She had shared more with him than anyone else she could remember, and at times had strayed dangerously close to the rocky beaches of truth. He was like a lighthouse in her life, always tempting her to the deadly shore with his kind words and self-inflicted jokes. What was worse was that texting with him made her smile, even happy at times. She knew it had to stop, but she just hadn't found the willpower to do it yet. *Maybe tomorrow* she thought as she sent a response.

EVA: Fine. U?
ADAM: Got my MFA today. Yay!

MFA? Of course he did. Adam was the whole package. He was smart and creative and...but she stopped herself. *Stop imagining things,* she scolded herself. *Don't create something out of nothing.*

EVA: Grats!

ADAM: What r u doing right now?

EVA: Nothing. U?

ADAM: Let's meet.

Zot looked up from a long butt scoot as Eva gasped, stifling her voice with her hand.

*   *   *

It was fortunate, Adam thought, that he had found his way to a stool with the long bar counter set out in front of him. If not, what would he have slammed his head repeatedly onto as the "Message sent" alert sounded on his phone?

"Stupid. Stupid. Stupid. Stupid. Stupid." Again and again he pounded his forehead on the lacquered bar top. Other customers eyed him uneasily, the way you look at someone when it's obvious that they've had too much to drink.

DING! The bell on his phone rang. He looked up in shock at the message displayed on the screen.

EVA: Where??

Chapter Two

If you have never been to the Financial District in lower Manhattan, there are a few things you should know. The first is that it is deceptively quiet at night. While other parts of the city live up to the old 'City that never Sleeps' adage, the Financial District seems to close with the stock market, becoming a quiet place to walk with a date on the boardwalk, or take a moonlit ferry ride along the Hudson River. The other thing you need to know is that although it is the wealthiest part of the city, it also houses some of the darkest back alleys and side streets. Clinging to the wall as she traversed one of these, was a bloodied and bruised Miyako.

Her hood was up, covering the large gash in her forehead. Crimson blood had begun to soak through the arms of her hoodie, revealing itself to the outside world. In the alleyway, there was a large gray pickup truck. It was old and battered, abandoned by its owner, and parked precariously close to the wall. Miyako approached it, reaching into her pocket to pull out her can of spray paint.

She leaned on the truck, grabbing at her ribs in pain. A scuffed leather briefcase with little gold clasps on the side, lay under the front of the truck. She pulled it out from its hiding place with her foot, and then kicked it open. Inside were several large folded up layers of white paper with black markings on them. With a wave of her hand, one of the papers flew into the air, unfolding mystically and then slapping itself hard against the brick wall.

Unfolded, the paper was the cut out of a creature drawn with dark black ink against a white canvas. It stood taller than Miyako and had a large, bulbous head. In the center of its round face was one large, Cyclopsian eye. Its hands were bulky with black lines running down them, culminating in two thick fingers and a thumb. Its feet and lower body were small in comparison to its torso. It was a creature built more for brute strength than mobility.

Miyako pointed the metal stem of her spray can at the center of the creature and with a slight press of her forefinger, sprayed a spot of red on its chest. The creature sprung out from the wall, blinking its large eye lazily as it breathed in life for the first time. It seemed bored with the idea.

"Grr." It responded as Miyako tilted her head towards the pickup truck. Lumbering like a faineant giant, it plodded up to the car and placed its hulking hands on the hood. It pushed. The car creaked, clearly not wanting to be moved from its post. With just a few big steps, the creature had displaced the truck, revealing a fabric-like tear in the brick wall. Beyond it was a pitch-black cave.

Miyako entered the cave, snapping her fingers as she entered. The creature watched her go and then walked to the wall, pulling the tear from the wall. In his hands, it was simply a crudely cut-out sheet of black paper. It grunted once more before shredding itself down its center and falling to the ground, lifeless once more.

✻   Ж   ✵

A floating origami crane, alight with a soft blue flame, was the only light in the darkness of the windowless room. It was by this light that Jasmine folded another of its kin at a crude wooden work desk. Jasmine was only slightly older than Miyako in years, but she was an old soul, calm, collected and wise. She was larger than most girls her height and had dark ebony skin. Her hair, naturally black, had been almost entirely dyed a bright crimson red.

Cough! Cough! She covered her mouth and caught her breath. She then went back to folding, meticulously tracing her forefinger once, twice, three times over the creases so as to make each crane an identical replica of the one that came before. She finished it by folding out its wings and finally its beak, giving it a face; an identity. And then, as if it suddenly became worthless, she threw it behind her, like a piece of garbage to be collected later.

"Eight hundred ninety-six," she murmured under her breath. The crane landed behind her, joining a collection of other discarded cranes, which had formed a little paper graveyard in a circle around her chair.

Thud. The slightest sound caught her ear. Jasmine stood instantly, and all the previously dead cranes were resurrected into a fiery army around her. Her chair fell to the ground behind her, its wood resounding on the cold stone floor.

Standing in the shadows, Miyako waved a hand nonchalantly at Jasmine. "It's just me."

The cranes fell peacefully back to the floor as Jasmine covered her mouth once again to let out a deafening cough, the phlegm in her throat gurgling with each heave. Her head felt light and her vision blurred as she took a step back.

"Sit down," said Miyako, looking on with worry. "You know you can't push yourself like that." Miyako righted the chair and motioned Jasmine back to it.

"I'm fine." Jasmine feigned health while still grasping at her chest, hoping that it would help it to allow air in once again.

Miyako took a less than fresh cloth from the corner of the room, and dabbed it around Jasmine's mouth, inspecting her face for further signs of the disease creeping through her lungs.

Jasmine's vision reasserted itself and with it came the full view of Miyako. She was bleeding, more than usual, after a night out. Her eyes were tired, and her face bruised. She was limping. "You're hurt."

"I'm fine," Miyako looked up at Jasmine, both playful and yet stern.

"Who did this?" Jasmine traced the gash across Miyako's face.

"Who do you think?"

The two of them exchanged an understanding look.

"Damn, she got you good tonight," said Jasmine, now examining a cut on Miyako's forehead.

"That's why I came back first."

"First?" Jasmine pulled back.

"I can take her, she's weak." Miyako grabbed at her shoulder. "Can't you just help me for once without second guessing every little thing?"

"Maybe you need to call it a night. You look—"

"No!" Miyako yelled, frustrated. "This has gone on too long as it is. She's getting closer every night. If she finds this place. If she finds you..."

"Miyako." Jasmine petted her arm lightly.

"This ends tonight, Jazz." They stared into one another's eyes for a long moment.

"Sit down," Jasmine stood, making room for her and grabbing one of the cranes from the floor as she went. She caressed it in her hands, invoking a soft golden glow from the paper. Miyako slowly removed her sweater, wincing at the pain as she did. Every muscle tensed. Places where the blood had coagulated and become one with the sweater tore anew, causing the pain to double.

"Gah!" Miyako finally dropped the bloodied sweater to the ground, revealing her tanned skin which was scratched and torn all along her back.

Jasmine placed her hands, glowing crane and all, directly onto the largest cut on Miyako's back. Miyako gulped down the pain. "It'll sting," Jasmine cautioned, too late. "But it will seal the wounds."

"I can take it." Miyako held steady, only her shaking hands giving any indication of the real agony she was enduring. A gentle warmth caressed Miyako's shoulder. Jasmine was kissing her, not a part of the healing ritual. The thought of two witches co-habitating was bad enough to make the Sorceresses of old roll over in their fiery graves, let alone the feelings they shared for one another. They had been together so long now that it had just made sense to take a taboo friendship and add an even more egregious physical element to it. They had shared their first kiss together. They had giggled as children when they held each other's hands for the first time. They had explored one another intimately and knew each other's bodies better than they knew their own. It had all been for fun, but Miyako sensed that Jasmine felt differently. She felt there was something more for them. This could never be. That was the one rule, wasn't it? Witches don't get to love. It was forbidden.

Never love. Never die.

Jasmine continued to use the heated cranes on every wound, bump and scratch until finally she stopped, leaning in so that her forehead touched Miyako's. She whispered over Miyako's shoulder.

"Go get that bitch."

*   *   *

Eva half walked, half limped her way to Lafayette Street and then made her way across Prince, trying to avoid the peculiar looks of late-night Soho wanderers. She had sent Zot flying home and had concealed her staff with a wave of her hand. Now she hastily applied concealer to the bruises on her face. In her excitement and anxiety, she had failed to notice her deeper wounds, which strangely seemed to be feeling better already. Her heart was racing a million miles a minute. She had talked with guys online, chatted, flirted even, but meeting was something she had avoided at all cost. Yet somehow, when Adam had asked her, she had said yes without a moment's hesitation. Maybe she was losing her mind or maybe she was just bored, craving something dangerous and new.

Her feet guiding her by memory, she soon found herself in front of their designated meeting spot, the Soho Room, a quaint little bar with a low-key vibe. She took a deep breath and adjusted her skirt, barely remembering to tuck her skull necklace under her sweater, before pushing open the glass paneled door.

She walked slowly past the bar, examining the faces of the forlorn drinkers, waiting for one of them to remind her of the dorky grin and black-rimmed glasses that she knew Adam for from his profile photo. Past the bar was a larger lounge, with seats and tables. There, sitting at one of them, fidgeting with his cell phone like it was a stress ball, was Adam. She eyed him for a moment. He was actually better looking in person, something she did not expect. What came across as naive and goofy in his picture, here seemed nerdy and neurotic. Was that something she was into? She pondered this only for as long as it took for Adam to look up. With a small start, he raised his hand to her. He stood, only slightly, before seeming a bit dizzy and then sitting back down.

"Eva?" Was she imagining things, or had she just seen his eyes cross slightly as he said her name?

"Adam."

"That's me." They smiled briefly at each other before shaking hands.

"Sorry it took me so long to get here," said Eva. "Trains were a mess." In the city, it was customary to use the trains as an excuse for any lateness where the actual story was either too long or too embarrassing. For Eva, both cases were true.

"It's fine." Adam motioned her to sit.

As she did, she couldn't help but smile. Tonight, Eva Grey was on her very first date.

*   *   *

Adam did not feel well. *Could she tell?* He wondered. The alcohol in his system had remained at a manageable level for most of the evening. But the anxiety of meeting Eva Grey, coupled with the extra shots he'd taken to work up the nerve to ask her out, had converged in his bloodstream. His pulse was increasing at an unnatural pace. The world around him was spinning, and he clutched at the table from underneath just to keep from falling over.

Eva was so pretty, he thought. He wanted to pet her hair. That might have been the alcohol talking. *Focus.* He just needed to pay attention to the conversation at hand. They were talking about her dog. A pug, right? He knew that from her profile. Eva's profile had been annoyingly nondescript. It had made him think she was hiding something and for some reason, this intrigued him. How many years had she had the dog? She'd just said, hadn't she? Her lips were so shiny, begging to be kissed. *Control yourself*, he thought, shaking off the feeling. He winked. Or did he blink? Maybe his eyes didn't close at all. *Get a hold of yourself, Adam. Ask her something. Ask her about her family.*

"So, what about yer mom?" he managed to get out. "She as hot as you?" Wait, that wasn't what he meant. "Er...pretty as you?"

Eva pulled back, a bit uneasy. "Excuse me?"

"What I mean is...um..." *Water.* He needed water. He needed to get something into his system that was not rum or beer or gin or whiskey.

"Adam," she placed a hand on his and winced as if feeling his pain. "I hate to ask, but are you drunk right now?"

Uh oh. "Am I? NO!" He waved a hand defiantly through the air. "You are!"

"Adam..."

He broke down, massaging his temple with his

forefinger. "Okay Eva, I'm gonna level with you. Did I have one drink before I came here? Sure. Five? Six? It's entirely pobbible." *That wasn't right.* "Plassible." *Nope.* "Poss-ee-ble." *Close enough.*

Eva scooted back in her chair. "Hey, it's Saturday night. I get it. But if we're gonna do this, maybe another night would be better." She began to stand up.

Adam lost all control. It couldn't end like this. Not when he had finally gotten the nerve to ask her here in the first place. With more force than he intended, he reached out to her. He slammed into the table, spilling the glass of water in front of him. As if in slow motion, he watched the water shoot through the air and land squarely across Eva's front. A look of pure shock spread across her face.

"Oh my God," Adam managed to blurt out. It was amazing just how sobering the look of anger on Eva's face was.

"Unbelievable."

"No, wait, I can..."

"I shouldn't have come here. I knew that, and I came anyway." Eva shook her head. "This is just the universe's way of punishing me." She started for the door, Adam stumbling out of his chair after her.

"Eva, come on, don't just—" Adam toppled into a nearby wall before he could finish.

"I have nothing left to say." Eva's lips tensed.

31

"Goodbye, Adam."

*   *   *

Eva was halfway down the block when she heard him call out for her. Adam had apparently collected himself enough to make it out the front door. She hesitated, not wanting to turn around. It would be so easy to keep going. He'd never catch up. She could round that corner up ahead, hop on her broom and be out of here before he knew what hit him. She'd erase his number from her phone, delete that stupid profile, and get on with her life. Wasn't she a bit old to be teasing boys on a dating site? Boys she could never even be with.

"Eva, just stop and hear me out for one minute!" Adam's slurring had stopped. Maybe he'd thrown up on his way out of the bar and gotten some of his sense back. Everything in her pleaded to run away. Instead, she turned to face Adam who, using a nearby wall for support, was edging towards her. "Oh," he blurted out, surprised. "I didn't expect you to actually—"

"You have one minute," Eva crossed her arms, giving him the coldest gaze she could muster. Even in his inebriated state, she still found him cute. *Stop those thoughts, Eva. Stop them now.*

"I'm..." His left eye twitched. "Sorry?"

"Seriously?" Her patience was drawing to an end.

32

She shifted her weight, ready to make her exit.

"Wait!" Adam pushed off from the wall. He struggled to focus on staying upright and not slurring his words. "Look at you." His voice was no longer pleading or drunk. It was weak, vulnerable even. "Now look at me. Really take a good long look at me." He shook his head. "You are SO out of my league, it's not even funny." He gulped down the shakiness in his voice. "It's sad." Adam moved towards her as Eva felt her shoulders softening, the glare on her face evaporating. "I don't do this, Eva. I go to bed before midnight. I never get drunk on Saturday night. I rarely even leave my house. I ACTUALLY stay home and read. How sad is that? And I certainly don't text girls in the middle of the night." He had been progressively getting closer to her and now they stood so close that they could stare into each other's eyes. "So yes, I drank a little...er...a lot. But thank God I did, because if I hadn't, I NEVER would have met you because I NEVER would have had the guts to ask you out in the first place."

For a long moment, they just stared at each other. A soft wind blew through the street. Several cabs passed by, dropping off fur-coated ladies and businessmen just turning in for the night. In the distance, a siren chirped a few high notes and then continued on.

"I've seen your profile." Eva broke the silence. "You being a stay at home guy who follows every rule in the

33

book is not news to me."

Adam let out a sigh of relief.

"Why don't we just start over," she said.

"I'd like that." He smiled at her. "So, what now?"

"Now?" Eva chuckled, "I think it's time we break some rules."

*   *   *

Shhhhh. The spray can emitted a low hiss as it filled a small bird shaped stencil with its crimson red ink. Miyako had been working quickly yet meticulously as she covered a wall from one end to the other with little birds. She had tagged the entire wall now, making it a collage of blood-red beaks and feathers. She pulled away, examining her work. She twisted her neck, allowing several joints to pop into place.

Her eyes opened wide as she swung her arm up. The birds ripped themselves from their brick birthplace so that they were suspended in air still dripping with fresh paint. Their wings beating produced a low hum as they swooped into a wide circle around Miyako, like a flock of blood-soaked hummingbirds. She smirked, taking in the adoration of her small army. Her eyes narrowed, and her pupils tightened as she gave the command. "Find her."

The flock erupted into the night sky.

Chapter Three

Adam was only six years old when his mother wisely decided to enroll him in swimming lessons. According to her, every young boy should know how to swim. On his initial attempt in the pool, he did fine, paddling and keeping his head above water like a natural. That was at first. Suddenly he started to lose his breath and sink slowly underneath. There were screams all around. His head dropped beneath the surface and though he grasped for the air that was only inches above him, he still sank, further and further, until everything went black.

He awoke coughing for air with a crowd of people hovering around him. His mother was by his side in tears. It was at that precise moment that Adam realized he was deathly afraid of water.

When Eva suggested a bit of fun and offered to blindfold him to add to the suspense, this fear of water was the furthest thing from his mind. She led him, and he followed willingly, just happy that she was still around. He had been standing for some time now when he heard a loud horn sound from somewhere ahead. Startled, he now felt the need to see beyond the blackness covering his eyes, wanting to make out the horn's origin. It wasn't a car. Too loud to be any sort of truck. His mind slipped to his early days in the city, standing at the boardwalk, watching the boats trudge by and hearing their—

"Was that a boat?" Adam's heart stopped. It was all coming together. Her master plan, her evil scheme, her diabolical undoing of him. She HAD read his profile and under 'Biggest Fear' she had read: Water. She had chosen the number one rule in his book to break first. Never. EVER. Get on a boat.

"I don't know. Was it?" Eva giggled next to him.

Adam spun around, having no idea where he was or what was around him. "Eva, I can't get on a boat. Don't make me do this. I'm not happy right now."

"Wow, you are such a big baby," she said, grabbing his hand. "Come on, time to board."

"No, no, no, no!" He pleaded with her as she dragged him onto a shaky platform and then further, onto hard metal flooring. "Eva, please. I'm begging you." They continued forward. Her grip on his arm was disturbingly strong, or maybe he was just weak.

"Remember when you were going to leave and never come back? How about we try that again?"

"You are so manly right now," Eva said, sarcastically.

"The second I get home, I'm taking 'fear of water' off my profile page."

"Too late for that."

Adam grasped at everything. Anything near him was fair game. Slick metal walls and railings, the matted surface of what he assumed was a flotation device. The wood of something reminded him of a lifeboat which he was sure he wouldn't make it into if the boat sank. "I can't BREATHE!"

Somewhere below, the engine roared to life and the floor beneath him shook as the boat pulled out to sea. His feet stopped working as he imagined the land getting further away by the minute. Eva dragged him through the ships underbelly by his hand, refusing to give up the fight. "We're going to die," he said. "We're going to hit an iceberg or another boat or a terrorist and we're going to die." *If we drown, I won't have to find a job.* He shook the thought from his head.

"Stop whining." In her voice, he could hear the sick joy she was taking from this.

He heard the creak of a door, and then a cold wind broke over his face. They were outside. He was finding a whole new series of reasons to panic when the blindfold was unceremoniously ripped from his eyes.

There, across the water, was the New York cityscape, sprawled out in all its glory. Lights radiated, creating ghostly reflections across the water. You could see everything, from the Freedom Tower to the Empire State Building and beyond. Hundreds and thousands of homes and lives reduced to fireflies in the night sky.

"Wow..." His breath steadied, and the world seemed to stop around him. He had spent so much of his life avoiding water, that he had never thought to try actually *taking* a boat ride. Now that he was here, all the panic and anxiety from before were replaced with an overwhelming calm. The water, and its haunting depths, were far below, out of sight and mind. All he could see was the sparkling view ahead and it mesmerized him.

"Pretty amazing, right?" Eva leaned on the railings, the only barrier between them and the water below. Adam put a single hand on the bar, not even realizing he was doing it.

"I've never seen it like this," Adam said in awe. "From afar. Lit up like Christmas."

"I just can't believe you've never taken a river cruise," Eva said, still grinning a victorious smile. "I thought that was something out-of-towners did the first week they moved here, when they're still in tourist mode."

"I don't do a lot of cruising."

Eva turned around to lean back on the bars, so she could look at Adam. She smiled softly. "I'll take that 'thank you' anytime."

Adam chuckled, still a bit queasy. "Maybe when we get back on land. There's still a good chance I'll throw up on you."

Eva snorted with laughter. "How romantic."

A drop of red paint landed on the deck next to them, but they were too busy laughing to see it. High above the boat, a lone red bird hovered against the blackened sky. It lingered only for a moment, unseen, above Adam and Eva. Then, with a heavy thrust of its wings, it zoomed back towards the city.

*   *   *

Diego stopped, still inside the man beneath him, as a sweet scent rolled past his nose. It was so familiar that it took him completely out of the room to a time long past. He hadn't seen or heard from the owner of that scent for years and yet, he knew it had to be her.

"Something wrong?" Jon asked, turning his head on the pillow. Or was it Jake? Diego couldn't recall. It didn't really matter though. This would not become a regular thing. It never did. Diego pulled out, rolling off the bed and throwing the condom in the trash. He reached for his clothes, rummaging through the pile for his underwear. "What the hell?" Joe sat up, disgruntled.

"I've gotta go," Diego pulled on his jeans, leaving his belt undone. He'd buckle it on the way out.

"Go? We just got here. You were the one that wanted to come here, remember?" Jack stood, naked, his erection dwindling by the second.

"Sorry, Jeff," he mumbled, buttoning his shirt.

"Jeff?" Apparently, he'd guessed wrong.

Diego threw on his jacket in one fluid motion and headed for the door, leaving Jared yelling obscenities behind him.

He practically flew down the stairs and out of the seedy little apartment building. Jack, Jeff, Jon, whoever he was, had clearly not been reeling in the cash. He dusted off his jacket, walking down the street at a brisk pace, the night air grabbing at the skin on his face. He eyed each alley he walked by for a fire escape with the ladder low enough to reach. The first was too high and the second building didn't even have one. The third had a dumpster placed just perfectly so that he could climb up to it and then ascend the ladder and subsequent stairs. He glided up the shaky metal staircase in hushed footsteps, as if it were the most normal thing in the world.

When he finally reached the roof, he took a moment to breathe in deep, finding the scent once more. Her perfume wafted through the air. Honey and peony. So simple. So elegant. So *her*.

If you had blinked you might have missed the transformation, for where once stood Diego, now stood a large black dragon with a long neck and an even longer tail. Its wings were sharp and commanding, leathery and expansive. It had two curved horns on its head and another on its nose. In between these were a pair dazzling green eyes, which glowed softly. It flapped its wings once, powerfully, and with a gust of air beneath them, took off towards the stars.

*   *   *

Adam and Eva strolled along a peaceful street in the West Village, in no hurry to get anywhere.

"Favorite book?" asked Adam. They'd progressively gotten to know more about each other as the evening had waned. Sure, some of the questions had been asked at one time or another over text, but now it seemed more real; more relevant.

"Pride and Prejudice," replied Eva.

"What a sap."

"Oh, really? What's yours?" She slapped his arm playfully.

"Do comic books count?" Adam couldn't even remember the last time he'd read a real book.

"No."

"Graphic novels?

"Still no."

Eva stopped, turning to Adam and pushing her hair behind her ear with one finger. "This is me."

Adam looked up. They were standing in front of a small staircase, leading up to the entrance to a three-story brick building. The romantic in him couldn't help but notice the absolute New Yorkian vibe he got from this building and the two of them, slowly approaching the end of their date, getting carried away in conversation, before it ended all too suddenly. He liked the whole idea of it, like something out of a Meg Ryan movie.

"I'm really glad you messaged me," she said, and meant it. What started out as an anxiety filled evening had turned out enjoyable. For a moment, she even forgot about the dire nature of her situation and the fact that what had transpired tonight could never happen again.

"I'm glad you made me face my mortal fear," chuckled Adam, nervously.

"Really?"

"Of course. Gives me something to tweet about this week." They laughed. "But," started Adam, "given my drunkenness at the start of the evening, I'm going to be a gentleman and NOT kiss you."

"Next time then?" She gulped down the pain at the

prospect that there wouldn't be a next time.

"Oh? There's a next time?" Adam grinned, feigning ignorance. "Tell me about that."

Eva placed a hand gently on his chest. He felt so warm. "You're better at this than you think."

She turned to the stairs, pushing down the despair boiling up inside of her. With each step, she felt her heart sink. *Don't look back,* she told herself. *Don't you dare look back.* She could feel Adam's eyes piercing her back, not letting her out of his sight. She knew he was waiting for her to go inside before he left. *He needs to know,* she thought. She shook her head, no. But he *had to.* Never before had a guy made her feel so normal.

Her heart raced as her feet finally landed on the top step. Her apartment was so close. She was near salvation, but the pressure inside of her was too much. She turned her back on safety and called out to him.

*   *   *

Adam watched her walk up the stairs, not letting his eyes off of her until finally she had ascended to the top. If he allowed his eyes to linger any longer, he knew he would indefinitely regret his decision not to kiss her. He could already feel remorse building in his mind. He turned away, ready to head down the street in search of the nearest train station.

"Adam, wait," Eva called, her voice shaky.

Adam turned back to her.

"I can't let you leave here with the wrong impression." Eva's lips shook as if she was holding back her voice. Adam let her words sink in. She was going to tell him that there was no connection, that they were not going to see each other again. He dreaded this part, but knew it was inevitable.

"Oh," he managed to mumble, "you mean..."

Seeing the heartbreak in his eyes grated on her soul. "No. It's not like that. I just—" Eva breathed in deeply and then sighed. "I'm a witch."

Weeks later, Adam would find himself running down a long subway track, contemplating which death would be more painless, a bevy of arrowed purple snakes or being run over by a late L train. In that second, he would remember this as the moment he could have walked away, leaving her behind avoiding all the trouble that would soon befall him. But he didn't run. He didn't even turn. He stared her down, a confused look on his face.

"A...witch?" It wasn't something you heard every day, that was for sure.

Eva took another long breath and then waved her hand through the air. A small cloud of purple smoke followed it and, swirling in on itself, manifested a long wooden staff with a purple orb at the end. Adam's mouth fell open in shock. Eva snapped her fingers and even quicker than it had appeared, the staff vanished with a puff of smoke.

"I'm a magic-wielding sorceress supreme of the fifth order," said Eva. Adam's head was spinning. Was he dreaming? This girl could not possibly be saying the words he was hearing. They were fantasy, the type of thing you saw in a role-playing game. Yet she was throwing them around like they were as normal as telling someone what you did for a living. "I am wanted dead by every witch in this city and then some." She hesitated before going on. "You and I can never be a 'we'. But for one night you made me feel...normal. So, before I say goodbye, I just wanted to say...thank you."

Adam's brain melted. His heart pounded. It was a feeling that was so overwhelming and made such little sense that the cloud in his mind seemed to clear for the first time in his life. He knew exactly what he wanted to do. No doubts. No fears. Adam ascended the stairs, moving faster than he'd ever moved.

"What are you—"

Her words were cut off as Adam pulled her in cradling her neck and the small of her back with his hands, which seemed unsure of themselves and their placement. He kissed her as though she was the last girl in the world. It had been some time since he had kissed a girl, but he racked his brain for memories from High

School and two drunken parties in college. He focused on being gentle yet firm. He could hear Diego in the back of his head. *Not too much tongue. Straight boys always use too much tongue.* There was no stopping his feelings now. Adam had been searching for one thing his entire life, and now he realized what that thing was: Eva Grey.

*　　　*　　　*

The air shifted and became colder as Diego flew further and further North, the city fading behind him. He flapped his wings, gaining altitude to see the expanse of the street below. On the horizon he could just make out the shape of a large tour bus, driving towards the city. It was a dark magenta, with jagged lines in neon pink and yellow, which ended in small arrows, pointing this way and that. It was a gaudy affair that was bright and offensive enough to distract anyone who might drive beside it.

He veered his long neck, propelling his large body down towards the Earth below. The bus got closer and closer. He descended towards the roof, which was rimmed with lights, making it look like a landing strip. He glided softly over the bus and then landed, his large claws scraping for just a moment along the metal, before he transformed back into a man.

He moved quickly along the roof, the wind beating at his face, before opening a small hatch near the front of the bus. He dropped in, closing it behind him.

Before he could even get a word out, two large men held guns to his head. His hands went up above his head. This was how it always was. "Freeze!" screamed one of the guards.

"Hands in the air!" screamed the second.

"Way ahead of you, boys," snickered Diego. He flashed a smile at a woman, sitting leisurely across a pink leather sofa behind the men. "Queen Victoria," He bowed his head slightly, attempting to not make any sudden movements. "It's been too long."

Vicky sat up in her seat, laughing to herself. "Down, boys." The men fell back, holstering their weapons. Diego noticed small purple lines on their faces, which glowed for just a moment at the command, and then vanish. He smirked, recognizing the signs of her mind controlling powers. Vicky was in her late 20's but used enough makeup that you'd never know. She had every facet of a Rockstar. Her hair was big, blond and curly, done to perfection, looking like she had just stepped off a photo shoot. Her lips were painted bright red, and her eye liner made her eyes deep and foreboding. She dressed like a trashy cowgirl, with denim shorts and a plaid buttoned shirt, tied up to show her cream white stomach. The ensemble was topped off with high-heeled, leather boots.

"Well isn't this a lovely surprise," she said, with a slight twang in her voice. "But honestly darling, the formalities have got to go. Thought we were past all that, Diego."

"Welcome back, Vicky," Diego shot her a wink.

"That's better." she gave Diego a long careful look before shifting gears; wide eyed and friendly. "You're looking fabulous as always. I imagine the boys are on you like moths to a flame."

"I was burning one of those moths when I picked up your scent. You should know he was very disappointed to see me go." They laughed.

"You always knew how to make a girl feel special."

Vicky motioned to a long couch next to her and Diego complied, pushing past the guards and sitting. "What brings you to town?" he asked.

Vicky rolled her eyes, already bored with the idea. "These weak-ass witches, what else? You know, there hasn't been a legitimate kill here for years. They toy with each other like cats who are declawed, batting at mice in a cage. Pointless." She reached her hand over to a small side table and snapped a piece of chocolate off a larger bar. She tossed the chocolate into her mouth. "Someone needs to show them how it's done, or I fear they'll go on like this forever."

The last kill had been Eva's, cementing her as the

most feared witch in town. Many considered her an overnight force to be reckoned with, unheard of one day, off on a witch killing rampage the next. And once it was done, she'd vanished back to her quiet life of potion making and sparring occasionally with Miyako. No one knew what to make of it but they sure as hell weren't going to ask questions of someone so hell bent on murder.

Diego nodded with a smirk on his face. "The Witch Queen has come to shake up the Big Apple. I like it."

"I've just had a thought." Vicky's eyes narrowed, a wicked smile crawling across her crimson lips. "Tell me, my wizardly friend, what would you say to helping me? It could be just like old times." She broke off another piece of chocolate and placed it gingerly into his mouth. He bit into it, allowing the tastes of marshmallows, caramel and chocolate to break over his tongue.

"Party with the hottest girl in town and take down some witches in the process?" Diego swallowed. "What more could a guy ask for?"

Vicky cackled with laughter. "Then buckle up Beautiful, cuz we've got work to do."

The bus sped down the highway, the lights of the city just peeking out over the horizon ahead. Fireflies, awaiting their impending doom.

Chapter Four

Miyako stood on the roof, her mind racing, trying to process the sight she now beheld. She had tracked Eva, following her bird's directions, to an aged apartment building in the heart of Soho. Across the street, Eva Grey, the baddest witch in town, her nemesis, was in full tongue war with a man. Not just any man. A normal, non-magical, non-wizard, non-sorcerer. He had as much right to be kissing her as a toad. Even less. After all, toads had healing properties. Maybe there was more to this man than met the eye, a reason he had managed to weasel his way into Eva's life. Miyako's side still hurt, and her wounds, though sealed, still pulsed with heat. Yet Eva looked as though nothing had happened to her earlier that night. It would be hard to take her head on like this, but maybe she didn't have to. Maybe this man knew something Miyako didn't.

She pulled her spray can from her pocket and drew

a line through the air. The red haze of paint curdled and spun itself into a long wooden broom. It was sleek and black with sharp bristles at the base and two metal foot rests, behind which were metal exhaust pipes, like those of a motorcycle.

The broom dropped into her hand as she re-pocketed the paint can. She jumped onto the broom and kicked at the foot pedal. Two jets of blue flame erupted from the exhaust pipes and Miyako rocketed into the street.

*   *   *

Adam finally pulled away, thinking he could live on those soft lips for the rest of his life. Eva's eyes blinked open, misty. She smelled so good. If she really was a witch, maybe there was a spell she could cast that would make this moment last forever. A soft buzzing filled his ear. Was this a side effect of kissing a witch? It seemed to be getting louder. Her eyes widened, and her face contorted. *Oh no,* he thought. *She hated it. I'm a bad kisser. That's the face that girls make when they think I'm a bad kisser.*

"Adam," she said, her face filling with panic. "Run!"

His chest crushed in on itself as something firm wrapped around him, tightly. It was bright red, like a lasso, but thinner in substance. "What the—" His feet

51

were off the ground and he was rising through the air, climbing and climbing. His mind flashed to being ten years old and forced by his best friend to get on the Tower of Doom, an amusement park ride that took you high up into the air and then dropped you, at full speed, back to the Earth. He recalled not liking this experience, as much as he did not enjoy what was currently happening. The street was vanishing beneath him and now he was soaring over New York City, heading downtown, block after block. He had to stop this. He looked up to see a small Asian girl on a broom, gripping a small canister. The spray can streamed the red rope that now held him captive. He suddenly became aware that he was screaming at the top of his lungs.

"AHHHHHHH!" He was struggling to get free. Why? He didn't know. Surely the only alternative was to fall to his death. "Oh God, oh God, oh God!"

"Stop squirming or I'll drop you," shouted Miyako from above.

"No no no no!" He called out. "No dropping! I'll do anything you want. Just don't drop me!"

"That's a good start," said Miyako. "If you really want to live—"

"I do I do I do!"

"You'll tell me everything you know about Eva Grey." Miyako glared down at him. "How did you bend her to your will? What are her weaknesses?"

Weaknesses? What was she talking about? Did witches *have* weaknesses? Was fire weak to water? Rock weak to electricity? He ran through a backlog of childhood video game knowledge, trying to understand what kind of elemental system witches might function under. How did this work? "I-I don't know," he spat out.

"Wrong answer." Miyako leaned into her broom and the rockets from the exhaust kicked into overdrive.

"Ahhhhhhh!" He was screaming again. They were coming up towards the edge of the island, the lights of the Brooklyn Bridge looming up ahead.

"Now let's try this again. What do you know about—" She was cut off as a large laughing skull, engulfed in purple smoke, rocketed past her, just missing her head. "Whoa!"

Adam turned his head to see Eva, trailing behind them, on a broom of her own. She really was a full-on witch. He didn't know whether to be impressed or terrified. Her broom was a bit more traditional than Miyako's, with a light wooden handle and yellow straw at the sweeping end. On the front, little Day of the Dead skulls and beads dangled as if guarding against bad spirits.

"Looks like your girlfriend is pissed," cackled Miyako.

"I think it might be too soon to use the word

53

girlfriend," remarked Adam, taking this moment to really consider the dynamic their relationship had reached that evening. "We've really only been on one date. Did it look like she was my girlfriend to you?" Miyako rolled her eyes. "I'm just asking your personal opinion."

Miyako turned her broom sharply, the red rope tugging at Adam's chest, jolting the air out of him and shutting him up. "Not only a mortal, but a noisy one," Miyako scoffed.

Miyako weaved the broom in and out of the massive brick towers holding up the bridge structure as skulls shot at her in rapid fire. Ahead of them lay Brooklyn, where Miyako knew there would be even less cover for a broomed rider. Best to turn back and use the city to make an escape. She leaned to the right, turning her broom in a wide circle. Ferries and skiffs glided peacefully over the water. Miyako dropped to a height which made Adam feel even more uncomfortable. He didn't even need to look down to know how close to the water they were. He could feel the spray clipping at his legs as they soared over it. Just behind them, he could see Eva, as she propelled after them at full speed.

As the base of the island came into view, Adam felt them begin to rise once more. The high rises of the Financial District loomed ahead. "I don't know Eva all that well, but I get the feeling she's not gonna let you get away with this."

"Maybe not, but I'm not gonna turn around and just let her kill me," said Miyako under her breath, her voice less confident than before. "I've got too much to lose."

"This can end peacefully," Adam said, thinking of the cop shows he'd seen where the police tried to talk down someone holding hostages. "Just sit me down somewhere. No one has to get hurt."

"Heh." Miyako gave a weak laugh. "You really don't know her very well. When it comes to witches, everyone gets hurt."

They lifted higher and higher, the Freedom Tower in view. They were going so fast now that Adam could feel the skin on his face pulling back as the air hit it. As they ascended towards the top of the tower, he felt something warm creep over him. He looked around to see that a purple mist was enveloping both of them.

"What is this?" Adam called out, gasping for breath as the smoke overtook him.

"NO!" screamed Miyako.

The smoke created a ball around them and then, shape-shifting, formed itself into a huge revolver. Looming in the air, just over the antennae of the tower, it turned to the Hudson River and with a loud *BANG!* it shot out Miyako's body, like a bullet. She vanished out of sight.

The cloud evaporated. Adam fell back towards the

earth below. He felt Eva grab him as she soared by on her broom before he lost consciousness, and everything went dark.

*   *   *

Light peeked in the windows as Adam's eyes opened groggily. The first thing he noticed was that there was an intense pain in his stomach, as if he had pulled a muscle. He rolled over, feeling the tinge of agony. *How had that happened?* he wondered.

After a night of bad choices, there are always a few minutes after you wake up where you can't remember it. Adam relished these moments as he continued to toss in his bed, wanting so badly to not let his body and mind wake up. Finally, he forfeited and sat up, only to find that his head was pounding. He grabbed at it with his hands. "Gah." It was almost unbearable.

He remembered graduating the day before. Still, how had that resulted in *this*? Had he really gotten so drunk the night before? That wasn't like him. Diego had been there. Maybe he knew what happened.

He worked his way off the bed so that he was standing, teetering there by his bed for a moment. With great anguish, he took his first step, the hardwood floor creaking beneath him. Something smelled wonderful, like eggs and potatoes, the kind of breakfast his mother would have made when he still lived at home. Life really only got worse when you moved out on your own. Bills no longer vanished from the mantle where they were stored, and food didn't magically appear on the table at the same time every day. He pushed open the bedroom door, and there she was. Dressed in one of his white undershirts which fell just far enough down her that it covered her underwear, Eva Grey stood, cooking over his tiny stove.

It all came screaming back to him. The date, the kiss, the crazy high-speed witch chase. It was all there, like a Pandora's box of memories, spilling mercilessly out on him.

"Morning," said Eva with trepidation, busily stirring the contents of one of his pots. "Thought you'd never wake up. You must feel awful." She grabbed a large mug with a dark green liquid gurgling around inside and placed it in his hands. "Drink this."

Adam took a sip. It tasted sour, the way dirty socks might taste if you were so inclined to put them in your mouth. "Guh, this is awful."

"It's my hangover cure."

"What's in it?" Adam flapped his tongue around, trying to get rid of the nauseating taste.

"Mostly frogs," said Eva, not even blinking at the thought. "And some parsley for flavor."

Adam gagged. "That's disgusting!" He spat back

into the cup, searching the kitchen desperately for something less amphibian to wash out his mouth.

"Don't be dramatic. Just drink it."

Adam did not want to drink more frogs. He searched Eva's face for a sign that she was joking but none came. She smiled, miming the motions of drinking as encouragement. Not wanting to disappoint her, he pinched his nose and took another sip. It didn't help. He swallowed, trying not to let his disgust show on his face. *If that girl had dropped me,* he thought, *I wouldn't have to drink frogs.* He sat the mug back on the table.

"How did you find my house?" he asked, curiously.

"Magic." She flipped over an egg that was sizzling in a skillet.

"Seriously?"

"Your ID was in your wallet." Eva winked at him, then went back to her cooking.

"So, let me get this straight," said Adam defensively. "You waited until I was almost murdered to get in my pants?"

"I thought we just talked about being dramatic." Eva flipped the eggs onto two separate plates.

"And you're in my shirt," he pointed, trying to figure out the latter details of the evening. "Did we—"

Eva turned to him, rolling her eyes. "Are you twelve?"

Adam looked away, embarrassed. Of course she

hadn't slept with him.

"Besides, I've never done...*that.*" Her cheeks flushed. "I'm not going to start with some guy who's passed out and smells like jet fuel and beer."

"So...the shirt?" Adam looked away, not entirely comfortable with Eva confessing her virginity to him.

"My clothes were dirty," she said, placing a hot soup-like substance into a bowl. "Besides, I've always heard boy's shirts were comfy." She placed the bowl on the table. "And they are."

"Mystery solved," said Adam, sarcastically waving his hands in the air to show mock excitement.

Eva moved several more plates to the table. There were eggs cooked sunny side up and a collection of peppers of different colors and variations mixed together as a salsa. There were avocados and pineapples, bacon and chorizo. It all sizzled and popped with heat, filling the house with smells of warmth and comfort. Eva opened a hand to the table, inviting him to sit.

"You have a lot of questions, I'm sure. Come eat, and I'll answer what I can.

"You made all of this?" Adam hesitantly walked to the table, hoping that there wouldn't be any more froggy surprises for the duration of breakfast.

"I used to cook all the time with my mom." Eva took a seat. "I guess you could say that was her gift she passed down to me. Do you cook?"

"Everyone has to cook once in a while...right?" he said, thinking of an app on his phone he frequently used to order takeout. "Plus, I'm a designer, so everything I make usually looks super professional."

"Oh?" remarked Eva, pulling a piece of bacon to her plate.

"Tastes terrible though."

They both laughed.

Adam hesitated, changing the topic to a more pressing matter. "That girl, the one from last night," started Adam.

"Her name is Miyako."

"I don't think she likes you."

Eva looked up from her coffee, concerned. "She wants me dead."

"Yeah, I got that. Why?" Adam was having a hard time getting himself in the mood to eat. Now that she had offered to answer his questions, he found he had dozens swirling around in his brain.

"Witches aren't like wizards. Wizards are born with as much power as they're ever gonna have. Some are meek, while others are godly, but it's set in stone." Eva took a breath. "But witches can become stronger. Much stronger."

*   *   *

Stephanie Jones ran through the trees, off the beaten path. Her mousey gray hair hung in a long-braided ponytail down her back. A few leaves had found a place to rest on her head, giving her a naturalistic appearance. Her skin had dulled with age, turning from a peach color, to a bland gray. She was so thin that every muscle and bone made a sharp appearance under her skin. This made her face jagged and hardened, like that of a solider.

Years ago, Stephanie had been considered the strongest witch in the city. She had been ruthless in her killing. She sought power and all the perks that came with it. One night she had entered a witch's home, taking her life. Upon searching the house, she found that there was a baby in the next room over. Hungry for power, she had killed the child, hoping to absorb the fresh gifts of an innocent. To her horror, the child had been mortal. She had broken the witch code to never harm humans. From the blood-soaked babe in her hands, she had looked up into a mirror, which hung above its crib. There, she saw not herself, but a monster. That was the last time she had killed another man, woman or child. She left the city, forfeiting her crown as one of the seven Witch Queens, and became something of a nomad.

In the past three years, she had found herself a nice quiet area to live in Forest Hills, near the park. Forest

61

Park was a well-kept secret in Queens; a small forest in the center of the fast-paced city around it. Tall sweeping trees and hills created a maze of woods that one could easily get lost in. She had hidden herself, avoiding the witch war that was Manhattan, choosing instead to live a simple life. At least, as simple as a girl could live in New York City. This had gone well for her. She would go into the woods to hunt every day and then take some of her game up to Flushing, to sell them to the seedier restaurants for money. The rest, she'd keep for herself and cook over a small stove. She somehow created a farmstead lifestyle in the heart of the city, and she was happy.

This morning was different. She took off into the woods, ready to find her first kill of the day, but as she finished an uneasy feeling had struck her. There was magic about, something that she had not felt since moving here. In the world, there were all sorts of magical beasts that weren't witches. Wizards and shamans, centaurs and giants, fairies and warlocks. They all fed off the same magic force and could sense each other's presence. It was the feeling most people had when they thought they were being watched. As she progressed forward, she slowed her pace, pulling an oversized boomerang from her back, ready to defend against any unwarranted attacks. For all she knew, it was a creature of the woods. Perhaps a Dire Wolf had taken up residence.

Stephanie pulled up to a tree, using it for cover as she snuck around it. She moved from tree to tree, all the while keeping a firm grip on her boomerang. It was as tall as she was and a soft beige color with little red ribbons hanging from either end.

Crack. Stephanie instinctively sent the boomerang flying. It zipped through the air, despite its size and weight. There was a loud thud as the boomerang hit something in a nearby tree, and then it spun around, readying its return flight. Stephanie caught the boomerang as a small sparrow fell from the tree limbs, dead. It plopped on the ground, its neck snapped clean in half, its skull impacted from the blunt force of the weapon.

Stephanie sighed and reluctantly let the tension out of her body. Just a bird. She was ready to turn back for home when she heard it.

Doom. Doom. Doom. Doom. It was low at first, like the lone bass line at the start of a rock song. It strummed evenly in 4/4 time. Stephanie turned slowly, trying to make out the sound. It was getting louder and faster. A cold wind hit her face as she turned just in time to see several jagged purple lines cutting across the ground towards her, like serpents, with arrows for heads, going in for the kill.

Stephanie turned to run. Her heart raced as she

descended the hill she had just come up, tripping over twigs and bushes and falling through the leaves. Every misplaced step resulted in her falling to her hands and knees. She could feel them start to bleed, the splinters stinging. She kept running. Ahead was a small cobblestone underpass. Maybe her assailant hadn't seen her yet and she could hide there. It was her only chance. Past that were the neighborhoods of Forest Hills and there, she would be out in the open.

Doom. Doom. Doom. Doom. The note seemed to be chasing her. She fell past the last of the trees and slammed onto her hands and knees in a pile of mud. A shadow crept across her and then moved forward on the ground. It was like a bird but larger, with a long neck and tail and a wide wingspan. *A dragon.* She was being hunted by a wizard, but why? She pulled herself up and ran towards the shelter of the underpass. A quick look back revealed the purple jagged arrows, closing in on her. She tripped again, her boomerang bouncing on the ground beside her as she fell. She reached out for it, but it was too late. Three of the jagged lines impaled the boomerang, raising it up, and then with a horrible cracking sound, tore it apart. Little wooden splinters rained down on Stephanie. She rolled on her back, using her feet and arms to back away from her pursuer, but it was no use.

Standing at the tunnel entrance behind Stephanie,

with a large purple and yellow electric guitar in her hands, was Vicky. She grinned deviously, clearly proud of herself.

"Please," Stephanie called out, still crawling backwards. How had this witch found her? And why? Stephanie had escaped the world of witches, swearing to never harm another. She had left them to their own devices. She was strong when she left, and there had been a clear understanding. She would stay out of their way as long as they stayed out of hers. She had found peace in a world where peace was forbidden.

"I need you, Stephanie," said Vicky, still grinning ear to ear, still strumming the same note on her guitar. The jagged purple lines were sneaking underneath Stephanie, silently moving across the pavement. "I need you to take a message back to the witches of this city. They need to know there's a new girl in town." Vicky licked her lips. "They need to know their days are numbered."

A message? Stephanie could do that. If it meant holding onto her quiet little world and her hunting and her fireplace, she could deliver a message. It was a small price to pay. "S so," she stuttered, shaking, "you're going to let me live?"

Vicky laughed. "Don't be silly."

DOOM! She played one last note on the guitar and the purple lines shot up from the ground, cutting through Stephanie's body, just as they had done with the boomerang. Her blood splattered the nearby wall, and her arms and legs went limp. The lines disappeared, dropping the girl's lifeless body in a heap on the muddy ground.

From the other end of the tunnel, Diego appeared. "Nice kill."

A wisp of white smoke leaked out of Stephanie like breath on a cold day, floating towards Vicky and wafting into her mouth. Vicky took a deep breath, absorbing the new strength she had acquired. "All thanks to your nose and expert tracking, darling."

"You flatter me," Diego smirked. "So, what now?"

"Put her somewhere they'll see."

Diego cocked his head, looking down at the body. "I know just the spot."

*　　　*　　　*

Adam looked over the table at Eva, dumbstruck. "To become stronger, we must ingest the strength of other witches. A witch's essence can only be consumed by the witch who strikes the killing blow." Eva said these words as if she had seen, and maybe even participated in this horrible tradition one too many times.

"That's terrible," said Adam, quickly losing his appetite.

"It's the way of the world," said Eva, shoving some egg into her mouth. "We're only rewarded for competition and murder. Punished for compassion and forbidden to love."

"What do you mean, punished?" Adam was suddenly hyper-aware of what she was saying. Forbidden to love? But then why meet him? Why go on a date in the first place? Wasn't the whole point of dating to fall in love?

"It is said that if a witch were to declare her love for another, she would lose all her power and be left defenseless." Eva cringed at the thought. "Another witch could then easily pick her off and absorb her essence. It would be suicide."

Adam thought all of this through and then asked the obvious, yet terrifying question. "So...you're telling me, you can never fall in love?"

"Never." Eva looked down at her plate, avoiding his gaze. "There are no love stories for witches."

Adam let out a breath as if he had been holding it. He felt something well up inside of him, and as it came to the forefront of his thoughts, he realized that what he was feeling was anger. Anger at himself for actually liking this girl. Anger at her for allowing him to entertain the idea, even though she knew it could never be. But most of all, he was angry that witches, who 24 hours ago he didn't even know existed, were now the main reason for his grief.

"What are we doing here, Eva?" he asked, yet it came out as more of an accusation.

"What do you mean?" Eva could tell he wasn't happy. He hadn't taken a bite of food in some time, and his face was starting to flush red.

"Why do you think I made that profile on Heart Heart Hug? To get rejected? To be toyed with by girls who have no business being there in the first place? Why?" Adam was standing now, his rage spilling out of him.

"Adam, I—"

He stood, walking to the window, trying to get control of himself. He wanted to fall in love. He wanted a family and kids. He wanted to not feel so lonely all the time. He wanted to share his life with someone he thought was perfect, and who thought he was perfect.

"You show up, daring me to challenge my rules and face my fears," he said. "But look at all the baggage you're carrying around. You break one rule, and you will literally wind up dead." Adam sighed. She couldn't fall in love with him, and he wouldn't be able to help himself. He was just that guy. If he met someone he liked, he started imagining a future together. "I think about meeting you for months, and now that you're in my life, you tell me you shouldn't be here in the first place." Adam stopped, taking several long breaths.

Eva fought back the wetness in her eyes. She nodded compliantly. "I'm sorry." She turned her head, not wanting to look at him. "Maybe I should go."

Adam walked to the apartment door and opened it, looking down. "I think so too," he said, reluctantly.

When he looked up to see her response, she had vanished into thin air, his shirt left behind on her chair.

Chapter Five

Eva stormed into her apartment, slamming the door behind her. It was a makeshift one bedroom, located in an inter-dimensional vortex between 11A and 11B. It wasn't much, but it was home. She had no windows, causing the room to be constantly dark, lit only by candles and the glow of certain potions which lit up as they brewed. Everything in the apartment was old or used or borrowed. There was a large apothecary cabinet to the side where she kept potion ingredients and a collection of teenage romance novels she had found on one of her hunts. She enjoyed reading these as a last resort for entertainment, late into the night, when books about golems and trolls had run their course. A large wooden table in the center of the room was home to several beakers and tubes with different sorts of liquids floating between them. Some brewed and bubbled while others were decidedly still. There was a small pink radio she had found in the garbage of an elementary school, which had little white kittens on it. Eva found this to be quite cute and had added it to her collection. Little vases of different shapes and sizes were spread around the room with flowers springing up from them in an attempt to brighten up an otherwise morose room. In truth, she was a bit of a hoarder, picking up anything of interest off the street and adding it to the décor of an already complicated Feng Shui design. Dishes were stacked high in her kitchen sink. Ropes with little stones and ornaments hung from the ceiling, imbued with incantations that warded off bad spirits, other witches or worst of all, the landlord.

Eva threw her bag to the ground and waved a hand across the room, lighting ten large candles so that the room was filled with a warm glow. She went to sit at her desk and put her face in her hands. How had she been so stupid? How had she allowed someone to get so close? He had kissed her, for God's sake. She was slipping. For a time, witches had seen her as the most foreboding, most vicious witch on the block but if this got out, she'd be a sitting duck. If even a hint of her having feelings for someone was known, every witch in the city would be searching for her, ready to take her down in her weakened state.

The worst part, the part that made her want to vomit, was how much she had liked spending time with

Adam. In her head, she replayed the events of the evening. She liked how he smiled and the way his skin felt when she had tucked him into his bed. She liked the way his clothes smelled and the way everything in his drawer was so neatly folded. She liked the way he alphabetized his kitchen and the way that even though he rarely cooked, he still had all the proper utensils to make a good meal. The structure in his life pulled her to him, but she just wasn't that girl. She never could be. She was a witch. A night wandering, magic gathering, cold blooded murderer.

She opened her laptop, tying her hair back to keep it out of her way. The screen came on, making it the brightest thing in the room. She opened her 'HeartHeartHug' profile and without a thought, clicked on Adam's page. There he was, the guy who had broken all his rules just to meet her. Her heart hurt. He had been so easy to talk to, so considerate. Sure, the date had gotten off on the wrong foot, but from there on out, he held doors open for her. He laughed at all her jokes. He had made her feel more normal than she had ever considered herself. With pain in her chest, she went to her account page and found the "Delete Profile" button. She hovered over it for just a moment, before clicking, erasing her existence from the site.

She closed the laptop and stood, walking over to the table. She eyed the potion she'd been working on for the past several weeks and then opened up an old leather-bound book, turning to her most recent dog-eared page. She started reading, hoping that if nothing else, her work could distract from the immediate feeling of regret welling up in the pit of her stomach.

*   *   *

Miyako's hand pulled the dark-inked pen quickly across the sketchbook, crafting panels and pictures. Etching out faces and hands. Writing words into little bubbles in order to explicate the story. She had been working on her own Manga, a stylized Japanese comic book, during the course of her college math class. It was affectionately called *Miyako Kicks Eva Grey's Ass*. Maybe the title needed some work, but Miyako thought it served the purpose.

On this particular page, Miyako was screaming at the top of her lungs as she hacked and slashed away at a near helpless Eva. Dark ink splotches dotted the page as blood went flying everywhere.

She had sulked her way home the night before and nursed her wounds, spending the rest of the night trying to cleanse herself of the Hudson River grime and muck, just so that she didn't look foolish showing up to class the next day, smelling like a fish. This had left her feeling exhausted and caring even less about school than usual.

"Miyako?" She looked up at the teacher standing at the front of the classroom. The eyes of all the students were fixed on Miyako. Jasmine had convinced her on their move to the city that one of them needed to get a college education, learn the ways of the world, if they were going to make it on their own. That responsibility had fallen to Miyako. She thought at first that it might be fun, pretending to be normal, but she soon discovered otherwise. Being normal was so unbelievably boring. Day in and day out, it was the same thing. She was accustomed to dealing with life and death situations, but these people fussed about who was dating who, and which guy they'd be hooking up with that weekend, and who got so drunk at that one party that they threw up. It made Miyako sick. Then there were the classes, filled with teachers who spoke to her like a helpless child. As if math was difficult, or history hard to remember. She was bored by the courses, and the textbooks she had finished reading and memorized in the first week. She was even bored by the school itself, its taupe walls lulling her into a near-comatose state.

"Would you mind joining us in the world of the learning?" the teacher asked spitefully. This woman, Miyako thought, was the worst. She had a large face with skin that sagged so that she had massive jowls, like that of a bulldog. She had thinning gray hair and always wore a blue blazer with a little owl pin. The owl wore a graduation cap and held a diploma, as if that made her special. The blazer only slightly covered her robust size and breasts which hung to her hips. She looked down her half-moon glasses at Miyako and the rest of the class, as if they were utter morons.

Rolling her eyes, Miyako closed her sketch book.

"Why don't you come up here and write out Pi for us." The teacher gestured at the board with a small piece of white chalk. "I'm sure you can at least manage the first few numbers. Especially since we are *clearly* boring you." So, this was how it was going to be, singling her out in order to make her a fool in front of the other students. Unfortunately for this old wretch, Miyako didn't much care for the opinions of the other students, or anyone else for that matter.

She slowly stood and walked towards the front of the classroom, making sure that her footsteps made as much noise as possible. Gently, she pulled the chalk out of the teacher's hands. Her eyes narrowed, giving the teacher a cold glare.

Steadily, she began to write on the board.

3.14

"A little nervous, are we?" asked the teacher. "Don't worry. Everyone gets hung up after the first couple of numbers. At least we have it in the basic form. Now, no more distractions. Please return to your—"

Miyako had already tuned her out as her hand continued to write numbers across the board.

$$3.1415926535897932384626433832795028841971693993751058209749444592$$

Number after number, she wrote, filling the first half of the chalkboard and then moving onto the other.

"That's enough, Miyako," said the teacher, clearly flustered. Behind her, she could hear the students shouting and cheering. Yet even this fell on her ears as simple background noise. She kept going and going until suddenly the teacher was grabbing her hand.

"NO!" Miyako shoved the old woman backwards, sending her falling across her wooden desk. Her dress flew up around her waist, revealing a pair of ripped pantyhose and her little pin detached from its blue tweed home. It clattered to the ground with a deafening ring, skidding along the floor until it hit the wall. The class went silent. Miyako paced back to her desk with conviction. Without another word, she grabbed her book bag, shoved her sketchpad inside, and walked out the door as the other students jumped up to help the teacher, who was attempting to get her bearings while screeching for help.

School, she decided, was not for her.

*   *   *

Just two blocks east of the secret hovel, there was a small park with little benches and a quaint garden. It was peaceful and soothing, with little cobblestone paths that crisscrossed between grassy patches and rose bushes. Jasmine sat on one of the benches, head back towards the sky, her eyes closed. She should have been folding cranes, but she needed to feel the warmth of the sun on her face. Their home was always so dark, with no windows or electricity. She needed the light to remind her that there was still hope, that life still existed. Miyako would have had a heart attack if she'd known that Jasmine took these little walks. It was for this reason that Jasmine had suggested school for Miyako. Not just something to stimulate her mind, but for Jasmine's sake as well. She desperately needed to feel the open air and the breeze despite all the risks that came along with doing so.

She took in a deep breath but was cut short, feeling her lungs tighten.

Cough! Cough! Cough! She grabbed at her chest, trying to find the air within them. She caught her breath for the moment, closing her eyes to focus. She gulped down the phlegm in her throat.

Her strength was fading. It was time to go back home. She stood slowly, taking her time. The cave was only a couple blocks away. She had made it here with no problems. She could surely make it back. She took an easy step and then another, finding her pace. She was going to be okay.

Then it hit. A hard pain in her chest. She grasped at her chest, falling to one knee. People walking by in the park stopped to look at her, concerned.

Cough! Cough! Ca-Cough! It felt as though her lung might actually explode.

"You okay, lady?" A middle-aged man in a bowler hat stood next to her, unsure of what to do in this situation. He reached out to comfort her, but Jasmine pushed him away, avoiding the man's gaze.

She quickly rose up from the ground, pulling a hood over her head. "I'm fine. Leave me alone." She took a step and then stopped, nodding to the man. "Thanks..."

Jasmine took off, still wheezing. Her day in the park was over.

*   *   *

Miyako stomped along 43rd street, full of rage. How had she thought for one minute that school would be a good idea? It was Jasmine's fault. She'd applied and pushed herself through the process for Jasmine. But why? She certainly didn't owe the girl anything. Their connection was an anomaly, something that existed because they had done it for so long that it had become normal. It was a distraction, therefore a weakness, which Miyako refused to acknowledge. Any time the thought piqued up in her head, she would deny it any power, avoiding it at all costs.

She rounded the corner into Times Square, pushing through the crowds of tourists who didn't know any better but to stand on a crowded sidewalk and look up. That was when she saw it. Pinned up on the Times Square Tower, like Jesus on the cross, was the mutilated body of Stephanie Jones, one of the greatest witches on the East coast. Her naked body hung with her arms outstretched and her feet bound together. Blood had dried on her skin where three large holes punctured her chest. Her head drooped to one side. Beneath her, someone had hastily painted in large green letters, "*Something Wicked, This Way Comes.*" It sent chills up Miyako's spine.

She gasped at the sight, covering her mouth. A few passersby gave her awkward glances as she composed herself so as not to draw attention. Why wouldn't they? After all, it was a message for witches. No mortal could see the body or the words. It was both a warning and a threat. Someone new had entered the arena, and she wanted everyone to know just how strong she was.

"Shit," said Miyako under her breath. She quickly tucked her phone away and headed out. She had to get to Jasmine, before someone else did. She ran down a vacant side street, sprayed out her broom and took off.

*   *   *

Diego stood over the bathroom sink, thoroughly washing the blood from his hands. Getting her body up there was easy. He had simply flown her up and then punched in the nails. The finishing touch was the writing, which he was quite proud of. He had been inspired to use the color green by a certain musical involving a wicked witch who wasn't all that wicked. Humans really had no idea how things were.

He rinsed the last remnants of blood from his hands, dried them, adjusted his collar and fixed his hair. He exited the bathroom of the small cafe, just as Adam was entering the front door. The cafe itself had auburn walls and long wooden benches for sitting, which bordered small circular tables. Several patrons chatted and worked at their laptops while shakily sipping at hot cups of coffee. Adam looked exhausted and not like his usual self. His book bag hung flimsily from his right arm, and his sweater and jeans looked like they had been thrown on, hanging awkwardly from his lanky body.

"There he is!" shouted Diego, hugging his friend.

"Hey," grunted Adam.

"Rough night?"

"And morning."

"Yikes," said Diego, turning to the counter. "Let me grab you a coffee. I think for once you might need it worse than me."

They sat at one of the tables, Diego on the bench and Adam opposite him on a rickety metal chair. They drank their hot beverages as Adam told Diego of his evening, stealthily omitting any mention of witches.

"Can't fall in love?" Diego scoffed at the thought. "What kind of crazy girl says she can't fall in love? Isn't that ideology usually reserved for gay men?"

"Ha ha," said Adam sarcastically. "This is why I can't meet women. They all turn out crazy...or married."

"I don't see what the big deal is," said Diego, shrugging his shoulders. "So, she doesn't want a real relationship. Sounds like the perfect girl. Isn't this what most men dream of? What's the problem with just having some fun for once in your life? Who's to say you can't just be friends? Why's everything got to be about love? I've got lots of friends."

"I don't have sex with my friends," said Adam, rolling his eyes.

"Yeah, I've noticed," teased Diego. They laughed.

"Guess I won't be seeing her again," Adam sighed.

"On to the next."

"You're a sick man." They laughed again.

The two of them continued to talk and drink until they had emptied their cups. As they said their good-byes, they hugged, then took off in opposite directions.

Diego mused on how much he cared for Adam. Adam was the perfect escape from his otherwise magic-filled life. It was nice, he thought, to have someone in his life that had nothing to do with witches or wizards or spells or death. Adam was kind of like a pet. They know nothing of what you do during the day but are always happy to see you when you get home. And as much as someone can care for a beloved pet, he truly did love Adam, clueless though he might be.

*   *   *

Jasmine sat at her table, slowly folding cranes. She had barely made it back, out of breath and feeling as though her feet couldn't carry her any further. Now that she was back, the urgency of folding the cranes became even more apparent. Fold after crease, she regained her breath, holding onto the steady monotonous rhythm of the task.

Miyako rushed in, her face red as her eyes darted about the room. "We're leaving," she announced, as if the topic was not up for debate.

"What?" Jasmine turned to her. "Why?"

"We aren't safe here anymore." Miyako was packing things in the room into a large duffel bag, only half looking at what was thrown in. Clothes, shoes, potions, books, all of it a jumbled mess.

Cough Cough! Jasmine tried to catch her breath in the excitement. "Just slow down. Tell me what's going on!"

Miyako turned to Jasmine, frustrated. "We don't have time for this, Jazz!"

"You're asking me to pick up my life, our lives, and just move without question?" asked Jasmine, the tone of her voice raising. "I'm aware of our situation. I'm not stupid, but if you want me to go, then make some time. Explain it to me. Use your words."

"There's a witch killer in town!" Miyako stopped everything. "We have to move. If we stay here, she'll find us."

Jasmine shook her head. "Every witch is a witch killer. I am, and so are you! What makes this one any different?"

"She killed Stephanie Jones."

The room fell silent as the two of them stared at each other. Jasmine sank back into her chair, realizing the full weight of the situation. "What?"

"And she didn't just kill her, Jazz. She hung her in Times Square with magic, so the mortals couldn't see. It was a message for witches. A threat only we could read." Miyako's arms filled with goosebumps at the thought. Jasmine couldn't remember the last time she had seen her this shaken. "She's coming for us. Every last one of us. This bitch means business."

Jasmine sat back as Miyako continued to pack everything in sight. "Where will we go?"

"Somewhere," said Miyako, trying to think, but failing. "Anywhere." She turned to Jasmine. "Can you walk?"

Jasmine thought back to her secret excursion, and how she had not made it far. She was even weaker for it. Even so, she nodded. "Yes." Jasmine coughed again. "I can."

"We have to stay on the move." Miyako frantically returned to packing.

Jasmine grabbed Miyako's arm, stopping her in her tracks. She pulled her close and kissed Miyako on the forehead softly. "Okay," she whispered.

They finished packing what few belongings they had which amounted to a large duffel bag of clothes and random items, another bag filled with paper cranes, and the briefcase which held Miyako's cutouts. They left the cave together, leaving behind a small candle on the desk to burn itself out.

Outside, Jasmine leaned against a dumpster as Miyako sprayed a large red bomb on the wall. It was only a large circle with a fuse on the top, but it would have to do. They grabbed their belongings. Miyako held Jasmine up, as they moved out of the alleyway. Approaching the west end of the next block, they heard the thundering sound of the bomb exploding, eradicating all traces of them. Wiping away their past up to this point and cracking open their future, the unknown.

Chapter Six

For a week, Adam had skulked around his apartment in his underwear. For a week, Adam sent in hundreds of resumes to countless design firms in the state, and when that didn't seem to pan out, he applied to out of state firms. For a week, Adam opened his 'Heart Heart Hug' app every time he felt a phantom vibration in his pants pocket, only to see that he didn't have any new messages. For a week, Adam thought out every little detail of his night and morning with Eva Grey, obsessing over every moment, trying to figure out how it could have ended differently. For a week, Adam looked longingly at every train that pulled into the station, thinking about how easy it would be to jump in front of it, and for a week, Adam had decided to give life at least one more shot.

Finally, while lying in his bed playing the same game on his phone he played every time he felt useless, 'Fruit Smash,' a call came in, inviting him to a job interview at a Design Firm on the Upper West Side. An actual, real life job. He pulled himself out of his depression and went to work on perfecting his handshake and finely pressing all of his clothes again.

The next day, he sat with his leg shaking neurotically, as he watched a suited man in front of him carefully pour over his resume. His eyes did not indicate any signs of being impressed. In fact, the man seemed a bit bored by the whole affair. The office was large with a view of Central Park. Several plaques and diplomas hung from the wall and there was a photo of the man awkwardly shaking Hillary Clinton's hand. Neither of them looked excited to be at whatever well-to-do gala they were attending. The desk was long and acted as a divider between interviewer and interviewee. There were little bobble-heads atop it as well as a picture of the man with his much more attractive wife, and various other office bric-a-brac.

"Graduated from Pratt," mused the man. "Good school." Adam sarcastically thought of how fortunate he was that men of his status could tell Adam how good his school was. As if the massive loans piling up at his house weren't validation enough.

"It was," Adam said nervously, "Is."

The man tossed the resume onto his desk, removing his glasses. "Tell me a little about your work history."

Adam sat up. Finally, a chance for him to talk about

himself, list his passions, convince this overly paid asshole that he was right for the job. "Yeah, of course." Adam adjusted his tie. "I recently volunteered at—"

"Not volunteer work," the man cut him off. "Real work. I see plenty of *free* work on your resume. I want to know what you've done that's actually worth knowing."

"Oh," Adam sputtered, churning over previous jobs in his head to see what might qualify to this man as 'real work.'

"Have you ever actually been paid to design something?" The man looked down his nose, judging Adam.

"Define *paid*," said Adam, his heart sinking.

The man let out a long sigh. "We'll be in touch."

*   *   *

STATUS UPDATE: Feeling crappy. Can't find work. No one hires people with no experience. #FML.

Adam, like so many others, used social media to update the world on his well-being in hopes of getting sympathy or maybe even some validation. At some point, we all needed friends to tell us it was all going to be okay, even if they had no real proof or reason for saying so. He stared at the phone as he walked down the bustling street, waiting for someone to like the post or maybe even comment. No one did.

He shoved his phone back in his pocket. Online friends, he decided, were the worst. As he climbed the stairs of his apartment building, he smelled the fresh scent of baking. The family in the three bedroom across the hall was always cooking and sometimes would even invite him over for dinner. It was always delicious, but he made a point to not overstay his welcome. He didn't want them to think that he was taking advantage. He unlocked his own door and pushed it open, to discover that those fresh scents were actually coming from his own kitchen.

Taking a sip from a small spoon over a pot, was Eva Grey. It was all so nonchalant, as if he often found her there when he came home. So much of the scene felt so right. Yet Adam did not fall for it. He knew that what he saw before him had to be some kind of trick or game. Some sort of witchery to lure him into a false sense of security.

"How did you get in here?" he asked, bluntly.

"Seriously?" she said, turning to him and smiling. He had missed that smile since the last time he had seen it. It was gentle and soft and kind.

"Right," he recalled. "Magic." He moved into the room, hanging up his jacket and sitting his bag down. "Let's try this one. *Why are you here?*"

"I saw your status," she said nonchalantly. So, she was still keeping tabs on him online. Not to say that he wasn't doing the same, but she rarely posted anything outside the occasional link to a cute pug video. "Decided to come make you dinner. Thought you might need someone to talk to."

Adam let out a long sigh. "That's really nice of you, but did you really think you'd be the right person for the job?"

Eva stopped and looked at him the way she'd felt all along, upset and unsure, just like he was. "Please, Adam..."

"We talked about this," he pushed on. "You can't be in my life."

"Christ, Adam!" She slammed a spoon down on the table. "This isn't all about you!" She took a deep breath, trying to calm herself. "You think I meet a lot of guys online? I don't. Not one. Not until you. I was scared too, the first time we met. Scared you wouldn't like me for who I am. Scared you'd run and tell someone or try to use me for my powers. But you didn't do any of that. Adam, we chatted for months before we met last week."

It was true. From the moment Adam had messaged her, they'd texted every single day. They shared favorite colors and favorite past times. When Adam was bored at three in the morning, he could always message her and know that she would send him a response. If he saw a particularly interesting piece of artwork, he'd send her a picture and she'd do the same, sending him pictures of the New York Cityscape from several stories up. He was never sure how she had gotten so high to take these snapshots until now. They'd taken selfies just to share with one another. They'd remarked at how they might be hearing the same screaming woman in the middle of the night or how they might have ridden the same train that day. Often times, Adam even thought he caught sight of her while waiting on the R train platform. Then, just before he could get a good look, she'd vanish into the crowd. They became friends before they even knew each other. Their first date hadn't even felt like a first date. It was more like two friends reuniting after a long time apart.

"Then, just like that, you were out of my life," Eva sighed. "I kept checking my phone for a message out of habit. I started to feel like a crazy person." Eva took a deep breath, collecting herself. "I guess I...missed you."

Adam was blindsided. He had been so busy thinking about how this girl had wronged him that he had completely failed to realize that she might not be taking things so well either. Did he honestly believe that just because she was a witch and couldn't fall in love, that she wasn't struggling with her feelings the way he was? He observed the grand feast before him.

"This looks great."

"I made tamales. It's a family recipe."

"Sounds wonderful." Adam gave a weak smile. "Let me open a bottle of wine. We'll have dinner...like normal people."

"Having dinner together won't make us more normal" Eva seemed unsure.

"Yeah, but at least then we'll be full and buzzed," Adam grinned. "Everything is a little bit less awful when you're full and buzzed."

Adam pulled a bottle of wine from the refrigerator and filled two glasses. Then they sat at the table, the mortal boy and the witch, eating tamales together as if this was the way things had always been.

*   *   *

Vicky stood, leaning on the railing of her patio loft as she observed the city below. Her silk camisole glided through the air behind her as a light breeze passed her. She breathed in the air and smiled. This was her city now. "You hear that?" She said to the shadow looming behind her. "That's the sound of a dozen little witches running scared." She turned as Diego moved into view on the patio and placed a gin and tonic in her hand. She pecked him on the cheek and smiled, heading indoors.

"What's next?" he asked, half excited, half anxious. He wasn't usually one to get his hands dirty, and the last job had been overly messy for his taste.

"I've got another project for you," said Vicky, approaching a large box at the side of the room. The loft was lavishly decorated in expensive furs and modern furniture. Abstract paintings that needed too much explanation to understand them, hung from the walls ominously.

"I can only hope this one doesn't require a full body scrub afterward," said Diego, half joking.

"Relax, sugar," she chuckled, opening the box. "Just a little PR."

From the box, she pulled a rolled-up poster. She carefully unrolled it and then whipped it flat, revealing the image. The poster showed Vicky, holding a guitar, with her band behind her and fans cheering and reaching out their hands for her. It read "Vicky Davis. One Night Only. The Veranda Theater." Underneath all of this was a tagline which Diego found to be quite accurate. "Be Wicked." Vicky presented the poster, smiling flirtatiously.

"You're doing a show?" Diego took the poster from her, giving it a good long look.

"Why, of course, darling. That's what we rock stars do, you know." She paced the room. "Besides, for what I'm planning, I'll need some new...fans." Her voice lowered, revealing a darker purpose.

Diego rerolled the poster. "PR it is."

"Put them everywhere," she ordered. "I need a sold out show if I'm going to make this work."

"Sounds like you're building an army," Diego said slyly.

"A star needs her fans. A commander needs her soldiers."

"Two birds, one stone."

"This is why I like you, Diego. So smart. So loyal." She ran a finger along his cheek.

Diego nodded respectfully and then went to the window. In an instant he transformed, beating his leathery wings, and took off over the city.

Vicky looked out the window at him as he went and snickered. "Good boy."

*   *   *

The food was delicious, and as Adam and Eva revisited previously texted conversations about their families and their likes and dislikes, favorite colors, worst childhood memory and future plans, it slowly disappeared from their plates. They did the dishes together, giving each other sideways glances all the while. But their night together was coming to an end. It was late, far past Adam's normal bed time. Though, now that he didn't work or go to school, what did it really matter what time he went to bed? They stood at his door, still full and buzzed, but keeping a healthy distance from each other. It was as if there was an invisible force between them. Like two magnets of the same polarization, repelling each other.

"I know I already said it, but my compliments to the chef," said Adam, rubbing his stomach. "And to your mom of course, for teaching you all the recipes."

"Thanks, I'll let her know," said Eva, tilting her head to the side.

"I thought you said she'd...y'know...died."

"She did."

"Right," said Adam, getting the hang of things. "Magic." Adam looked down, trying to hold himself together. "This was fun."

"Yeah." Eva was also looking down. "It was." Eva reached out and gently touched Adam's arm. He resisted the urge to pull away. "And no one ever said witches can't have friends. We can be friends, right Adam?"

Adam thought about this for a moment and then let out a heavy sigh. "It's just that—" he trailed off.

"Oh." Eva sighed, understanding his hesitation. After all, she didn't imagine being friends would be nearly as easy as it sounded.

"No, wait. Let me explain." Adam felt as though he'd been working to keep his true feelings inside all night, but now they came pouring out. "I feel like there are two sides fighting this battle inside of me. One part is screaming at me to walk away. That part knows that sooner or later, I'm going to get hurt by all of this. No matter how hard I might try, I won't want to be just your friend." Adam stopped, biting his lip.

Eva looked at him with the smallest glimmer of hope in her eyes. "And the other part?"

"Oh, that guy," chuckled Adam weakly. "He thinks you might just be the best mistake he could possibly make."

Eva smiled, her bottom lip quivering. She stepped to him, leaving the door ajar and hugged him. He was so warm. He wrapped his arms around her and for a long time, they stood, neither wanting to be the first to pull away. Eva had never hugged a man before, but she was surprised at just how safe she felt. Adam could smell coconut in her hair. It was intoxicating. He could feel her breath as her chest rose and fell. *Stop shaking,* he thought, but it had been a long time since he had hugged a girl, let alone one he liked this much. He focused on something else. *Baseball?* That was no good. He knew very little about sports.

She pulled back, her arms stopping at his shoulders as she looked into his soft eyes. She sighed, trying to force herself to look away. "I should go," she said.

"Yeah," said Adam. *Does your voice sound higher than normal? That's how you sound when you're lying,* he thought. *Pull yourself together, Adam!* "You

96

should."

"I really should go," she repeated, her hands still on his shoulders.

"You really should," he said, his hands still holding the small of her back. "Or..." he froze. *Are you kidding me?!* His subconscious was screaming at him, begging him to let her go.

"Or?" She asked. She was frozen in place, not wanting to leave but not wanting to make the first move. She'd never even kissed a man until last week. Hell, she didn't even know what a first move looked like.

"You could..."

Eva didn't let him finish. This time it was she who kissed him. They held each other tightly, exploring each other's lips, allowing this kiss to last much longer than the last. "Okay," said Eva at last. "I'll stay. Just for tonight. I'll stay."

"Uh...yeah," said Adam, even more nervous now.

She gingerly placed her hand in his and led him from the living room to his bedroom where she stopped, looking at him with worry. "I've...never done this before."

"I've *barely* done this before," he replied.

"It's just that...I don't want to disappoint you," she looked away. She couldn't believe that she, the great and powerful Eva Grey, was feeling nervous about *this* of all things.

"Well you are in luck," said Adam, placing a hand on her cheek. "Because I have very low standards."

They laughed as they kissed again. He slowly unzipped her hoodie, fumbling with the zipper, which kept getting caught on frayed fabric, and she unbuttoned his shirt, looking down several times from their kiss to see what the hell she was doing. They trembled in each other's arms, moving to the bed, checking in with one another now and then to make sure the other was okay. They laughed when things didn't go exactly as planned and begged each other not to stop when things did. Maybe everything in their relationship was impossible. Maybe this could never happen again. But for this one moment, they were one person, their souls connected.

*　　　*　　　*

It was so late into the night that one might consider it morning. Diego traversed the city, rooftop to rooftop, alleyway to alleyway. He stapled the posters on walls and telephone poles and billboards using an industrial sized staple-gun. With his massive wings and eye for marketing hot spots, he made quick work of the task. He had graduated a year ahead of Adam with a degree in Public Relations. Even before he finished his senior year, he was a hot commodity amongst clubs and bars in the city. He had a knack for getting people to go to something that was only mediocre. He knew how to make the unwanted and drab appear exciting and new.

As he walked down the street, only a few posters still in tow, he pulled out his phone, quickly checking missed texts and status updates of the day. It was someone's birthday, and another was feeling optimistic about a new house for rent. But the one that stood out was Adam's. It was in reference to Adam's depression at not being able to find a job. Diego smiled and shook his head. As soon as he was done with Vicky's request, he would drop by Adam's place, he thought, maybe bring some beer and cheer the guy up. He pulled out a poster and stuck it to a brick wall. *Chik!* The large staple drove it in.

SLAM! Suddenly he was pushed up against the wall by something grappling around his neck. He grasped at the bricks in front of him for a moment before getting his breath back. With a quick shove backwards, he transformed, pushing his captor back with the strength of a dragon. Turning his long neck, he saw a white and black creature, made of paper, crash into the wall behind him. He spun his body, glimpsing a small girl leaping over him in the corner of his eye. A fast-moving stream of red clocked him over the head and then tightened around his neck disorienting him. He was ripped from his feet and hurtled into a nearby wall.

With a loud crash, he slammed into the wall

sending bricks and dust falling from it. He slowly stood up on all fours, his body in pain from the blow. He turned his large head and saw his assailant for the first time. Miyako stood not far from him, her spray can in hand, taking long deep breaths. She was furious.

"*Go home, little girl*," snarled Diego, his dragon voice deep and foreboding.

"Who is she? Why did she kill Stephanie? And why is a wizard helping her?" spat Miyako. She had been on her way home when she had seen the wizard putting up posters. The words on the posters had shot a tingle up her spine, reminding her of the morbid scene of Stephanie's body. Miyako didn't believe in coincidences. She knew this wizard and Stephanie's murder were connected somehow. "Don't your kind have enough problems? I hear your school was burnt down by one of your own. Maybe you should be checking in on that instead of messing with us."

"*I have my own reason for helping the Queen.*" Diego raised his neck, attempting to look large and imposing to the girl. "*I don't need a child questioning me.*"

"You think I'm a child?" Miyako smiled. "Fine. Get ready to tell your friends how you got your ass handed to you by a kid." Miyako lunged forward at incredible speed, a whip of red shooting from the can in her hand. Diego took a quick breath and then shot a blazing stream of fire at her. Miyako dodged, jumping off a nearby wall flying over the flame. She got in one good hit as the red paint whipped Diego across the face, merely scratching his thick skin. He spun around, catching her with his tail, sending her skidding along the ground, back down the alleyway. He charged towards her, taking his opening. She desperately scrambled to get back up and stand her ground. He was almost on top of her when another paper creature, this one far larger than the first, dropped down in front of him, guarding Miyako.

"Where did you come from?" shouted Diego.

"Never leave home without backup," barked Miyako.

WHAM! The creature slugged Diego across the face with one of its large club-like hands.

Diego spun, slapping the creature into the wall with his tail, and then shot a ball of fire at it, incinerating the creature, burning a hole through the wall. Diego turned back to Miyako, but she was already gone.

He transformed back into a man and leaned on the wall, catching his breath. He walked back down the alley and picked up the remaining posters, now scattered along the ground. It was time to finish this errand and go see Adam. Maybe he'd be interested in a drink. The evening definitely warranted it.

*　　　*　　　*

The first light of morning peeked through the window as Adam collapsed next to Eva, sweat dripping down his chest and face. They both breathed heavily, as if they had just gone for an all-night jog.

"Wow," whispered Adam.

"Yeah," agreed Eva.

"So much for being *just friends*'" chuckled Adam, wiping the sweat from his forehead.

Eva felt a pang of guilt at the words. She was formulating a response in her head, something to let him down easily when a third voice entered the air.

"Adam, wake up," the voice called from the living room. The front door closed behind it.

"Oh God," sighed Adam, anxiety rising in his chest. His best friend Diego was about to walk in on him naked in bed with a girl. He quickly stood, moving to the bedroom door.

"I'm here to cheer you up, ya big Debbie Downer," Diego called from the living room. His voice was getting closer now.

"I'm a little busy actually," said Adam, tripping over the sheets on the floor and falling back into the bed.

Eva laughed, finding the whole situation fairly hilarious.

"Folding your shirts for the third time does not count as busy," laughed Diego, now just outside the door.

Diego pushed open the door and gasped. "What the—"

Eva pulled the blanket over her body, her eyes going wide with fear. "Diego!?" she screamed in surprise.

"Wait," said Adam, confused. "How do you know Diego?" he asked Eva.

"I've got a better question," snapped Diego, his face turning red. "What the hell are you doing in bed with my sister?"

Chapter Seven

Ten Years Ago

Even at a young age, Eva had known that she enjoyed anything that involved combining elements to create something new. She loved to cook, smelling the aromas of a fresh baked concoction, or tasting the sultry seasonings of a savory new dish. She loved the idea of making something from nothing. So often, it was a witch's duty to destroy and mutilate, but Eva found it quite rewarding to create. She figured this was something that made her quirky.

Even more than cooking up a leg of lamb, she enjoyed dabbling in the brewing of potions. It was an older art form that not many witches still held on to, but she was obsessed. There was something compelling about finding an old recipe, scouring the city for just the right ingredients and then, after a long search, finally heating up her cauldron and bringing a century-old mixture to life.

It was late afternoon in South Brooklyn. She was scouring dumpsters and rooftops for Wolfsbane, Hearth root and fingernails of one who "has left this plane, yet still bears life." Potion books were so vague and foreboding. That's what made it a challenge. She had taken the fingernail clippings off a drunk sleeping next to a dumpster. She assumed he wouldn't miss them. She was rounding a street corner, passing by a cute little cafe, when she noticed a large warehouse.

There is a look that buildings have when no one has entered them in a long time. They look ancient and grown over. They look as though time has forgotten them. To Eva, the building looked like a rich cornucopia of secrets and treasures, untouched by the other witches of the city. She looked down at her watch, realizing she didn't have much time to get home before dark. She weighed the pros and cons.

Eva was fifteen now and had only recently started going out on her own, but the overbearing attacks of the witches of the city meant that she only went out searching for ingredients during the day. To go out after dark would surely mean death. Once or twice she had come into contact with another witch and had just survived by the skin of her teeth. Since then, she had become much more cautious. She peered into her bag, noticing the lightness of it. She had barely found anything worth getting excited about today, and there was no way she would be trying out her new recipe with so few ingredients. She took a deep breath in and then out, centering herself. She headed for the warehouse.

Getting in was easy enough. She broke the lock on the gate with a simple wave of her hand, better than flying over which might warrant unwanted attention, and then did the same to the front doors. She pulled a small notebook from her bag and began to make a map of the building as she walked through it, so as not to get lost. That was the last thing she needed. The inside looked like something out of a zombie movie. There were discarded papers and boxes, upturned desks, and chairs on their sides. There were doors locked with large metal chains, and dead leaves had found their way into the building and now layered the floor. She took to her search, checking cabinets and desk drawers, uplifting floorboards, and rifling through closets. Nothing.

What seemed to be minutes rolling by, were actually hours. She lost track of everything, focused in on this massive place and the secrets it held. Surely there was something here that warranted finding, otherwise why would she have come at all? Her mother had always said that a witch should follow her instincts, that they were imbued with the ability to simply know when something magical was close by. Eva had known at the sight of this place that there was something important here. She just had to figure out what. Outside, the sun was setting, but Eva didn't care. She was obsessed now.

In the corner of her eye, something glimmered. She turned to see a door unlike any other in the building. Where the other doors were thin and wooden, this one was thick and metal, like a safe. She stared at it for a long moment, trying to figure out what could be behind it that would warrant so much more security than the rest of the entire warehouse.

BOOM! Something slammed into the other side of the door. Eva jumped in surprise, taking a step back.

"Hello?" She said it quietly, not entirely sure she really wanted someone to answer. There was a long pause.

BOOM! The door shook again. Eva took a step towards it, waving her hand through the air and pulling her staff from a cloud of purple smoke. She gripped it with two hands in front of her, preparing to guard against any unwanted attack that might come from the door. She edged closer. There was a long brass handle on the door that had rusted over with time. It looked like it had not been touched for a very long time. She reached for the handle.

BOOM! She pulled back only slightly this time, and then reached out again, gently touching the handle. It was ice cold, as if something frozen was waiting for her inside. She pulled on it, but it didn't budge. She bit her lip, thinking for a moment. She waved her staff at the door, whispering an incantation under her breath. Still nothing. She thought of another spell. Still nothing. Spell after spell, nothing seemed to affect the door. There was clearly something in there that was not meant to be let out or to be found and by the looks of it, something magical had contained it. Otherwise, at least one of her powers should have worked. The thought of something so dangerous excited her. She put a hand to the door, letting the cold run over her.

BOOM! Something slammed into the door, this time leaving a small indentation, as if a large fist was punching the other side. Eva pulled back.

"It's okay," she said, hoping that whatever was behind the door could understand her. "I'm not here to hurt you. I want to help." She looked down at the orb in her staff and noticed that the revolving purple spiral had lightened. "I'm going to try something," she yelled through the door. "Just stand back, will you?"

Eva held up her staff and touched the orb to the surface of the door. There was a sound, distant at first but it grew quickly. It was like the scream of a tea kettle as the water starts to boil. As it built, the orb began to glow with a brilliant purple light. The leaves and discarded papers on the floor began to swirl, as if a gentle breeze were pulling them towards Eva. The light intensified to such a brilliant glow that Eva was forced to look away.

KRACKOOM! The door exploded open, sending metal and debris everywhere, the paper and leaves shooting back towards the surrounding walls. Eva fell back, slamming onto the hard-tiled floor as an overwhelming cold poured from the room. She waved her hands vigorously, trying to dissipate the dust in the air. She coughed as she stood, looking through the haze. Cautiously, she stepped forward into the icy mist. She crossed the threshold, her staff out in front of her at the ready in case whatever was behind the door tried to get the jump on her. The orb glowed gently and as the dust settled, she gasped in horror.

Decayed bodies lay frozen by the stinging cold of the air of the room. The smell was pungent and overwhelming with toxicity and death. "Ugh!" screamed Eva, pinching her nose. She rifled through her bag and pulled out a small vial, drinking the contents in one gulp. She released her nose and took a deep breath. She smelled nothing. It was not a potion she used often but, in this case, she was glad to have it.

The bodies looked as though they had been left there for more than a few years. The flesh on all of them was torn off, and black streaks of dried blood lined the floor. The most curious thing though was what sat at the center of this long-ago massacre. A little pug dog, with little wings on its head, panted so heavily that it sounded like a small pig. Eva chuckled at the dog.

"Are you what's been making all this racket?" She knelt down, petting the dog. It pushed its head into her hand happily and then fell back on its rear end. It scratched at its neck, the chain jangling. It whined, as though the chain were an irritation. "And what do we have here?" She gently caressed the lock around his neck, looking it over for any sign of its true power. She turned it over, finding a small rune on the bottom. She knew the rune from her studies and there was no mistaking its meaning: *Demon.* "Hmm," she said, thinking aloud as she looked over the little pug. She pulled at the lock, trying to lift it from the dog's neck, but it wouldn't budge. She waved her staff at it, whispering a few choice incantations under her breath. Still nothing. The lock and chain seemed to be as much attached to the pug as its own tail.

"I imagine there's more to you than meets the eye, little guy." She scratched under his chin. He closed his eyes in approval. "I tell you what. You stick with me, help me out if I get in a pinch while I'm ingredient hunting, and I'll work on finding a way to get this thing off of you." She lifted the pug's head to look at her. "Deal?"

Suddenly the pug lunged at her, head butting her. She fell backwards and passed out only for a moment. When she awoke, she knew three things. There was a pug with egregiously bad breath licking her face. His name was Zelerot. And somehow, some way, they now belonged to each other.

Today

Zot sat, tongue hanging out, tail wagging, on top of a large metal trash can. Above him on a slat wall hung a poster that was so bright, so gaudy, he had actually forgotten what he was doing while he flew through the city and stopped just to stare at it. He had been staring now for exactly four hours. He was easily entertained. The poster depicted a blond woman who might have been very beautiful underneath the heaps and pounds of makeup that layered her face. She wore an outfit that was not enough to be called clothes, but just slightly more than what one might consider underwear. In her hands was a large electric guitar which she appeared to be strumming with fervor. Zot licked the air. *What did that stringed thing taste like?* he pondered.

His ears perked up. He was attuned to Eva's emotions. Her heartbeat and the slightest flux in her emotional state would be felt by him no matter how far she might be. He leaned forward, licking the poster goodbye, promising to return, with a longing look in his eyes, and then took off into the sky.

He zipped over the city, his little wings flapping

desperately to keep him airborne as he homed in for a trace of his master. She was getting closer and closer. Somewhere below, a cyclist received a drop of what many New Yorkers refer to as "mysterious city drip." This one just so happened to be a dribble of drool from Zot's over excited maw.

He made a straight shot for the room that housed Eva, completely forgetting the concept of windows just long enough to slam into one. *Squish!* His face flattened against Adam's bedroom window. His eyes smeared across the glass, catching a glimpse of what was going on inside.

*   *   *

Adam and Eva were standing. Adam's boxers hung loose around his waist as Eva pulled the comforter of the bed over her. Diego's face was still red with fury.

"Why didn't I tell you?" questioned Eva in disbelief. "I haven't even seen you, Diego. It's been four months since you took off. Again!"

"I am your brother!" he shouted back, losing the composure that was so key to Diego's demeanor. "I deserve to know if you're seeing a new guy. Especially if it's my best friend."

"I really think we all just need to calm down," said Adam, his hands out as if he were being held up by the police. "I think we should all just go grab some coffee and discuss this like adults."

"Not now, Adam!" screamed Eva and Diego in unison.

Thud! Thud! Thud! They all turned to see Zot repeatedly slamming his face into the window. He'd been trying to get in throughout the course of the yelling match, but now he discovered that he rather liked the way the window felt as it smushed his face.

"Dammit, Diego," grumbled Eva. "All this yelling, Zot thinks I'm in trouble." Eva shuffled to the window, opening it and allowing Zot to float in. He nuzzled her cheek and she kissed his head, smiling. "You came to protect me, didn't you? Yes, you did! Yes, you did!"

Adam eyed the odd dog and the lock around its neck. He bit his lip, looking over at Diego. "So," he began uneasily, "How have you been? Did you ever call that guy you met at the bar? John? Joe?"

"Too soon, man," snapped Diego.

"Right," said Adam, pulling back.

Eva turned back to them as Zot collapsed on the bed, rolling around in it. "I think you should leave," she said, her eyes narrowing on Diego. "Now."

"Whatever," he snapped back.

Diego turned to go but stopped. "Oh yeah, almost forgot." He reached into his pack, pulling out one last poster. "I'm doing PR for a show. Wasn't gonna invite you but now I think it might do you some good." He threw the poster on the bed, giving Eva a cold stare. "I hear she's something of a showstopper." With that, he stormed out of the apartment, slamming the door behind him.

For a long moment, Eva and Adam sat in uncomfortable silence.

"I did not see that coming," mumbled Adam, not sure what the proper reaction was. Who should he be mad at? Eva, for failing to inform him of her brother? Had he ever even asked? Was it something that just never came up in conversation? Clearly, he should be mad at Diego for failing to inform him during one of their many drunken nights. Then again, is there ever a good time to tell someone your sister is a witch? "I don't think you mentioned a brother."

"We're not very close," grumbled Eva.

"Wait." A thought occurred to Adam. A thought he was afraid to entertain, even though there was no way of avoiding it. "If you're a witch—"

"He's a wizard," she said, turning to Adam with a questioning look. "Guessing you two aren't that close either."

"He's my best friend," said Adam, feeling more and more ignorant by the second. "I've known him for years."

"The secrets we keep, huh?" Eva sighed a laugh.

"Don't worry, I've known him my whole life. He still manages to exceed my expectations for what an ass he can be." Eva threw Zot up into the air, his little wings kicking into action as he floated out of the room into the rest of the apartment. "Go play," she said softly to the dog.

"I'm not really allowed to have dogs in the apartment," said Adam uneasily.

"Not a problem."

"It's not?"

"He's not a dog." Eva winked at Adam whose face filled with concern. She got back into bed and padded her way across it, kissing him softly on the lips. "Now, where were we?"

Adam felt apprehensive. The morning had proved more informative than he had expected. Shouldn't one take the time to take in all of this? Was it inappropriate to jump right back into bed after such an earth-shattering revelation? Was he really going to become one of those people who dealt with his feelings through sex?

"Really?" he questioned her. "Now? Even after your brother barged in like that?"

"Are you saying you don't want to?" She peered at him, batting her eyelashes in a faux-pouty fashion. How was a man supposed to say no to that?

"Oh, I want to," he blurted out. "I really, really want

115

to." He kissed her, pulling her close to him, and then everything faded into the background as the covers were pulled over them.

* * *

Diego strutted, angrily through the city streets, bumping into more than a few passersby who refused to look up from their cell phones as they hurried to work. "Watch where you're going!" one man shouted. "What's wrong with you?!" another woman screamed. He got to a street corner crowded with tourists taking photos of an empty green wall. *A green wall! Really? That's all it was!* He shoved the whole group out into the street and one of them was nearly hit by a city bus.

It wasn't until he reached his destination that he actually realized where he'd been going the whole time. The Veranda was one of those old theaters which have been around so long that they have become a part of history. If a band was notable, it had probably played there at some point early on in its existence when most people still had not heard of them. It had become a breeding place for the new and different, the eclectic and the untested. For this reason, it seemed odd that Vicky would choose such a place for her concert. Her music was neither new nor different. It was basically the culmination of every pop song, bad 90's commercial jingle and cell phone ringtone brutally mashed together and then played for an audience. Therein lay the secret to her success. It was so bad, so completely unlistenable that you couldn't help but try it out, and once you heard her sing, you were hooked forever. This was the nature of her guitar-based spell casting. She could kill you quickly or take her time, but you would love her regardless.

As Diego entered the auditorium, Vicky was seated in a large red folding chair, shouting orders at several men, who were quickly building the stage of her show. He couldn't help but notice that all the men were shirtless with hulking muscles and drenched in sweat. It looked like the type of ad that parents would be squeamish about their daughters seeing as they passed it in a mall.

"Not there, you imbecile!" she yelled impatiently. "Over there!" She pointed to the opposite side of the stage as two of the men hefted up a large wooden slab and hauled it in the opposite direction they'd just come from. Diego noticed little purple lines crawling across their faces, gently pulsating so that if you weren't looking for them, you wouldn't even notice they were there.

"We need to talk," said Diego, sternly approaching her.

Vicky's face brightened. "Hello darling," she batted her eyelashes at him. "Take a seat. Enjoy the pre-show, as I like to call it," she chuckled.

"Why does your crew look like a pack of male strippers? asked Diego. "Not that I mind."

"Setting up a show can be so drab and stressful. I like to spice things up." She winked at him. "And you can't deny the view."

"You really can't," mused Diego, forgetting his anger for just a moment. He shook his head to refocus. "But that's not why I'm here."

"Tell me."

"I know I told you I didn't need anything in return for helping you." He took a deep breath. "But circumstances have changed."

Vicky smiled, thinking just how adorable it was that Diego thought he had a choice in the matter of helping her. "I think I know what you're going to ask, but the answer is 'no' darling. You wouldn't want my kidneys anyway. Their chock full of smoke and liquor, and a whole list of things I'd rather not mention." Vicky grimaced at the thought.

"What? No." Diego quickly wiped the look of disgust from his face. "My sister has started seeing this guy."

"Your sister, the witch?" Diego could see a hunger in her eyes.

"She's off limits." Diego snapped.

"Yes yes, I know," she said, rolling her eyes. It was

clearly an inconvenience to her that she was not allowed to murder Eva Grey.

"I need her to 'unsee' him," Diego's voice was stern.

"Hmm," pondered Vicky. "You're going to have to work extra hard for a favor like that."

"Done." Diego felt the slightest warmth on his face, but it vanished as quickly as it came.

"Such a good boy." She pulled her cell phone from her pocket. "I'm texting you a list of names. See to it that our paths cross. I'm gonna need all the strength I can get for this show. It'll be my biggest yet."

"Yes ma'am."

"But first, why not take a couple of these fine young men in back for a little break," Vicky waved at the stage where the men were hard at work. "All work and no play, you know."

"Maybe next time," sighed Diego. "I hate to mix business and pleasure."

"Oh darling, when will you learn," she smirked. "This business *is* pleasure."

*　　　*　　　*

A crumpled-up newspaper blew by Jasmine as she sat on the hard pavement, huddled up against an abandoned store front. A blanket lay on top of her knees to help keep out the cold, but it wasn't nearly as effective as she had hoped. She shivered as she folded another crane, her shaking fingers pinching over the creases one at a time, perfecting it.

Clink! A man dropped a coin into Jasmine's bag as he passed by. It was the first time she really felt the direness of her situation. She had fallen so far that people were now taking pity on her in the form of charity. It had been a long time since she'd lived in a traditional home, but at least with Miyako, they'd had a roof over their heads to keep out the elements. Now, they didn't even have that.

Cough! She spit a hunk of phlegm to the ground as another woman dropped a dollar in her bag. It didn't matter what others thought. What mattered were the cranes. She went back to folding.

Miyako appeared from across the street. She approached quickly, her hood over her head. She seemed paranoid, looking around as if to make sure she had not been followed. She pulled a bedraggled sandwich from her pocket, pushing in from the sides to make it look less flat. It didn't help the sandwich's shape, but as far as Jasmine was concerned, it was the thought that counted. Miyako had been trying to shield her from their situation in every small, innocuous way she could think of.

"Hey," said Miyako, kneeling down next to Jasmine. "I got dinner."

"Bought it, or stole it?" asked Jasmine, already knowing the answer.

"Does it matter?" Miyako shot her a harsh look.

"We aren't thieves," said Jasmine. *Cough cough cough!* She covered her mouth in vain, hoping it might lessen the severity of the disease.

"Time to reassess your morals," said Miyako, ripping off half of the sandwich and handing it to Jasmine.

It had been some time since they had eaten and could be even longer before they did again. They both took a big bite, trying to relish every taste as it hit their taste buds. It was a ham and turkey sandwich with little bits of lettuce and olives and a light vinaigrette on top. The whole thing was folded into a white hero. Nothing special, but they enjoyed it all the same.

Miyako glanced over at the large bag filled with cranes, and then at the still unfolded papers, unfinished in Jasmine's lap. "How many?" she asked, before taking another bite of the sandwich.

"This is nine hundred and two," said Jasmine, brushing the crumbs of the sandwich off of her blanket.

"You'll get there," said Miyako. She smiled, placing a hand on Jasmine's cheek. Jasmine jumped at the touch. She often showed affection to Miyako, but these days it was rare that it was reciprocated.

"I hope so," said Jasmine, softly. She smiled.

"You two ladies looking for a good time?" A man appeared, hovering over them. He wore a suit, the shirt untucked and the tie pulled loose. He had probably gone out after work and had one too many drinks.

Jasmine and Miyako looked up at him with disdain. "Get lost, loser," said Miyako, her eyes narrowing in on him. Jasmine turned to her, seeing a darkness build inside her that she'd only seen in the worst of circumstances.

"Awe, come on, might be some dinner in it for you." The man grabbed his crotch and winked at them. "I'd rather have the dark one, but little Miss Fortune Cookie's hands will be nice everywhere else."

"Miyako, no!" screamed Jasmine, but it was too late.

Miyako's spray paint can was pointed directly at the man's pelvis and before Jasmine could stop her, a beam of red paint shot up and through the man, exploding his groin and any hope he had of ever having a 'good time' again out his back.

"GAH!" Screamed the man, grabbing at parts that no longer belonged to him and falling to the ground in pain. "You bitch!"

"Jasmine, get your things, we're leaving," said Miyako, standing over the man as he flailed on the ground, still trying to grab for a body-part that was halfway across Washington Square Park by now.

"Don't kill him!" screamed Jasmine, hastily packing all of her things into a large duffel bag.

Miyako leaned over the man, cocking her head to the side as she looked at him. "What the hell are you?" the man cried.

"I'm the girl you're gonna think about every time you see a woman you want to have sex with," whispered Miyako to the man. Tears now flowed freely down his face. "You'll want them. And then you'll think of me, the girl who neutered you so that no woman would ever have to feel threatened by your dick ever again." Miyako leaned down so that she was speaking into the man's ear. "Don't wave a wand at a witch. Chances are, hers is bigger."

Miyako stood and turned back to Jasmine, who was still reeling. Around them, people were starting to point and stare, some screaming, others on their phones, most likely calling the police. She grabbed Jasmine's hand and they took off into the night, disappearing before the other people on the street could stop them.

Chapter Eight

The first week of any relationship is almost always the best week of the relationship. Eva and Adam saw each other every day, going to movies and dinner, dancing and theater. Their lives melded together almost seamlessly. Since Eva's primary source of income was trading potions for money, a profession she did from home, she was always free. And given Adam's current state of unemployment, it was much easier to say 'yes' to seeing her than to focus on his lack of a job.

The sun began to set as they lounged on the long benches of a small amphitheater along the High Line path. The High Line was an abandoned train track lofting over the streets of the Lower West Side which had been co-opted into an artistic urban park, elevated from 14th street up to 33rd. One could walk blissfully along it, taking in the flowers and urban architecture while chatting and grabbing some gelato.

They picked up a couple of small boxes of sushi and sat with chopsticks in hand, eating leisurely through their spicy tuna and mackerel. Time seemed to fly when they were together. There were never enough hours in the day and saying goodbye was always hard which was why they usually skipped that part and just ended up staying at Adam's place every night.

"Hanging out with you has been really fun," said Adam, swallowing down another piece of fish. "But I really need to start looking for a job. You won't want to stay with me if I'm homeless."

"I always forget normal people have to work day in and day out," said Eva, pondering the idea of it. "I don't think I'd handle it very well. Then again, it would be nice to not have to worry about being murdered every day."

Adam chuckled. "I'm glad you think normal people don't worry about that."

"What does Adam worry about? I wonder," she said, squinting her eyes at him and smiling.

"Mostly the future."

"Oh?"

"I worry about finding a job, falling in love, getting married, kids, what schools they'll go to. It's like a perpetual stream in my head of worry and doubt, and when I reach the end, it starts all over again." Adam looked up at her and gave a weak smile. "Sorry."

"It's okay," said Eva, thinking on what he had said.

"I don't really think about any of those things."

"How do you avoid it?" Adam grabbed another piece of sushi from the plate and shoved it into his mouth.

"I've got plenty to worry about in the here and now," said Eva casually. "Not really time for anything else."

Adam looked down, trying to force himself not to read too much into her words.

"My mother thought about the future a lot. She was always concerned about where Diego and I would end up." Eva sighed. "And look where that got her. Attacked in her own home while she was filling out school paperwork for Diego."

"That's how she died?" asked Adam.

"No," said Eva. She looked out over the other people walking along the path around them. "I killed her."

Adam blinked a few times, the sushi on his chopsticks falling back to where he'd grabbed it. "Excuse me, what?"

Eva looked at him, shaking her head. "I'd rather not talk about it."

"Oh," he said, hurt. "O-okay." For the remainder of the meal, they ate in silence.

*   *   *

The music throbbed to a fast beat as Diego entered the dance club. Laser lights flooded the room and a scent fueled by sweat and testosterone filled his nose as he breathed in. All around him, men in different degrees of undress jumped up and down to the song, some dancing by themselves, while others rode up on a partner, or sometimes two. There was a stench of cigarette smoke and liquor in the air that coalesced into something that he found quite soothing.

It had been a rough week. Discovering his sister was dating his best friend had started it, but the killing spree with Vicky that ensued had really driven home the point that his life was going in a terrifying new direction. He had never been big on cold-blooded murder like many wizards of the world were. Yet doing it for Vicky sent an odd rush through him.

Is this really me? But the thought vanished from his mind just as it came. He centered himself. He had come here to do a job. Though, Vicky had always told him that work was best when mixed with play. He wandered up to the bar where a tightly-muscled man nodded to him.

"What you havin', pretty eyes?" Diego smiled at the compliment. The bartenders here knew how to get the tips.

"Jack and coke," said Diego, leaning against the bar. From his pocket, he felt a vibration. He pulled his phone out to see that Adam was calling him. He scoffed and hit the 'ignore' button, replacing the phone into his pocket. He wasn't ready to deal with that mess just yet.

Next to him sat a girl with black hair, tinted with green at the bangs. She was on the heftier side and had pale skin. She laughed at two other men who were recounting their story of a weekend away at Fire Island, a gay friendly vacation spot known for its huge parties. The two men practically had heart attacks as the new Lady Gaga took over the room. They squealed and took off into the crowd to dance, leaving the girl drinking alone.

"Gay guys really are the worst," said Diego. The girl looked up at him, a confused expression on her face.

"Why do you say that?" Her voice had a raspy quality to it.

"We bring you out here to our club, tell you our boring-ass stories and then the second Lady Gaga comes on we vanish." The bartender handed Diego his drink. Diego slipped a ten onto the counter and took a sip. The alcohol flushed over his tongue, shocking his mouth to life. "Fucking assholes."

"A girl's gotta know what she signed up for when she comes to a place like this." She turned her body to Diego now, smiling at him.

"And what did you sign up for, exactly?"

"A little music. A little fun." She pushed her hair

out of her eyes. Was she flirting with him? Seriously? Diego had never quite understood behavior like this. Maybe it would make sense if she thought he was straight. But here? Now? You'd be crazy to draw that conclusion.

Not that it mattered. This wasn't personal. This was business. He took the rest of his drink in one swallow. "So, let's have some fun!"

*   *   *

Night had settled in. Miyako walked through the Union Square farmer's market with her hoodie up and her eyes peeled. There was a time in her life when living on the street and stealing food would have seemed impossible, like something out of a storybook where a girl eventually becomes a princess after a life of hardship. Her mother once read her books like this before bed, and it all seemed so fantastical. Yet here she was, wandering the street, her stomach rumbling with no end in sight. She wouldn't become a princess at the end of this. In fact, she knew that at this rate she was going to starve until another witch found her and finished the job. The only thing that kept her going was keeping Jasmine alive long enough for her to finish the crane spell.

It was getting near closing time for the market.

Usually she came earlier, when the stalls were crowded with shoppers. The farmers, who were much better at growing fresh fruits and vegetables, or baking bread, or culling livestock, then they were at manning a cash register, might miss her taking a loaf here and an apple there.   Unfortunately, Jasmine had had a coughing attack even worse than usual, and Miyako had refused to leave her side until it had subsided. Now she was out with the stragglers of the night, people who were picking up groceries they'd forgotten earlier, or just getting off of work and heading home. At this time, the stall owners were tired from the day, but they were also less distracted by the hordes of people asking for different produce.

She wandered close to a booth operated by a larger woman. She was starting to pack up her jams and jellies of different sorts as an elderly couple peered over their glasses to inspect the merchandise. Miyako evaluated the booth. The woman would be easy to get one over on, but was a jam or a jelly really worth putting this woman out? A woman who probably slaved over the concoctions all week and then had hefted them here from the Bronx. Was it worth making her day that much harder? Miyako decided not and moved on.

A man at the next booth was serving bread over a large glass case. A few men and women still stood at his booth picking over the last of his selection. Miyako watched as a young pregnant woman handed the man a ten. The man turned for a quick moment and then turned back to hand her the change, and by Miyako's count, shorted the girl by a dollar and fifty cents. She'd found a target deserving of her crime.

She approached slowly, letting her hood creep over her face so that her eyes were darkened by its shadow. A young couple wandered in front of the stall, giggling drunkenly as they pointed at the different loafs, trying to decide which one looked more appetizing. Miyako snuck in behind them. In one fluid motion, she reached out and grabbed a loaf of pumpernickel, sheathing it in her sweater. She continued walking, as if nothing had happened. She did not look up or make eye contact with anyone for fear of giving herself away. Stealing was something new to her and she had not yet mastered the art of relaxing her face so as to not appear guilty.

"Stop her!" came a cry from behind her. "She's a thief!" Miyako's eyes went wide, transfixed with fear. She turned to see two police officers from down the square, their conversation cut short by the call of the man, who was pointing directly at her. "Don't just stand there! Do something!" The officers took off at a run.

Miyako lunged forward, heading for a group of hippie drummers on the opposite corner of the street. She plunged through them, knocking over more than a few, and then headed into the middle of University

Street. She turned to see the officers still tight on her tail. A honk came from just ahead of her. She turned again, a small car baring down on her. She jumped, stepping up and over the car and then rolling back to her feet on to the street behind it.

She had to get out of there and fast. She considered pulling out her spray can and taking off with her broom, but the officers were too focused on her. They'd notice her taking off into the sky even if their brains wouldn't allow them to see her broom. Then it would end up on the news, painting a target on her as someone foolish and careless for all the other witches in the city to see. Not to mention the psychotic one who had murdered Stephanie.

She ran into an alleyway off the street, pulling her spray can from her pocket and shooting paint crudely onto the wall. She then yanked the can back, exploding the bricks into the alley and creating a heap of dust and rubble at its entrance. It would slow them down, but only for an instant.

Luckily, an instant was all she needed. She jumped up onto a dumpster and then shot another line of red paint up. It attached itself to the roof of the building like a grappling hook and then pulled her upwards. She soared past the roof and, in mid-air, drew the outline of her broom underneath her. She grabbed the handle as it materialized and with a loud crack and burst of fire from the tail end, she took off, leaving the police digging through bricks exclaiming in disbelief: "She's just a little girl!"

*   *   *

Sweat poured down Diego's face and chest, his shirt long lost in the crowd as he continued to dance with the girl, who had introduced herself as Lexie Gibbs. The men worshiped her and danced with her as if she were just another one of the boys. At least until they found another man to grind on. Lexie soaked in the attention. She didn't care who was dancing with her as long as someone was. Diego stayed by her side the whole night, even doing a shot from her cleavage, but time was starting to run short and he was starting to tire of the farce he was putting on. He could feel an unease rising in his stomach. Maybe it was the alcohol. Could it be that he actually felt bad for what was about to happen? Or did he just need to throw up? He couldn't tell.

"I'll be right back," he yelled in her ear over the thumping of the music. "Don't get lost!"

"Honey, I've *been* lost!" she yelled back, laughing drunkenly into his face.

Diego grinned and then pushed through the horde of men, heading towards the bathroom. He needed to relax. He could feel every muscle in his body tightening at the thought of what was about to happen to that girl.

The bathroom was a dark affair. The rooms were barely lit with a midnight blue glow that seemed to radiate off the gleaming skin of the men standing against the wall. Some kissed passionately, while others had their mouths elsewhere. Diego's eyes traced the outline of the room, trying to adjust to the new lighting. A man in the corner with blond hair and blue eyes grinned at Diego, making fierce eye contact.

Diego pushed through the room to reach the man in the corner. They got close, not even speaking. Diego could smell the alcohol permeating off of the boy's breath. Sweat rolled down the boy's face and bare chest. His eyes were slightly bloodshot, and it was clear that alcohol was not the only thing in his system. The boy ran a hand down Diego's bare chest. Diego stopped him with his hand, glaring into the boy's eyes with a look that spoke a firm 'No.' The boy looked back at him with a pleading look.

Diego didn't have time for semantics. This was not a time for foreplay or the feigned belief that this was anything more than sex in a bathroom. Diego gently grabbed the boy's blond hair and shoved him downwards.

As the boy unzipped Diego's jeans, Diego saw himself in the mirror. He had lost weight in the past couple of weeks. How had that happened so fast? It was the first time he'd really looked at himself recently. As Diego tried to relax, he couldn't help but notice what looked like purple veins sneaking along his cheeks but at second glance they'd disappeared, as if a trick of the light. Diego closed his eyes and forgot about what he thought he had seen. In the other room, The Cure's 'Love Song' started playing.

*   *   *

Lexie bobbed her head and kicked her feet to the song. She had always loved The Cure, and 80's new wave in general. It was always a treat when one of these clubs decided to get off of its Top 50 high horse and play something she could really dance to. She often came out to the gay clubs on the weekends and allowed men to rub up against her in order to get a hint of what being with a man was like without actually having to engage in it. As a witch, she could not afford the risks that came with male companionship. This had been her personal compromise.

Two long delicate combs sat atop her head with their sharp teeth holding up her wild black and green hair. They'd been poking her all night, like nagging children. She pulled them from atop her head, allowing her hair to fall all around her face, giving her a new dangerous look. All the men around her cooed and screamed. She whipped it around to give them something to talk about. She placed the combs in her pocket.

She danced and danced, allowing the music to take her to a time long past. A time when she was younger, and things seemed simpler, even though in truth, things were never really simple for a witch. She felt alive, like electricity was being pumped through her veins.

"Having fun?" Diego had reappeared from behind her. His face was flushed with a red glow.

"Yeah, and clearly so are you," she winked at him.

"Heh," Diego grinned. "Wanna run out and grab a smoke?"

"Sure." Diego grabbed her hand and headed for the door.

As they walked out into the alley behind the club, designated for those who wished to take a smoke break, she could feel the cold night air wash over her. The breeze was a stark contrast to the heat-induced sweat of the club's interior. Diego quickly re-put on his shirt, which he'd recovered from the club's floor, buttoning it and pulling down his cuffs to shield his arms from the chill.

"Milady." Diego offered a cigarette to her. She placed her lips on it and pulled it from his hand. Suddenly, he snapped his fingers and the cigarette lit at the end.

Lexie took a long drag and then pulled the cig from her mouth, gingerly. "I knew there was something special about you. I could feel it."

"I don't know if I'd go around telling wizards they're special," came a soft voice from behind her. "They'll start to get a big head. And let's face it honey, these boys are already getting enough head."

Lexie whirled around, her heart skipping a beat. Standing behind her, in boots, shorts, a tied-up shirt and cowboy hat like it wasn't the slightest bit cold, was Vicky. An overly bright electric guitar was strapped to her back. She stared at Lexie, a frigid look in her eyes.

"Oh shit," whispered Lexie under her breath.

"Sorry, Lex," said Diego behind her, not sounding very sorry.

She whirled around and slapped Diego across the face. "Fuck you!" In one quick movement, she pulled the combs from her hair and shoved them towards Diego. A blast of blue electricity sent Diego flying backwards, his body slamming into a set of metal trash cans at the end of the alley.

Lexie turned back to Vicky, who was now holding her guitar low at her waist and strumming a single note. *Doom! Doom! Doom!*

"You killed Stephanie, didn't you?" accused Lexie.

"Someone had to," snapped Vicky. "You witches aren't even trying here. Partying with boys, hunting in

137

the woods. We should be ruling this world, not hiding in it. We don't need to live their life. They need to live *ours."*

A long purple tendril with an arrow at the tip shot out at Lexie. She swung one of the combs so that a blast of electricity hit the tendril, knocking it away. "The humans are peaceful. We have no need to rule over them anymore. Don't you see, Queen Victoria? There can be peace!"

Lexie now had one comb in each hand and held them like claws. "So, put down your weapons," cackled Vicky. "Let's see where peace gets you."

Another set of purple tendrils shot at Lexie. She lunged into the air spinning so that she hit all of them with the electrical blasts of her combs. She moved like a ninja, flexible and fast. She began to run towards Vicky, deflecting blast after blast from the guitar. "It doesn't have to be this way!" she screamed. "I don't want to kill you, but I also didn't swear off killing like Stephanie. If it's you or me, I choose me."

"Do it then!" screamed Vicky, her hat falling to the ground below as she pulled her fingers maniacally over the strings of the guitar. "Kill me and prove your worth, Lexington Gibbs, Witch of the Second Order. You were born a witch, now act like one!"

Lexie was almost to her now. She lunged into the air, her combs over her head, ready to make the final blow. Suddenly her whole body was grabbed from the air by the tight grip of black claws, digging into her flesh. "Gah!" She screamed out as the dragon pulled her away from Vicky, throwing her to the pavement so hard her body rolled along the ground before skidding to a stop. She could feel blood pouring from her side.

In front of her, she could see Diego transform back to a human as he came to stand next to Vicky, who smiled proudly. "Finish her," he said coldly.

"Yes, my pet," said Vicky. "I shall."

"Someone is going to end you, Vicky." Blood trickled from Lexie's mouth as she spoke. "There are witches stronger than me in this city. Some even stronger than Stephanie. They just don't know it yet. But the second they do, you are so finished."

"Even if there is a witch like that," said Vicky, "It'll be too late. I'm going to kill all of you in this pitiful city. I'll be stronger than any witch before me. If this witch you speak of is out there, she'll be dead in no time." Vicky smiled, darkness rolling in her pupils as her fingers strummed along the guitar. "Just like you." *Doom!*

Long purple tendrils stabbed into Lexie's hands and legs, holding her in place. The last pierced her chest, sending blood across the alleyway. Lexington Gibbs was dead.

Chapter Nine

In the past few weeks, Jasmine and Miyako had slowly been working their way uptown. From their little hovel in the Financial District, they had moved to Soho, then up to Union Square, then on to Bryant Park. Now they had made it far enough North that they were taking refuge under a network of bridges and rock structures, in the heart of Central Park. It was more difficult than the other areas they had stayed. Guards and police officers made it impossible to stay in one place more than a couple of nights in a row. Yet somehow the fact that they were constantly on the move made them both feel a bit safer, even if they were staying within the confines of the park. It also felt like a calm oasis, safe from the terrors of the outside.

By day, Miyako would head south to Hell's Kitchen

in order to loot through dumpsters, or to grab food from unsuspecting tourists who were busy trying to both eat their food and decipher a map at the same time. She would sneak by and snag their meal from their hands, then continue walking as if nothing had happened. By the time they realized their lunch was missing, she was down to the next city block.

Meanwhile, Jasmine took to short walks within the park and folded her cranes out in the light of day. She would walk up to the historic castle and watch people look on in wonder. Sometimes she would go out to the lake and envy the happy couples on the swan boats. She'd close her eyes and dream of her and Miyako in one of these boats. In one fantasy, they would be laughing and then she would kick up water onto Miyako's face. Miyako would appear grouchy at first, until she finally splashed water back at Jasmine, and the water war would continue as they laughed on and on.

At the end of their day, Jasmine would walk Miyako home, somewhere on the Upper East Side, and she would kiss her before Miyako said goodnight. It wasn't real, and it never would be, but Jasmine had found that her imagination had been quite soothing in these times of distress.

Word on the street was that several more notable witches had fallen to a rogue witch. Some spoke of a deep rumbling sound that accompanied her presence, others had even mentioned the sound of a guitar. The reports were scattered and infrequent, and most people who spread these stories ended up dead within a few days, deterring others from talking.

Today, Jasmine had found a spot atop a long set of stairs with a little cement seat and a large cement table. She sat down and pulled a little piece of paper from her bag, ready to make her first crane of the day. She worried that she was drawing too much attention to herself. Several people who frequented the park had started referring to her as the 'crane girl.' Even some of the guards recognized her now and would wave to her. The thought had occurred to her that this was surely going to paint a target on her, but she hoped that no one would correlate the folding of paper cranes with sorcery.

She folded the paper into a small square. A few tables over, an elderly couple was looking on, eagerly trying to see what she was making. Jasmine didn't mind. She had become very accustomed to onlookers while living in the park. Everyone wanted to know what you were up to, and if it was something worth watching. Everything was a potential show, and everyone was looking for that next slice of New York entertainment. She folded the paper over again, running her thumb along the creases in order to make them harsher.

A young girl walked up to the table and peaked her eyes over the edge at what Jasmine was up to.

"What are you doing?" the little girl asked. She had curly brown hair and glasses that were much too large for her face. Jasmine had always been amused at how forward and unafraid children were in the face of something new and different before they learned to be scared of everything.

"Leave her alone, Gilly," came the call of her father, a taller Italian man with thick, hairy arms and a gruff beard. His wife, a stately woman with firm shoulders and a slack jaw, looked on slightly concerned with what her daughter might have gotten herself into now.

"It's okay," said Jasmine, smiling at the couple. Their gaze softened. Jasmine looked back to the young girl. "I'm making something magical."

"What kind of something?" asked the girl.

Jasmine got close to the girl now, as if she was sharing a secret with her. "The kind that makes people live longer. Very dangerous." Jasmine grinned sideways at the girl. "Wanna see?"

The little girl thought about it for a moment and then grinned from ear to ear, nodding her head in excitement.

Jasmine began to fold the crane again, asking Gilly to hold the paper in certain places for her and showing her how to firm up the creases. They folded out the wings together and Jasmine allowed Gilly to shape the beak. When it was finally done, Gilly looked on in amazement.

"Wow," she said, turning the crane over in her hands, her head trying to piece together how a sheet of paper had become this delicate thing. Her parents now stood over her, looking down with humbled smiles on their faces. "It's so pretty." She turned to her parents. "Mommy, Daddy, look!"

"It's very nice," said her father, patting her on the head. He looked up at Jasmine. "How much?"

Jasmine started in surprise. "What? No, no. There's no charge."

"Please, allow me to pay you for this." The man pulled a black leather wallet from his pocket.

Jasmine waved a hand through the air. "Please, sir," she said, stopping his hand with her own as he reached into the wallet. "No charge." She looked into his eyes. "It's only paper." She stood and threw her bag over her shoulder. She looked one last time at the little girl and winked at her, then walked away just as the sun was beginning to set over the park. The couple headed in the other direction, Gilly in tow. She held the little crane as if it were the most important thing in the universe.

*   *   *

Cheers of excitement went up as a large white screen was hoisted up at the front of the field. The sun had finally set low enough that the movie could be projected onto the screen. Now all those who had come out on this breezy night to the South Street Seaport with their blankets and snacks could watch and enjoy the show. Free movies in the park had become a staple form of entertainment in New York City and were a regular event at several parks across the island. Adam had taken advantage of the beautiful weather to take Eva out for a unique outdoor date. After all, watching a movie under the stars, while relaxing with a packed picnic screamed perfect date material, and Adam was all about that. Especially after their haunting conversation on their last date, he thought it best that this time involve less talking.

Adam always felt uneasy when first getting to know a girl, like he was holding his breath. He chose each word carefully and timed each joke so that there was never an awkward silence. But now he felt he could let that breath out a little bit. They had started to learn the small quirks about each other that people usually kept to themselves. He told her how he always washed his hands twice, and she shared with him that she never put her keys down in the same place and thus spent hours looking for them every morning. Through their flaws, they were seeing each other for who they really were and to Adam's surprise, Eva's flaws made him like her even more.

The movie began, and he reached for her hand,

something which had started this past week. It rested so easily in his palm, as if their hands were created as a pair. The first time he had done it, she had jumped as if it was taboo, but now she gave it to him without any fuss. She leaned her head on his shoulder comfortably as the movie played, and he could feel her body relaxing into him. It was strange for Adam as someone always so emotionally and mentally wrought with anxiety, to be seen by someone else as a source of support, even tranquility. The fact that Eva saw him this way made him able to believe he could be that person.

The movie was a comedy about two people with a similar mental disorder who drive each other crazy, until at long last they have no choice but to admit their love to each other. It had received rave reviews when it was first released, but Adam had failed to see it when it was still in theaters. Before now, he wasn't much for going to the movies, as it had usually meant going alone. Now, he was finally able to enjoy them.

He expected this was how his love story with Eva would play out. In fact, he likened his love for Eva to the love stories he saw in movies. He expected they'd go back and forth on the issue until finally she just had to admit that she loved him. Sure, she'd lose her powers, whatever that meant. But they'd be together and have one, maybe two kids, and live happily ever after, despite him being neurotic and her being a witch. It was just the way things were supposed to be.

After the movie, Eva folded up the blanket and placed it in a little satchel, while Adam packed away any scraps of trash from the picnic. Like the rest of the people who had come out for the film, they made their way off the grassy hillside. They decided to walk along the boardwalk, looking out at Jersey City across from them. Its view was less impressive than New York's but still beautiful all the same. Little skippers and a large cruise ship wafted by on the water, going much faster in reality than they appeared to be in the distance. Adam once again grabbed Eva's hand as they walked. But now that they were out on their own, away from the crowd, she seemed more hesitant. She pulled away.

"Can I show you something?" Eva looked at Adam nervously.

"Of course," Adam said, unsure of what to expect.

She waved a hand through the air, a familiar cloud of smoke forming, intertwining amidst her fingers. It shifted and bent becoming a ghost of her staff, until it solidified into hard birchwood. "Look." She pushed the staff out at him.

"I've seen it," said Adam. "Remember? The first night we met."

"I know you saw it then, but now I'm asking you to look." She gazed at him, reassuringly. "Really look." She placed the staff into his hands.

147

It was heavier than he imagined it would be. The wood was soft, not a single splinter or knot protruding out. He ran his hand along its smooth curves. Eva was watching him, encouraging him with her eyes. He traced the lines in the wood up to the top of the staff, where the wood split into three and wrapped itself around the purple orb. He stared into the orb, noticing for the first time the slow-moving mist that undulated within. It looked like a micro version of a great storm and if you watched long enough, you could see a little flash, like lightning.

"Every witch has one," said Eva.

"A staff?" Adam's eyes remained transfixed on the orb.

"A magical item. Our powers are useless without it. In the olden days they were known as runes or artifacts." She rolled her eyes as if it were something everyone knew. "Every witch chooses her item, but if you ask me, it chooses us. And sure, there are fads. For a while, everyone just wanted to use wands, and then it was staves, and then crystal balls. But just like everything else, they come and go."

"So why a staff?" posed Adam. "If you see it as just a 'fad.'

"A staff is like the Frank Sinatra of magical items," she said, as if it were obvious. "A classic is timeless." She chuckled to herself. "Can you imagine choosing a cell phone as your item? Those girls are going to regret that like a bad tattoo someday." She nudged him with her elbow. "Not like we can go to the store and get an upgrade."

Adam laughed, not fully understanding the joke. He looked back to the orb and for a split second he thought he saw something in the purple smoke. It was so faint and quick, but he knew exactly what he'd seen and as soon as it computed in his brain, it vanished back into the orb. He looked up at Eva, confused.

Eva grinned at him and grabbed the staff. It disappeared in a puff of smoke. She took his hand gently. He could tell she was nervous, that being affectionate still did not come naturally to her, but he had to at least give it to her for trying. "Look, about the other night..."

"Oh," remarked Adam, trying to act as if he hadn't been dwelling on the fact that she had told him how she had killed her own mother and then refused to speak of it. "I didn't mean to pry."

"I don't want you to have the wrong impression," said Eva. Her smile had faded, and she now looked pensive and sad. "I didn't murder my mother."

"Oh, so..."

"Some witches came after her," started Eva. "My mom was tough, but there were so many of them. She fought back and ran them off but by the time I got there, she was beyond saving. She was laying there on the kitchen floor and I wanted so badly to help her." Eva's eyes were elsewhere, remembering the gruesome sight. "She told me I had to end her life. See, a witch's power is transferred to the witch who actually takes the life. If she had died from bleeding out, one of the witches who attacked her would have taken her soul."

"You saved her soul," said Adam, mystified.

"I guess you could say that. In doing so, I became as strong as she was." Eva sighed. "But I didn't stop there. I was angry. I went out and I found all eight of the witches who had attacked her." Eva sniffed, wiping her eyes. When she looked up, her face was stiff, like that of a soldier. "And I killed every last one of them."

"Yikes," said Adam, not knowing what the proper response to something like this was.

"From then on, I was the most feared witch in the city. I never had to kill again because no one had the balls to challenge me." She grinned. "Except Miyako, that is."

Adam pulled his hand from hers and placed it on her cheek. He smiled at her.

"Do you hate me now?" she asked, avoiding his gaze.

He turned her face to look into her eyes. "I could never hate you, Eva. Though, if I'm being completely honest, I am a little bit terrified of you."

Eva smiled. "Good, you should be." She turned towards the city. "Come on," she said. "Let's go back to your place."

As they walked they chatted, but Adam had a hard time focusing. He couldn't stop thinking about what she'd said. He'd known she had probably killed before but now it was out there in the open, like finding a lover's sex tape they made with their ex. And then there was the orb. *Did I really just see that?* he thought. *I swear I saw myself running down the subway tracks in my underwear.* It was so odd. He laughed it off and turned his attention to where they would eat dessert, forgetting about the vision entirely.

*   *   *

Miyako felt it as she was walking home with her catch of the week, a couple of bagels with a cream cheese spread and half a bag of baby carrots. Something sent a tingling sensation down her back as she looped through the back alleys, moving towards the park. She had known from an early age that she had a special affinity for picking up the 'scent' of magic, and lately she had felt it getting stronger. She could feel an imbalance in the city. Something which started off as a hint, like a sprig of parsley added onto a salad, but now it had become an overly salty mess. Whatever this thing was, it was growing in power. And Miyako did not see it as a coincidence that witches were turning up dead all over the city, starting with Stephanie Jones. This was no ordinary imbalance, it was a witch and Miyako had a good idea of who to blame.

Now, she could feel it all at once, stronger than before, baring down on her. She was close. The witch killer, the girl from the poster, the threat looming over Jasmine and Miyako's life, was within a city block.

She shoved the food into her pockets, making sure it was secure. She snuck around a dumpster and there on the corner of the block were brightly lit neon letters reading 'The Veranda.' It looked like an old broken-down concert joint that someone had bought, renovated and then given up on for lack of money or concern. A small sign under the neon read 'One Night Only - Vicky Davis.' Miyako squinted her eyes. It was a name she knew from the posters she'd seen around town but there was something else familiar about it.

She was young compared to most of the city's witches, and her mother had not had much of a chance to teach her the hierarchy of the witch world. But the name reminded her of Victoria Davis, one of the current queens of the witch world. She'd seen the name on the poster the night she'd scuffled with the wizard, but now, at last, she made the connection. She thought it through and determined that a witch queen was a pretty good suspect for a power vacuum of magic in the city as well as a suspect for countless witch murders.

She pulled out her can of paint and sprayed it upwards, grappling to the roof of the building next to her. She rolled onto the harsh tar of the roof and then crouched as she sprinted across the building. She leapt to the next rooftop and landed atop the Veranda, the neon lights illuminating the way. At the center of the roof was an outcropping with a little door. She pulled on it. Locked, obviously. She sprayed the knob red and with a flick of her wrist, yanked the door from its hinges, sending it flying across the roof. She looked around for a brief moment to make sure no one had become aware of her. Sirens and chitter-chatter below were the only sounds in her ears. With her paint can at the ready, she descended into the unknown of the Veranda Theater.

*   *   *

Diego sat in a chair as Vicky performed up on the stage, practicing for her big show, which was coming up in less than ten days. She had been screaming at the drummer and the guy on keyboard. Not wanting to postpone the show and find new instrumentalists, she decided to take her aggression out on a stage hand, beating him to a pulp with a spare guitar. They were just barely making it through her latest hit single, "Get With

You." Diego noted that it was an obscenely shallow song about Vicky wanting to 'get with you.'

He looked down into his hand at his phone at a picture of Adam and himself which sat on the screen. They were both wearing large backpacks as they hiked the Catskills last year. They both smiled grandly at the camera. Diego recalled asking an elderly couple to take their picture, and how he had loudly proclaimed Adam the love of his life in order to make everyone involved as uncomfortable as possible.

He smiled briefly thinking of that moment, forgetting the current circumstances. It seemed like forever ago. Now, his life was consumed by death, murder and the blood of young girls. The scariest part of all was that he didn't feel bad. Sometimes he wondered why that was. He shook it off and hit the 'Edit' button on his phone. He quickly cropped the picture, cutting himself out of the image, leaving only Adam. He selected the picture and texted it to Vicky.

The bass player skipped the chorus and started playing the third verse. Vicky turned, rage in her eyes, as she picked up a mic stand and hurled it at the bassist. The man ducked just in time to not be impaled by the long piece of metal. "Failure!" she exclaimed at the man, who was struggling to hold back tears. "When you were born, and your mother looked at you, that's what she probably said, Eric. Failure!" Vicky wandered back to the center of the stage, removing her phone from her pocket. She eyed it for a moment and then looked up at Diego, in the audience. "This him?"

Diego nodded.

"No problem," said Vicky, winking. "I eat boys like him for breakfast." She went to find her place in the song and made sure that she was still standing in the spotlight. Diego laid back in the chair. He looked up to see boards and scrap were falling from the ceiling, and the lights looked as though they were hanging on by frayed threads. And in one of the ceiling holes sat the girl who had attacked him in the alleyway.

He froze as their eyes met. Even from far away, there was no mistaking that they were staring each other down, deciding who would be the first to move. It lasted longer than it should have, his muscles rigid as if his brain had just blown a fuse.

"Vicky!" shouted Diego. The girl darted out of sight. Diego jumped, transforming in mid leap and calling out "Vicky!" one more time before his head became that of a great black dragon. *"There's a witch in here! She's spying on us!"* His great wings flapped as he headed for the ceiling. He slammed into the rafters, wood and scrap metal falling down towards the pit of the concert hall.

He clawed his way through the gap and then lunged through a shaft. He could still smell the girl, her fear rank in the air. She wasn't far now. Vicky always had all the fun when it came to killing witches. This time, it was his turn.

*   *   *

Miyako lunged through the rooftop door, spraying a line in the air and jumping onto her broom before it had even fully finished forming. The exhaust pipes exploded with fire and she took off into the air, the wind baring down on her.

She had seen it all. The wizard was working with the witch all along and not just any witch, a Witch Queen. One of only seven in the world and very powerful. Miyako felt the immense energy emanating from her. She could sense the bodies of the dead witches somewhere underground. She could see the power of the purple lines across every face in the room as Vicky controlled them. She had seen the face of evil, and now she understood for the first time what it meant. It didn't matter where she and Jasmine chose to hide, whether it was an alley or a park or the moon. This witch would find them sooner or later.

There was an explosion behind her as the dragon shot through the building's roof, choosing not to take the door like a civilized person. Wizards were pigs. A fireball shot by her. She dodged just in time. She could feel the immense heat of the blue flames. The dragon

156

meant to kill her this time. She pulled up hard on the broom. It was an overcast night, rolling clouds filled the sky. This would be her one and only shot.

She zipped through the air, rolling out of the way of two more fireballs. She turned and shot a few paint balls at the creature. The first two missed but on her third, a roar of agony filled the air as the paint burned a hole into the dragon's side. He flapped harder, snapping at her angrily. He shot a huge stream of fire and she barreled away from it, but not soon enough. The end of her broom ignited in flames. She balled up the sleeves of her sweater and quickly hit the flames to pacify it. She turned again, this time banking into the lowest of the clouds. It was far colder now, and the precipitation of the clouds made it hard for her to navigate as the little drops of water pelted her. She sifted around, trying to decipher which way was up.

Another fireball shot by her, allowing her to see a bit into the distance. The attack was well off her tail, and she got the feeling that the dragon was just as lost in this mess as she was.

"*WHERE ARE YOU?!*" The dragon's voice boomed, and short flashes of lighting cracked through the air, ripping through the clouds. "*We will find you little girl. We will find you and we will RIP the FLESH from your BONES!!*" Another flash of lighting crashed through the clouds around her. She had to get out of here. Between the lightning, the fire and the dragon, she found herself in a tranquil death trap of cumulus. She pulled up on the broom. *"Wouldn't you rather get it out of the way now? I can make it end so much more peacefully. It won't hurt. At least not THAT much."*

The clouds were getting darker and the blackness began to surround her, bearing down with its rain and cold. She shivered, her whole body soaked. She gripped the broom hard for fear that she would tumble from it, no longer able to hold on to the slippery handle. Everything around her was pitch black, and it felt as though she was racing head first into an abyss of nothingness. Maybe the dragon had caught her, and she was dead and just didn't realize it yet. Perhaps this was the path to Hell.

Suddenly, light broke over her. She had come out on top of the clouds, and the stark white moon now glowed down on her amidst a bed of stars. It was like nothing she had ever seen. For a moment, she forgot that she was being chased. The air felt so cool and wonderful on her damp skin. She let it sink in only for a breath, then sighed out the anxiety that was coursing through her veins. She couldn't stay here. She was a sitting duck on this plane of pillowy white. She let her broom float down into the shelter of a patch of cloud that looked particularly soft and bent her body forward, hugging the broom with her arms. She clicked her heel on the pedal, turning off the exhaust pipes, allowing her to simply float silently. Nearby, she heard the desperate flaps of the dragon, who had finally decided to check the top of the clouds. In the hush night air, she could hear everything, every turn of his body and flap of his wings as he looked for her. She could hear his desperation.

"No," he growled. *"No. No. NO!!* He flapped around in rage. *"Where the FUCK did you go?!"* Finally, he let out a massive roar as if it might help, or possibly because in his primal state he simply couldn't handle himself. *"Grawwwwwwwwwr!"* Several flaps of his wings again, and Miyako felt a shadow bear down on her as he flew right over the top of her. The clouds shifted, but only slightly. Not enough to reveal her. The flapping continued but began to get softer and fainter, until finally it fell away into the wind.

She stayed there for a moment, knowing the coast was clear and that it was time to go, but not having the strength. Not yet. A tear fell from her eye and was followed by several more. She allowed herself to cry for the first time in years. She sobbed, whimpering into her sleeve, her other arm propping her up on the broom. She cried until finally she was able to pull herself together. She pushed her arm across her eyes, wiping them clean and leaving only the red on her nose and cheeks. That would vanish by the time she returned home. She allowed herself to feel everything that had been plaguing her for the past several weeks and months and years. She allowed herself to give into it only for a while so no one could see how weak she felt inside. She turned her broom and left her hiding spot in the clouds, leaving behind her fear.

Chapter Ten

It was the first night that it seemed summer might actually decide to show up. In New York, it was customary that one day could be freezing cold, forcing one to wear a tight array of coats, scarves, sweaters and hats, while the next day could suddenly be bright and warm. Eva was glad to breathe in the warm, fragrant air. It was the perfect time of year. The chill had finally dissipated, but the humidity of Summer had yet to make its mark.

She was on her way to Adam's house. She'd lost track of how often she went to his place now. It became a home away from home. He'd even given her a place to keep her stuff. He mentioned that he was worried that it might be too soon, but she didn't really have any frame of reference to know what 'too soon' was. It came out of convenience really. If she was going to be there all the time, why not have some clothes available so that she didn't have to schlep all the way back to her house. Besides, Adam's place was cleaner than hers and smelled nice. She was used to the smell of potions brewing and concocted elixirs smoldering over a fire, but it was nice to be somewhere that smelled of coriander and grapefruit and all the things that boys' mothers apparently taught them were good to smell like if you wanted a girl to like you. Adam was also tidy. He'd often make the bed before she even got back from the shower and he always organized her drawer. At first, it had been a bit off-putting to know that he was going through her things but eventually she had seen the kindness in it and, of course, things were easier to find.

She rounded a corner near St. Marks and made her way down the street, trying to slow her pace, forcing herself to not be excited to see him. What was she, a child on Christmas morning? He was just a boy. Eventually this would all have to fade. She knew she was living in a fantasy and that it couldn't last, but she liked it here. She felt comfort in the fact that she had laid out the ground rules with Adam, letting him know from the beginning that this could never progress beyond the point of "liking each other very much," for fear of losing her magic and consequently, her life. She was proud of the fact that they were on the same page, even if she did sometimes think it was a lie she told herself to make it all okay. After all, the looks Adam gave her when he thought she wasn't looking hinted at a feeling much stronger than 'like.'

She walked through the park near Adam's house, a shortcut she'd discovered a few days ago that cut out nearly ten minutes of walking time. It wasn't the nicest park in the city, filled with screaming children by day and desperate men by night, wasting away on benches. But it wasn't congested, and she liked that she didn't have to push past people just to walk at a normal pace.

The park was particularly quiet tonight. As she walked, she noticed that not even the trees swayed. Everything was still. She was suddenly hyper aware of just how little movement there was in the world around her. She slowed her pace and then stopped altogether in a small clearing where several paths met. There were several benches around the circle but none of them were occupied by even a single vagrant.

"*No.*" A voice echoed from the trees like a low growl. Eva spun around. In all her weeks with Adam, she had almost completely forgotten that she lived in a city of witches and that those witches were out for blood. She'd even heard that witch corpses had started showing up all over the city and yet, she ignored it. How had she been so stupid, so careless? Of course, it was her luck to have walked into a witch's territory. This park and its seclusion reeked of witchdom. "No, no, no, no, no." The voice was all around her. Everywhere and nowhere.

She spun around again, waving her hand through the air and grabbing her staff from the purple cloud which formed. She quickly circled the ground around her, creating a rune that glowed with a white opalescence, illuminating the clearing. Little glowing spots appeared on the ground, summoning portals for her skeleton army.

"NO!" From the bushes nearest Eva, a girl lunged at her, wielding an enormous scythe that must have been four times as big as its owner. She swiped at Eva, who put up her staff just in time to stop the blow. *CLANG!* The metal hit the birchwood of her staff and sent her flying backwards, ricocheting against the cobblestones of the park's pathways. Two skeletons emerged out of the ground, guns blazing. The girl disposed of them with a single swing of her scythe.

Eva spat a glob of blood onto the stone and looked up at the girl, sizing her up. She knew this girl. Zyla Rond must have only been sixteen years of age. She had dark skin and long ratty hair. Her clothes were torn and tattered, and her bloodshot eyes were housed by dark circles as though she had forgone sleep altogether. Her scythe was massive, looming next to her like a great beast. The long curved blade protruded from the long-snouted skull of an extinct wild animal, affixed to a short, bent staff. Zyla panted heavily as she looked down on Eva.

"Not me," she said, her eye twitching nervously. "You won't take me."

"I don't want to," said Eva, shaking her head, thinking only of Adam on the other side of the park. He was probably checking his watch compulsively by now, wondering what had caused her to be late. Had the L train experienced train traffic yet again? "I'm just passing by."

"Is that what you said to the others?" Zyla looked deranged, as if her world was filled with a darkness that shoved out any light that was once there. "Is that how you got them to let down their guard?"

"Zyla..."

"You don't know me!" screamed Zyla, swinging the great scythe at Eva. She stumbled backwards, the blade just missing her head. Landing back on the ground, she realized she had not been fast enough. Blood trickled down her knee where the weapon had nicked her. Not a fatal blow by any means but definitely not preferable. "Thirty-eight girls!" she yelled. "That's how many lives you've taken," Her face pulsed with redness as she berated Eva, who was using the time to catch her breath. "But I will NOT be thirty-nine!"

Zyla charged at Eva, her scythe spinning through the air. Eva whipped her staff upwards, shooting out two laughing skulls engulfed in purple smoke. They exploded on contact with the young girl, knocking her backwards. Eva took the opening, lunging through the smoke and bearing down on Zyla, slamming the staff hard against the blade of the scythe. A loud metal clang rang throughout the park.

"I didn't kill those girls," said Eva. "You've got the wrong witch."

Zyla pushed off of her, flipping backwards, out of reach. "You LIE!" She charged again, swooping the blade haphazardly through the air. Eva deflected it again and again. The metal 'tings' and 'schwings' played like a symphony of sword play as Zyla backed Eva into a nearby tree. Two more skeletons hurled themselves at Zyla, but she split them apart with the massive hunk of steel. She swiped at Eva, cutting a gash in her shoulder, spattering more blood onto the pavement. She laughed maniacally, drool dripping down her chin. She lunged into the air, swinging the scythe above her head.

Eva's eyes went wide. In her mind, she saw Adam waiting for her, saw him counting the minutes until it became later and later. She saw him calling her over and over to no avail. She saw him deciding to take a walk and coming upon her dead body in the park. She saw his tears and his pain. It was too much for her to bear. It welled up inside her like a bottomless pit of sadness. With all the power she could muster, she jutted the orb-end of her staff into the air.

"AHHHHHH!" she screamed. A massive ray of

light, the likes of which Eva had never before seen herself produce, shot out from the orb, throwing Zyla backwards, her weapon only inches from bashing in Eva's skull. The girl slammed to the ground on her side. A loud *Crack!* announced a broken bone or two. Eva pushed herself up from the tree behind her. Blood was still in her mouth, and she felt the bruises she'd incurred beginning to take their place.

Weakly, she waved the staff through the air. A purple cloud spawned an old, silver revolver, the likes of which were usually seen in movies about the old West. The barrel was long and slender, and a little revolving chamber allowed for six bullets. The words *Never Love, Never Die* were engraved on the side. She grabbed the gun out of the air and pointed it at Zyla, who was slowly pulling herself up from the ground. Her scythe had plunged its tooth into the dirt of a nearby patch of grass. It was too far away for Zyla to get to now, not if she wanted to stay alive.

"It's over," said Eva, wiping her mouth. "Just let me pass, and I swear, I won't come back through this way."

Zyla's breath was short. She grabbed at her left arm in agony, tears rolling down her eyes. "Did you make the same offer to Lexie before you killed her?" Zyla shook her head viciously, as if trying to shake off a sound that Eva couldn't hear. "That bitch was mine. I was the one who was supposed to kill her. You took that from me!"

167

"Just. Let. Me. Pass." Eva enunciated, keeping the gun squarely pointed at Zyla.

"Go to hell, bitch." To Eva's surprise, Zyla took off at a sprint, not for her weapon but directly for Eva. Her teeth looked like the jaws of a wild animal, going in for the kill. Her eyes were tiny and pinpointed on their target.

"Stop!" yelled Eva. "Zyla, STOP!"

Zyla lunged at Eva, snarling as her hands stretched out like claws towards Eva's throat.

BANG!!!

Zyla's body dropped lifeless to the cobblestone. Blood seeped from a small bullet wound in her forehead. Her eyes were open wide. The blood quickly pooled around her.

Eva dropped to her knees. She waved two fingers over Zyla's eyes, closing them. A wispy white aura bloomed from the girl's mouth and wafted through the air into Eva's lips. She breathed in the new power and then let out a remorseful sigh. From above, Zot dropped down next to her, panting heavily and looking around at the commotion.

"You're a little late," said Eva, petting his head. She shook her head and continued to sit there in the small clearing for a time. Adam could wait a bit longer. At least she would show up alive.

*   *   *

Adam had made dinner. Stuffed chicken breasts, which he hadn't known how to make, filled with blue cheese and sun-dried tomatoes, which he hadn't known where to buy. He then blanched some asparagus, which he didn't know was something you could do to asparagus, and had finished it all off with mashed potatoes, which he'd made once when he was ten. He'd laid it all out on the table with care, setting the forks, knives and spoons in their correct order. He'd looked online to figure out what order that was exactly, but he did it all the same. He lit candles and put on slow music, and then he waited.

Now, the food was getting cold and Eva was nowhere to be seen. He had wanted to do something romantic for her despite how she felt. He knew that they had talked about how they could never be more than friends, but he felt that she was starting to let that rule slide, and tonight he planned on making sure that they were ready to move forward. He just wanted them to be on the same page. In a sense, he was asking her to be exclusive, which in the city was something you had to ask before it could be official.

After ten minutes past the time he had asked Eva to arrive, he had become annoyed. He'd texted her a blatant "Where are you?" Twenty minutes in, he texted her a picture of the food, adding a filter to it for extra dramatic effect so she really knew what she was missing. At forty-five minutes, he began to worry and now, an hour and thirty minutes past, he was terrified that something had happened to her. He called her cell several times and was nervously pacing the living room when the doorbell rang.

He was fully prepared to chew her out, to tell her how much time he'd spent on dinner and how much she'd hurt him by not being there or even calling. All of this disappeared as he opened the door. Standing there, breathing deeply as she clutched her arm, was a beaten and bruised Eva. He noticed the cuts on her face and the dirt and mud all up and down her clothes. Her leg was bleeding and the sleeve of her shirt was caked with blood from the inside. Not only was she physically damaged, but the look in her eyes was that of someone who had lost a piece of herself.

"Adam," she said softly. "I'm so sorry I'm late." He let out a sigh and pulled her into him, holding her tightly in his arms. "I'll get your clothes dirty," she whimpered, trying to resist even though she was too weak.

"Who did this?" he whispered into her ear.

"I ran into a witch on the way here," she sighed. "Something had her all riled up. They're out of control. I don't know what's happening." She was shaking.

Behind her, Zot hovered with what Adam thought actually seemed like a worried look on his face. He nodded at Zot who flew into the apartment, going to the sofa to land and scratch his ear with his back leg.

Adam gently grabbed Eva's hand. He walked through the house with her, passing the food on the table and the candles and the perfectly placed flatware, and led her to the bathroom. As she stood there helpless, he removed her shirt, taking care to pull the shreds of fabric, one at a time, from the dried blood on her arm. He lifted it over her shoulder slowly, and when her hair was finally untangled from it, he threw it off to the side. He looked down at her body. There were bruises forming all over her stomach and back, and the large cut in her arm required immediate attention. Her face, too, was swelling, and the blood around her nose and the edges of her mouth had dried solid.

He sat her down on the edge of the bathtub, for fear that she would fall over. He unbuttoned her jeans and pulled them down for her, lifting each leg one at a time in order to remove them. He started the shower. The sound of the water hitting the ceramic tub made Eva jump slightly. He held his hand under the water, allowing it to warm but not become overly hot. Reaching out for her hand, he led her in.

"Your clothes..." she murmured. He had not removed any of his clothes and the water was now soaking straight through them, but he didn't feel it. All that mattered was her wellbeing. He was focused on it, obsessed even. He regarded her as a greater being, put onto a pedestal of power in his mind. His one purpose in life was to care for her. He grabbed a little purple sponge at the side of the tub and soaked it in the warm water. He then started with her arm, wiping away the blood a little at a time. When it was gone he moved down to her stomach, side and legs, slowly caressing her skin with the sponge, squeezing out the blood between each pass and then going back to her. Minutes turned into hours as he inspected and cleaned each and every wound.

Finally, he focused on her face, dabbing the blood away and pulling water through her mud-soaked hair. He turned her, so the water could rinse the dirt off. When at last he was finished, he turned off the water and stepped out, still soaking wet. He grabbed a towel and wrapped it around her. He led her out of the bathroom and into his room where he laid her on the bed. Her eyes were soft with exhaustion as she looked up at him.

"I'll be right back," he whispered in her ear.

"Adam," she said, grabbing his arm lightly, "Thank you."

"Shh. You should get some rest." He walked to the kitchen and removed an ice pack from the freezer. From a small drawer, he pulled a few band aids of varying sizes and some gauze pads left over from the time he had cut open his leg while hiking. He then returned to the bedroom to find that she had already fallen asleep. She snored gently, her damp hair falling perfectly over her neck and shoulders. He went to his dresser and changed from his soaked clothes, throwing them to the side, into a T-shirt and shorts. He then sat on the bed and applied the band aids and gauze pads to her cuts. He pulled the blanket up over her and placed the ice pack on her swollen eye. He held it there well into the night. Eventually he let it fall to the side as his eyes drooped shut and he fell asleep, his arms wrapped around her. A distant low buzzing could be heard from Eva's cell phone, discarded in her jeans on the bathroom floor.

*   *   *

Diego stood on the rooftop of the Plaza Hotel overlooking Central Park, holding his breath. The smell was unbearable. He held the phone to his ear, rhythmically tapping the case as the ring tone played. No one answered. The ringing stopped, and a voice spoke in its place.

"Hi, you've reached Eva. I'm out and about but tell me who you are and what's up or text me." Her voice disappeared with the sound of a loud *BEEP!*

Diego sighed. "Hey Manita," he said with a heavy breath. "Look, I'm sorry about what happened that day. I've just been friends with Adam so long and...you're my sister, you know?" He bit his tongue. "I miss you,

173

bruja." He peeked behind him for a moment and grimaced, then went back to staring out at the city below him. "I think you guys should come to the concert on Friday." He touched his face where Vicky had slapped him after he had returned without Miyako's body. It still stung to the touch. "It's going to be a blast and I think you'd both like it a lot. Anyway, I'll see you guys there...I hope. Tell Adam I say hi." He gave a soft smile. "Love you."

He removed the phone from his ear and tapped the 'End Call' button. He returned the cell to his pocket and hesitantly forced himself to turn around. Thirty-eight bodies lay, piled one on top of another. Some were still clothed while others were naked. Some had all their limbs while others were missing arms, legs or even heads. The stench given off by the bodies stung the nostrils and made him wince.

Several large discarded red canisters that once contained gallons of gasoline lay off to the side. He reached into his pocket and pulled out a small metal lighter. *'Sacrifices must be made.'* That's what Vicky had said upon sending him to dispose of the witch bodies by fire. He didn't really understand it. He flicked the lighter, a little flame springing from it. He gave it a long look and then threw it into the pile of witch bodies, like throwing away an old newspaper.

The fire spread quickly and within seconds, the

entire mountain of corpses was ablaze, flickering flames of death and mutilation into the night. Diego transformed and took off, not wanting to be near this hellish image for any longer than he needed to be. The bodies would burn well into the evening until there was no more flesh or gas left for fuel. They would then dwindle, leaving only black ashes in their place.

*   *   *

On a little hill on the north side of Central Park, Vicky sat in the grass breathing in the first night of spring. She let the air into her lungs and then breathed it back out again. Her guitar lay in the grass next to her. In the distance, she saw the flames go up on the rooftop and she smiled. It was all coming together. When she was little, a froggy-looking prophet who moonlighted as a clerk at an office supply store had told her that she would become the most powerful witch the world had ever known, but that her demise would come from another who knew a secret she couldn't even fathom. Vicky had determined that if there were no witches left then there would be no one to know a secret that could destroy her. Now all the witches of this city were either dead or dying, and soon the last would fall in her final plan.

As the fire flickered in the distance, she felt the hill

beneath her grumble and shake as if something long gone from this world were starting to awaken. She patted the grass as a master praises their dog. Her pet was glad for his sacrifice, happy that she had saved up so many bodies to burn for him. Beneath her, she could feel his strength growing as the smoke listed over the park and the trees and earth absorbed it.

"Soon, my pet," she said. A couple walked by and gave her an awkward glance, before facing straight ahead and continuing on their way. "Soon."

She laid back and closed her eyes, letting the grass cool her bare arms and legs. She fell asleep on the little hill with the knowledge that everything was going according to plan.

Chapter Eleven

Twelve Years Ago

Tiny hands fumbled over the already crudely folded piece of paper. While this might not have been their first time doing this, they certainly had not perfected the art. They would make a fold and then pause, as if trying to figure out their next move. Sometimes they would even go back a step, unfolding the last crease in order to do something different. Eventually, two small wings were fashioned, and a tiny beak was adjusted, forming the shape of a finished, albeit battered, paper crane.

Miyako was seven years old and was enjoying having her new friend over to her house for the first time. They'd met at the park the previous week. She had asked the girl to play with her in the sandbox and was glad to find that they got along quite well. She hated the way that the girl sat alone off to the side of the park, not having any fun. It simply wouldn't do. If one went to the park and didn't have a good time, they should not have gone at all.

She had already learned so much about her new friend. Her name was Jasmine, and she was eight years old. A full year older. Miyako happened to think this was quite impressive. This girl must know a lot more than she did. She had also learned that Jasmine lived with only a foster mother, and that they did not have much money. Miyako's mother was quick to point this out to her, though Miyako failed to see why this mattered. Her mother had plenty of money and still seemed extremely unhappy.

Miyako handed the finished crane to Jasmine, smiling proudly. Jasmine reached for it, touching the wings delicately as if they might break off if she was too aggressive.

"Done," said Miyako.

"It's so pretty," exclaimed Jasmine, pushing her thick curly hair out of her face so as to see it better. Miyako liked the way that the light reflected off of Jasmine's dark skin. She found it to be beautiful.

"You can have it, if you want," said Miyako, offering the crane up to Jasmine.

Peering into Miyako's bedroom was her mother, who was short but strongly built. The first lines of gray had started to permeate her hair, and her lips were permanently pursed in disapproval. She wore a black pants-suit and appeared all business. Next to her was her own mother, Miyako's grandmother. The old woman looked even more displeased with the situation at hand. Her hair had fully grayed and her back bent so much that she needed to lean on a long wooden cane. She peered over half-moon glasses which were fastened to her head by a little beaded string. Several large beaded necklaces hung in a gaudy affair around her neck.

"Are you sure it's wise," her grandmother proffered, "to let them play together?"

"They're just children, Mother," said the younger woman, rolling her eyes. The charm of her parent's old-fashioned ways had waned long ago. "The girl has no family. The chances of her being one of us are a million to one." She looked back to the two girls seated on the bedroom floor as they giggled together. "Let them have their fun."

Miyako's mother was quick to give her daughter anything that would make the girl like her more. They'd had a tenuous relationship ever since Miyako had accidentally walked in on her mother brutally murdering her father. But she felt there was no way around it. Some shamans just had it coming. She expected that Miyako would never again look at her without a little bit of hatred in her eyes.

Jasmine examined the crane in her hands, observing every fold, crease and crevice and then looked up at Miyako nervously. "Can you teach me to make one?"

Miyako grinned proudly, glad to be so highly regarded by her new friend. "My mom says that if you make a thousand of them you can get your wish. But they all gotta be perfect for the wish to come true."

Jasmine pondered this. What kind of wish? she wondered. Could it be anything? Even if it was just a small wish, that was still very impressive. "How many are you up to?" she asked.

Miyako put her hand on her chest valiantly, clearly proud of her accomplishment. "I'm already on my twelfth one."

Jasmine clapped for her, smiling in amazement. "Wow! That's a lot." Jasmine had seen the care and time that had gone into making just one perfect. She couldn't even imagine how long it would take to make twelve, let alone a thousand of them.

"I know, right?" Miyako beamed.

Jasmine thought about her situation. Miyako had shared something personal with her. She thought it only fair to do the same, to return the favor. "My foster mom says I have cystic fibrosis." She'd been diagnosed at a very young age, and the doctors had gone into terrifying details of how the disease usually progressed. She had heard how mucous would slowly fill her lungs and then spread to her other organs, and how she would have trouble breathing until eventually the disease would probably take her at a very young age. It had all sounded a bit terrifying, so terrifying in fact that her mother had left her at an orphanage, unable to bear the thought of losing her later on.

"Sounds scary," said Miyako, biting her cheek and looking at the girl with concern.

"Do you think...the cranes could fix me?" asked Jasmine.

Miyako smiled again, believing anything possible. "Of course!" She pulled out another piece of paper and handed it to Jasmine so that they could make the next one together. "But you better start now. It could take a while to get to a thousand."

"Maybe even years!" said Jasmine enthusiastically. In that moment, Jasmine and Miyako determined that they would be life-long friends, and their journey to create one thousand cranes would bond them together. After Miyako's mother had left the doorway, Miyako pulled a small short pin from under her bed.

"I saw my mom do this once when she thought I wasn't looking." She held Jasmine's large hand and jabbed at the middle finger. A little trickle of blood seeped from Jasmine's skin as she let out a breath of pain. Miyako did the same to her own finger and then touched their wounded fingers together. "Now our fates are part of each other."

"Friends forever," said Jasmine.

"Friends forever," echoed Miyako. They smiled at each other for a long while before forgetting the cranes and going to play with stuffed dinosaurs and princess castles.

Two Years Ago

"Are you sure your mom is out?" asked Jasmine. Her hair was much shorter now and straightened. It was dyed red at the tips. She ran a finger along Miyako's stomach as they lay in bed together.

"She said she'd be out all night," whispered Miyako, leaning over to kiss Jasmine. She breathed in the raspberry lip balm on Jasmine's lips. They kissed passionately. Jasmine slid her hand up Miyako's shirt, caressing her gently before removing it entirely. She threw it to the side of the bed and then proceeded to kiss Miyako's neck and collar bone. She kissed down Miyako's chest and stomach, unbuttoning her jeans and reaching her hand down into them, slowly.

Miyako let out a gasp of pleasure. Jasmine returned to Miyako's lips, kissing them more forcefully now as her fingers were warmed by the heat inside of Miyako. Miyako moaned softly. She grabbed the back of Jasmine's neck, her finger nails digging into the skin there. Jasmine whimpered. All around them, the cranes were floating with little flames emanating from them, a side effect of Jasmine's arousal.

"What the hell is going on?" They both froze, looking up. Miyako gasped, buttoning her jeans and haphazardly pulling on her shirt.

"I thought you were supposed to be out!" snapped Miyako. The cranes went dark and fell to the ground, lifeless.

In the doorway, Miyako's mother stood, her face flushing with rage. "I came back for my keys. And good thing I did. Not only is my daughter a sexual deviant, but with another witch, no less."

"Mom, just slow down. I can explain—"

"You hid this from me!" Her mother moved into the room, waving at the cranes on the ground angrily. "And for how long?"

"Mom, I—"

"How long have you known, Miyako?!" They stared at each other, no one in the room daring to move.

"Since we were little. Jazz took to the cranes. The paper is her connection to magic." Miyako sighed.

"Miyako, don't—" started Jasmine.

"She already knows anyway," said Miyako, tears in her eyes. "She can manipulate it, use it," she mumbled to her mother. "We were trying to get to a thousand to cure her."

"And how many do you have now?" Miyako's

mother crossed her arms.

"Nine hundred eighty-five," said Jasmine. "We're almost there." She smiled, hoping that maybe the woman would take pity on her.

"I see," said the stern woman. She pulled a small wand from her coat pocket, fingering it gingerly in her hand. She held it up and then pulled it through the air slowly.

"NO!" screamed Miyako, lunging for her mother. But it was too late. As the wand pulled through the air, every single crane in the room tore itself to shreds, leaving only bits and pieces of themselves behind on the floor. Little tearing noises rang out in the room like a chorus of paper death.

"Oh God!" gasped Jasmine, putting her hands to her mouth. She jumped at the woman. "How could you?!" Tears poured down Jasmine's face. Miyako's mother dodged out of the way, grabbing a handful of Jasmine's hair just as she fell to the ground.

"Aiieeeeeh!" Jasmine howled in agony as Miyako's mother dragged her out of the room and threw her down the stairs to the first floor of the house.

"Mom! Stop! You're hurting her!" shouted Miyako, chasing after them. Her mother jumped from the banister and landed over Jasmine, looking down on her with utter hatred. Miyako ran down the stairs, tears pouring down her face.

"She's a witch, Miyako!" yelled her mother, pointing at Jasmine who was shaking on the floor. She held up her hands defensively as if to shield an oncoming attack. "And not only have you allowed her to live, you were in bed with her!"

Miyako grabbed her mother's arm, crying. "Mother, please!"

"Enough." Her mother stepped away, leaving Miyako standing over Jasmine. "I've allowed this to go on for far too long. Your grandmother tried to warn me, rest her soul, but I wouldn't listen. I only ever wanted the best for you."

"Mom, I—" But her mother no longer heard her.

"It's time to make things right." Her mother's eyes fixed on hers. "Kill her." Miyako felt her heart plummet to her stomach.

"Mom, no!" Miyako put a hand over Jasmine, warning her to stay down.

"Kill her and take her power for your own," said her mother, her voice distinctly soft in the silent living room. "Time to grow up."

Miyako looked down at Jasmine, who lay on the floor trembling in fear. She knew what she had to do. She could feel it building inside of her. She knew how much she wanted to fight it, but she realized just how unavoidable her fate was now. She went to a small chest at the side of the room and pulled out a crudely drawn paper cut out of a large black and white figure. It was round and stood about six feet tall, with large fingers and little feet. In the center of its face was a single large round eye. She slapped it onto the nearest blank wall and then, pulling her spray can from the air, sprayed a circle of red on its belly. She whipped the can back, letting the creature spring from the wall, breathing in new life.

Grr. It grunted its approval at having been born. Miyako's mother smiled as Miyako stepped back to the center of the room, the creature beside her. Miyako sighed a long breath.

"I'm sorry," she said, "but she's right."

The creature suddenly turned, wrapping its clubbed fingers around her mother's neck. The older woman's face filled with shock as her hands grabbed at the fingers, trying to rip them away. "GAHHHHH!" she wailed, her wand clattering to the floor. Miyako picked it up and without a second thought, snapped it in half and tossed it aside.

"Guess you know how Dad felt now," Miyako said, no emotions in her voice.

Jasmine shuddered as she backed up to a wall, wanting to be as far from here as possible. She had been sure that this would be her last moment on Earth. She had accepted death but now, it seemed, life was giving her a second chance.

Miyako stepped over to Jasmine, her mother still gasping desperately for air and hitting the creature to get free. She reached out a hand and Jasmine took it. Miyako pulled her to her feet and hugged her. "Are you okay?"

"Yeah," she said.

The sounds of her mother struggling faded until finally her body went limp, and only when Miyako nodded did the creature release the body to the floor. A soft white essence emerged from her mother's mouth and floated towards Miyako. She breathed it in and gave her mother one last look. Then she turned, guiding Jasmine to the door.

"We're on our own from here on out, Jazz," said Miyako grimly.

"I know," said Jasmine. "What about the cranes?"

"You'll have to start over," said Miyako. "I'm sorry."

"It's alright," said Jasmine, pressing her forehead up to Miyako's. "As long as we're together, I can make a million of them."

"It's going to be okay, Jazz. You're going to be okay. I promise."

"I trust you."

They left the house together. The creature tore itself apart and then fell lifeless to the ground, covering Miyako's mother like a large white blanket.

Present Day

Miyako had staked out for a week as the preparations for Vicky's concert came together. She had become more careful now, keeping to the shadows. It seemed that the great amount of power Vicky acquired had come at the cost of not being able to sense when a witch was close by. She didn't even flinch when Miyako was near. Over the last week, Miyako had formulated a plan. She had to take Vicky down before she found Jasmine. Miyako would catch her on the night of the concert when she was distracted by the excitement of the crowd.

She watched from a nearby rooftop as Vicky berated the owner of the theater for not having met all of her demands. Miyako had seen enough. The concert was in a couple hours, and she needed to see Jasmine one more time before it started. In case something went wrong.

She left the rooftop, making for the ground and then the entrance to the subway. After her encounter the prior week, she'd moved Jasmine and herself underground. Living in the subways had proven much more difficult than living in the parks or even on the streets. There was a darker side of poverty and despair underground. The first day, she'd had to fight off several men who were attempting to steal their food, and after that she started sleeping with one eye open to watch out for anyone who would try to take advantage of them.

It was a world of beggars and performers. Men would form groups to sing in quartets, going from train to train collecting money. They seemed so happy and communal, but as soon as no one was looking, they would yell at each other. Some simply stood at the edge of the platform and sobbed. On the fourth day, she witnessed a girl jump onto the tracks, allowing the F train to take her life. Miyako couldn't help but wonder how long it would be before she chose to succumb to the same fate.

She rushed down the stairs into the underground labyrinth, passing by people heading home after a full day of work. Having no money for a metro card to gain access to the trains, she jumped the turnstile, and then headed down the platform towards where she had left Jasmine that morning.

From a distance she saw Jasmine, seated on a long wooden bench. Her body was limp, and her head hung to the side. A paper crane lay half-finished at her feet. Fear filled Miyako. Her heart began to race.

"No," she said, picking up her pace as she started to run through the stragglers from the previous train. Miyako reached her. Jasmine was still. Not even a muscle twitched. Miyako looked on in horror. "Jasmine!" She grabbed Jasmine by the shoulders and began to shake her. Tears welled up in her eyes, which she forced back by squeezing them shut. "JASMINE!!!"

Jasmine's eyes fluttered open as the violent shaking continued. "Wh-What?" She shook her head, coming back from the dream she'd been having and grabbed Miyako's arms to stop the incessant jostling. "What's going on?"

Miyako finally loosened her hold, looking up at Jasmine's open eyes and concerned face. She let out a long sigh of relief as she fell to the floor, kneeling as she caught her breath. "Oh, thank God," she sighed. "I thought you were—"

Jasmine pushed her red hair back, blinking her eyes to adjust to the light. "I must have fallen asleep." She placed a finger under Miyako's chin, raising her head to look into her eyes. "Stop worrying. You know this girl ain't going out on a subway bench. I'm going out in style."

"I just—" Miyako looked away, forcing more tears back.

"Besides, I can't leave you here all alone." Jasmine smiled softly. "I lo—"

"No," interrupted Miyako. "Don't say it. Don't you dare use that word. You know what happens if we do. You're weak enough as it is." Miyako stood, trying to ignore the pain in Jasmine's face. "I came here to tell you I'll be going out tonight." She stopped Jasmine before the words even left her mouth. "You can't come.

I need you to stay here. Stay safe."

"Where are you going?" asked Jasmine suspiciously. Miyako had become more detached lately, often coming back to her with bruises and cuts, which she refused to explain. She seemed as though she was losing a little bit more of herself every day.

"It's better if you don't know," responded Miyako, a slight tremble in her voice.

"Miyako..." For a long moment, they sat in silence.

"I know who's killing all the witches," said Miyako, still not able to make eye contact. She sounded meek and frail. "I have to stop her, before she finds—"

"Stop," whispered Jasmine. She grabbed Miyako's hand. "You don't get to rush headlong into a fight you can't win, for my sake."

"It's too late for that," said Miyako, dejected. She pulled away, turning to walk back the way she'd entered. She used the sleeve of her sweater to wipe her eyes and then opened them with new conviction. This was it, the endgame. Either she would die, or Vicky would. It felt as though her whole life had been leading up to this moment, to this concert. It was fate. As she walked up the stairs, she noticed one of Vicky's posters hanging on a wall. She ripped it from the wall, tearing Vicky's face in half. She was merely paper, easily shredded. And paper, Miyako mused, was her specialty.

Chapter Twelve

As night fell, a crowd of crazed girls, eye-rolling boyfriends, under-dressed women, and over-boozed men arrived at the Veranda theater eagerly awaiting admittance.   Within that crowd, were Adam and Eva. The doors remained closed as everyone chatted amongst themselves.

"I hear she has a whole outfit made out of googly eyes."

"I hear she spent more on her jewelry than the Prince of England spent on his wedding."

"I hear she punched a bear in the face on a dare."

"I hear the bear died!"

The crowd was full of energy and felt alive with anticipation.

"Why do we have to go to this thing again?" asked Adam, who was not eager to see either Vicky Davis or Diego, whom he hadn't spoken to since their unfortunate last meeting. Adam had tried calling his friend several times after the intrusion but was always sent to voicemail. He knew that it was a shock to see his best friend with his sister, but Adam thought there wasn't anything a few laughs and some drinks couldn't fix between them. Surely Diego would come around.

"My brother gave us the tickets. It's his roundabout way of apologizing for the other day." said Eva, not entirely sure she wanted to be there either. Her wounds had healed quickly, almost too quickly, she thought. She had been sure she would be recovering for at least a few weeks if not months, but her cuts had sealed shut and only the slightest hints of the battle with Zyla remained. She was leery of why this might have happened but chose not to question such good fortune. She was still finding it hard to look at Adam, not knowing how to thank him or even talk to him after that night. Never before had someone seen her in such a destroyed state and yet, he hadn't run or even flinched. He'd nursed her back to health. She didn't quite know how to react to such an act of kindness.

Adam looked around at the women who were wearing too much makeup; their boyfriends, who looked bored to tears and only there on the slight chance that they might get some action later; and the other men, clearly gay, who were there on the slight chance of turning one of the bored straight men for the night.

"This is definitely Diego's crowd," he said into Eva's ear, hoping that only she would hear him.

"You mean trashy?" Eva asked, a look of disgust on her face.

"I was gonna say authentic," he replied.

The crowd let out a loud cheer. At long last, the doors to the theater opened wide and the crowd pushed forward, like cows moving towards their untimely slaughter. Adam and Eva took one step at a time, scanning their tickets and then entering the large auditorium. There were several seats in the back, but they headed for the large open space in the pit. Young girls were eagerly clawing at the stage. The stage itself was covered by a large, hanging white sheet which hid anything beyond it. It rippled from time to time, causing another false start cheer from the crowd.

"It's packed," noted Adam, looking around at the space which was surely filled far beyond the legal capacity. It felt as though people were everywhere, practically hanging from the rafters, just to see some pop star he had never even heard of.

"Diego always did have friends in high places," said Eva, who seemed almost as surprised as he was.

Adam observed the crowd. There was no shortage of beautiful women, but he found that they didn't even catch his eye the way they once would have. He would have stared at them longingly and then become depressed, realizing he could never get someone as beautiful, interesting or cool as they were. Now, he only had eyes for the girl standing hand in hand next to him. Eva Grey had become the center of his world, a light in a dark tunnel of missed opportunities, bad dates and failed attempts at love. He felt as though they had known each other for years, as if they had grown up together. Their lives had crashed headlong into each other that fateful first night, but now it seemed so natural, as if there was no other way life was meant to be lived.

"Hey," he said, getting her attention. Her thoughts were lost in the crowd around them.

"Yeah?" she asked, looking back at him. He smiled, saying nothing. "What is it?" She poked his stomach where she knew he was ticklish. He giggled and pushed her back.

"Stop that!"

"You know you like it," she laughed.

"I'm trying to tell you something important."

She pulled back, her smile fading. "So, spit it out."

"This last month has been incredible," he started. "It's all seemed a bit like a fairy tale."

Eva shook her head. "You almost died the first night we met. I almost died last week. I'd hardly call that a fairy tale. Don't you think you're embellishing things a bit?"

Adam pulled back, the smile on his face slowly

fading.

"What you're saying is sweet," said Eva, placing a hand on his arm. "But I'm worried that you're so caught up in your feelings, you can't see this for what it actually is."

"Eva—" Adam's face filled with hurt, each of her words stinging his ears. "I'm falling in love with you."

SLAP! Eva's hand flew almost instinctively across his face. The crack of it echoed around them. Several people turned to take in the drama happening right beside them.

"Holy shit!" shouted Adam, grabbing his face in pain.

"What the hell is wrong with you?" asked Eva, her eyes piercing Adam.

"Me? You just hit me for saying I love you!" Adam was yelling now. "I think you need to reevaluate *Wrong*."

"l told you, I can't say those words." Her voice was shaking now. "I can't feel them. I can't think them. Are you trying to get me killed?"

"You spend every night at my house. You stare at me when you think I'm not looking. You want to say you can't feel love but I'm sorry, it's bullshit." Adam's face was red. "I know what we said in the beginning, but things have changed."

Eva shook her head, getting a hold of her emotions.

"You've created this world in your head where I'm not a witch and we're going to run away tomorrow and have a family." Eva put a hand to her chest. "I don't get those things, Adam. Somewhere in this world is the witch who will kill me. Maybe you can live in a fantasy land, but I can't afford to."

She turned, tears threatening to pour down her face. Adam reached out for her arm. "Eva, wait!"

Eva pulled away, giving Adam a cold glare. Her bottom lip quivered with anger. "Don't." Eva pulled back into the crowd. "I'm getting something to drink. Don't follow me."

Adam stood in the crowd of crazed teens and hopped up men, sighing in disbelief, alone in a sea of strangers.

*　　　*　　　*

Vicky stood with her guitar in hand, staring out into space through the white sheet in front of her. She could hear the crowd just beyond it. She took a deep breath, taking in the smoke, alcohol and hormonal fervor. She could feel every muscle in her body tense and release.

"Your fans are waiting, Vicky," said Diego, sidling up beside her. "And they'll make a fine army."

"I feel something out there, Diego. It's so faint. But I think a witch is here." She closed her eyes and took a deep breath. "Why is it so faint?"

"Probably just my sister," said Diego. "You told me to have her bring Adam."

"I can't guarantee her safety if she gets too close," said Vicky, a flicker of hunger in her eyes.

"You promised not to hurt her," said Diego sternly. "Neither of them gets hurt. You just make him forget about her."

"I'll try my hardest to spare her, Diego," she said, staring him down. "Just like you did when you caught that little bitch who was spying on us."

"But, I didn't—" Diego froze.

"I know." She winked at him and then turned to the white curtain as he backed into the shadows. Out of sight. Out of mind.

The latches holding the white sheet detached as it fell in front of her. The crowd exploded with screams and applause. Vicky smiled as the spotlight hit her face.

*　　　*　　　*

"Eva!" Adam called out for her as he pushed through the crowd, but it was too late. The roar of the audience drowned out his calls.

"WOOOOOO!" The cheer went up as they surged forward, trying to get a better look at the star, but Adam's eyes were turned away from the stage. He was

198

searching the crowd for any sign of Eva's long black hair. A girl, clearly intoxicated, shoved him forward. He dodged out of her way as he continued to call out.

"Ladies and gentlemen!" announced a voice overhead, coming through the heavily outdated PA system. The sound of the voice only excited the audience more. They were like a pack of wild animals, feral and rabid for any taste of the show to come. "Please put your hands together for VICKY DAVIS!!!" The volume of the crowd seemed to quadruple as they surged forward, yet again, hands in the air, all their mouths open and screaming. A boy next to Adam was an emotional wreck. His whole body was shaking from being so overwhelmed.

"AHHHHHHH!" The cries were deafening and just when Adam thought it couldn't get any louder, he heard her voice speak softly into the microphone.

"Hello fabulous people," she said. Even though everything up to this point coming through the sound system had been muffled and almost incomprehensible, her voice rang out clear and true. There was something sickeningly sweet about it. It was unavoidable. Without even knowing exactly how or why, Adam turned to look at her. "Are you ready to make some noise?"

The crowd let up a blaze of applause and cacophony. She was the most beautiful woman Adam had ever seen. Her hair was perfectly curled in a shade of blond that most women only dreamed of, and she wore a tube top that left almost nothing to the imagination. Over this, she wore a sparkling jean jacket with several large jewels on it. She had on jean shorts and calf-high red cowboy boots. Completing her look was a cowboy hat, and Adam couldn't resist becoming aroused by gawking at her. Her whole body seemed to sparkle and glow, like an angel.

Her hand traced over a single low note and then began to strum it. *Doom da doom. Da Ting Da Doom.* The drums picked up behind her and before long, the bass was putting in its own rhythm but try as he might, Adam couldn't take his eyes off of her. *Doom da doom. Ting da doom. Ting Ting da doom.*

What Adam couldn't see were the jagged purple arrows rushing along the floor underneath him, snaking their pointed heads up each audience member's legs and curling into their skin. Soon, the audience was bouncing to the same rhythm, swaying in synchronization. It was as if they had all learned the same dance routine in advance. All but Adam.

Vicky leaned into the microphone, her hand still pulling over the strings.

"I wanna 'Uh Uh' with you. I wanna get, get with you. I waaannnaa be, be, be with you babay."

"Eva!" Adam called out, his eyes still glued to the

stage. He didn't know why he couldn't turn away. His eyes were permanently affixed to Vicky. "You're missing it," he said, to no one in particular. "The music is terrible, but I...can't...stop...listening..."

A second spotlight suddenly shot through the crowd, and to his surprise, shined directly on Adam. Vicky Davis, the one and only, stared right at him, as if she was singing to *only* him. "What the—" The shock took him out of the trance, but only for a moment.

"Sing with me!" Vicky commanded. As the crowd sang along, they began to part, as if she were Moses and they were the sea.

"I wanna 'Uh Uh' with you. I wanna get, get with you. I waaannnaaa be, be, be with you babay."

She smiled at Adam and then took a step off the stage. To his surprise, the crowd caught her boots, holding her up perfectly, as if she were walking on air.

"I see your face, amongst the crowd, it's callin' to, to me."
Doom da ting. Doom doom.
"I see your eyes, your face, your mouth. That's where I wanna be."

She began to step down, the crowd grasping her

feet, taking her slowly closer to the floor like a staircase. A clear path lay between her and Adam.

"I want you, baby, yeah. I want you in me, on me, through me, WITH ME!"

And then the crowd exploded with the song as only the bass and the drums remained.

"Uh, I wanna. Uh uh, I wanna.
Get, I wanna. Get get, I wanna.
Be, I wanna. Be be, I wanna be with you. With you.
With youuuuuuu!"

Her boot hit the floor gently as she continued her approach. Adam was unaware of the little purple arrows permeating his face, pulsing with excitement.

*   *   *

Eva took her third shot and then turned to the manic crowd behind her. The guitarist had disappeared. Something had felt off all night. This usually happened when she was around a magical creature or sometimes a witch, but she had let it go. After all, with this many people, there was sure to be at least a couple of witches. There was no way they could pinpoint each other in this crowd. She swallowed the alcohol and put her suspicions out of her mind. The singer was atrociously bad. Eva was taken aback at how synchronized everyone's movements were as she perused the room. They all jumped at the same time, waved their hands on cue, stepped right and then left. It was all so precise, she thought, but then again, she hadn't been to many concerts.

"Get, get with you. I wanna, get, get with you." Eva couldn't take it anymore. She needed to talk to Adam. She had let her temper get out of control and it wasn't fair to him. After all, he was only doing what came naturally to him. He had fallen for her the way mortals always fell for each other. She should have seen it coming, should have broken things off with him a long time ago. Instead, she had allowed things to devolve to this moment. She needed to close things off for good and she could only hope that he wouldn't hate her for it. In time he would heal and hopefully so would she.

She pushed into the crowd, ready to confront him, but they were surprisingly unwieldy. They made no room for her and no matter how many times she yelled "Excuse me," it seemed to fall on deaf ears. Finally, overtaken by frustration, she began to actively shove men and women aside. "Move!" She berated them. "What's wrong with you?" She tripped over a man who was jumping on cue and almost fell to the floor.

"Dammit, I said MOVE!" On and on she trudged through them. "Adam!" She called. "Adam!!!" She pushed and shoved her way deeper and deeper as the song intensified. She had to be getting close now. She took a deep breath and plunged through the sea of people.

* * *

Vicky was within arm's reach of Adam. "*Be, be with you.*" she sang. "*Get, get with you.*" Adam's eyes pulsed to the rhythm. He was powerless to her. He wanted her. Every muscle in his body ached to touch her, to get with her, to be with her. Somewhere far away, he could hear Eva calling to him, but none of that mattered now. The only thing he cared about was Vicky Davis. He loved her with all his heart. He wanted to never be apart from her. "*Be, be, be, be...*" Vicky stepped right up to Adam and smiled. "*With you...*" Her face edged near his. Her hand left the guitar on one final note and then grabbed his chin, softly but with a firmness that demanded obedience. "*Babay.*"

They kissed. Her tongue ran along his and he pushed his mouth into hers, grabbing the back of her neck. He wanted her right there on the dance floor. He went to reach his hand under her shirt, but she pulled back, whispering in his ear. "Meet me backstage," she said, and then left him, starting up the next song.

He turned, his heart still beating rapidly, his body shaking, to see Eva, standing at the edge of the clearing the crowd had left for him. She stared in disbelief. "Adam..."

"Yes," said Adam, his voice dead and monotone. "I am Adam."

"You said you loved me," she said, tears forming in her eyes. "You said—"

"I love—" started Adam, and then he smiled. "Vicky Davis."

As Vicky sang the next song, Adam turned towards the backstage door. Eva stormed out of the Veranda, wiping the tears away from her face and damning herself for ever thinking that anyone could feel anything for her besides hatred. She had been stupid and now she understood, this time for certain. There were no love stories for witches. There never were, and there never would be, and she, Eva Grey, was no exception.

Chapter Thirteen

The music was loud and obnoxious, vibrating through the streets in muffled tones just outside the Veranda. Miyako stood on the roof of a nearby building, overlooking the concert hall. Her hood was up, casting a shadow over most of her face. A gentle breeze blew past her, causing her hair to flutter.

From the front of the theater, a familiar face appeared, bursting through the double doors at full speed. It was the last person Miyako had expected to see. In fact, she was surprised that the girl was even still alive, but then again, Eva Grey was not one who would have been taken down easily. She seemed upset, wiping away tears as she stormed across the barren street. Miyako wasn't sure what compelled her to jump from the roof. Maybe it was the need to know what had happened. Maybe she felt that through all of their fights and rivalry, she was somehow related to Eva.

She landed squarely in front of Eva, who jumped, startled by the witch's sudden appearance. Eva's demeanor did not falter. Even at her most distraught she still gave off the air of someone not to be messed with. For a long moment, they just stared each other down; both sizing up the opponent, yet neither of them reached for their weapon.

"What are you doing here?" asked Eva finally, breaking the silence.

"I'm here to kill a witch," said Miyako. She had never been one for subtlety.

Eva shook her head, annoyed. "So kill me already."

"Not you," said Miyako. Her face lifted to look at the Veranda behind Eva. "Not this time." Eva didn't seem to understand. "Christ, you're slow."

"What are you talking about? Who pissed you off?"

"I'm here to kill that bitch with the guitar."

It all began to piece together in Eva's head. She remembered the tight feeling in her stomach, knowing that something magical was nearby. "She's...a witch?"

"She's THE witch," responded Miyako. She began to circle around Eva, her anger coming to the surface. "Stephanie. Lexie. Ariel. Erin. The list goes on and on. She's been picking us off one at a time. Pretty soon she'll have killed off every witch in the city, and then what? The country? The world? She's hungry for power and the more she gets, the less chance we have of stopping her."

"I know you're young, Miyako," said Eva. "But this is how things are."

"No!" snapped Miyako. "We kill each other, sure, but there is a balance. The moment one magical entity becomes too strong, it changes everything. Spring coming late this year? Her. Dormant volcanoes beginning to affect the water in their surrounding towns? Her. Snails invading Florida? Her. It's going to get worse and worse, Eva. The stronger she gets, the more out of whack things will become. It's all connected. We risk everything by letting her continue. We risk the world. We risk the humans finding out about us."

"How do you know all this?" Eva asked.

"I can feel it," replied Miyako. "I've always been better at pinpointing magical distortions than most witches. You could say I've got a finely tuned Hagdar."

Eva's eyes lit up. "Oh! *That's* how you always got the jump on me."

"Really? You're proud it took you this you long to figure that out?" Miyako rolled her eyes. "No wonder you're dating a mortal. You can be stupid together."

Eva gasped, remembering how she'd last seen that mortal. "I left him with her."

"Who?"

"Adam."

"You're a shitty girlfriend."

"Oh, God," Eva smacked her forehead, suddenly understanding. "She's controlling him. She's controlling ALL of them."

The music and cheers and rhythmic thumps of the concert stopped all at once. The street fell silent. Eva and Miyako turned to the Veranda with bated breath, waiting for the noise to come back but it didn't. It was as if they had both gone deaf. Somewhere in the distance, a siren wailed, giving them the reassurance to breathe again.

"This isn't a concert at all, it's a recruitment. That's what this was all about," Eva said, turning back to Miyako. "She just made herself an army."

"Shit," said Miyako. "What do we do?"

Eva stared at the building for a long moment, thinking about all the parts in play. "She's got everyone in there under her control. She'd be less likely to use them against us if she was distracted somehow. Still, we'd do best to avoid the crowd. She's sure to have guards, and then there's Diego to consider."

"He's mine," said Miyako, her fists clenching.

"Sorry, I already got dibs," replied Eva, her own frustrations bubbling up. He'd invited them, after all. He knew this would happen, and he'd let them walk into a trap willingly.

"That asshole tried to kill me," objected Miyako.

"That asshole is my brother."

Miyako considered this and then rolled her eyes. "Fine." She looked up at the building. "She's probably got all kinds of defense spells up in there by now. The only chance we've got is to get her outside."

"And how do you propose we do that?" pondered Eva.

"Take away her newest play thing. Something tells me she's the kind of girl who enjoys the thrill of the chase." Miyako grinned.

"That 'play thing' is my boyfriend," said Eva, faltering. "*Was* my boyfriend. I don't really know at this point."

"You're kind of a stupid witch," offered Miyako.

"Yeah, that thought has crossed my mind."

They both looked up at the Veranda, taking in deep breaths while they considered what they were about to do. They were going to sneak into the lair of the greatest witch in the western hemisphere and purposefully try to piss her off. It wasn't a great plan but at least it was something.

"I've always wondered what it'd be like to work with another witch," she said.

"Don't get used to it," snapped Miyako.

"Obviously."

Without another word, they walked headlong back into the theater with determination, ready to make sure Vicky Davis did not get an encore performance.

*   *   *

Vicky's dressing room was an array of every shade of pink and purple that one could possibly imagine. Her mirror was adorned with flowers and tiaras and various gifts that had been thrown to the stage during her performance. Her dresser housed mountains of chocolates and little wrapped packages which had been sent to her by mail. There were pictures of her everywhere you looked, making it look more like a shrine than a dressing room. There were two rooms, a main room, where all her clothes hung, and her dresser and mirror sat, and an adjoining room, with a large heart-shaped bed, and a washroom connected to it. She had clearly made her own adjustments to the original setup.

Upon entering the room with Adam, she ordered him to strip. He did so willingly, taking off his clothes down to his white briefs. She then ordered him to stand with his back to a wall as she clasped a pair of handcuffs on his wrists, locking him to an overhanging metal rod. Adam smiled as she did so.

"You are SO pretty," he said, leaning in to try and kiss her, but she pulled back.

"Awww," she cooed, patting his cheek with her soft hand. "You just might be the sweetest little slave I've ever had." She moved over to the dresser and sat her hat on it. She turned back to him and winked. "I'm gonna change into something more comfortable."

Adam giggled at the thought and would have fallen over from going limp if his hands hadn't been restrained above him.

"When I get back, you and I are going to have a chat about that little witch of yours." She walked over to him and tapped him on the nose. He grinned from ear to ear.

"Anything for you," he said, longingly.

"Good boy," she said. She moved into the other room, started the water, and slipped into a warm bath. A reward for a hard day's work. Her army was assembled and ready to move at her command. There was only one piece of her plan left to execute. Before long, she would awaken a goliath from days long past and her reign over the natural world would begin. She breathed in the lavender bath salts and closed her eyes, happy with the way everything was playing out ever so perfectly.

*   *   *

Eva looked back on her life as a witch, trying to recall a scene more haunting than the one she now beheld. Nothing came to mind. The concert hall was dead silent, yet all of the concert goers were still there, motionless. Their eyes were wide open and staring blankly towards the stage. They stood in lines, as if in a strict military formation. On each of their faces, glowing purple arrows pulsed in unison.

"If that doesn't make you want to run away screaming," whispered Miyako, "I don't know what would." They moved slowly around the crowd, not sure if sudden movements would startle them. The last thing they wanted to do was cause an unnecessary barrier between themselves and their target. They moved to the stage. It was barren. All signs of the show, which had been raging only moments earlier, had vanished, along with all the musicians. The drum set and speakers were left like relics of an old war.

"Think they know what's going on?" asked Eva, looking out over the crowd. They stared up at Eva and Miyako.

"Hard to say," replied Miyako. "But I'm not hanging around to find out. They headed for the back of the stage and shot around a corner, stealthily looking for any sign of trouble. They came into a well-lit corridor and allowed their eyes to adjust to the light.

"There," said Eva, pointing to a sign over a staircase reading *Dressing Rooms*. "Guessing she'll be pampering herself after all the hard work."

"Hard work?" scoffed Miyako. "Bitch can't even sing."

"Eva?" They both looked to see Diego moving down the opposite hallway towards them. His eyes stopped over Miyako. "And...*you*."

"Go," said Eva, just under her breath. "Get Adam, I've got this." Eva began marching down the hallway towards Diego.

"I'm glad you made it, actually," he said, trying not to show alarm. "How about it? Good show? Music is a little whatever, but the lady does know how to entertain."

POW! Eva punched Diego squarely in the jaw. He went tumbling backwards down the hallway.

"Go!" she yelled to Miyako.

Miyako did not need to be told again. She ran for the stairs, descending out of sight.

Diego picked himself up from the floor, wiping the blood from his lip. "Do you know how much work I had to do to protect you? Do you have any idea?" He looked up at her, fire in his eyes. "Now she'll kill you, just like the rest."

"Oh Diego," said Eva, shaking her head. A purple cloud loomed in the air as she pulled her staff from it. "You're really long overdue for an ass kicking." She whipped the staff around, cutting under his chin and sending him flying backwards once more. As he slammed along the floor, his body transformed, growing thick and scaly. The black color spread down his back and arms. His neck stretched out and little horns jutted out of his face. By the time he hit the ground, he was a fully-formed dragon. He stood tall, his long neck hovering over her.

"Back down, sister," he growled, smoke rolling off his tongue.

"Not a chance in hell." They charged at each other.

*   *   *

Miyako barreled down the stairs, forgetting that she was trying to be quiet. The sight of Diego had dredged up all her feelings from the night he had chased her into the clouds. Now, as her heart raced and sweat dripped down her forehead, she fled not because Eva had ordered it, but because her body had willed it. She hit the floor at the bottom of the stairs, her eyes closed as she caught her breath. She bent over for a moment, placing her hands on her knees as she forced the memory to leave her body. Slowly she stood and opened her eyes.

In front of her, seven large muscled guards, in all black, stood with their eyes glued to her. They all had meaty heads and barely any neck and their shirtsleeves were rolled up to reveal thick biceps and a few brightly colored tattoos. They all wore sunglasses and had small purple arrows engraved in their cheeks. They seemed as shocked as she was by the intrusion. The stillness seemed to last an eternity, as Miyako and the guards exchanged awkward glances. Finally, one of the guards broke the silence.

"Get her!" he shouted, and the full force of the seven men descended upon her.

She moved on pure adrenaline, pulling two crumpled pieces of paper from her pockets and hurling them at the walls to either side of her. They unfolded, slapping themselves into place, two massive black and white creatures. Her spray can spun around in her palm and then shot a flurry of red in a circle around her, tagging the two creatures and sending the first of the guards backwards. The creatures stepped from the walls and grunted towards the guards. They stepped in front of Miyako, guarding her as one of the men neared her end of the hallway.

"Move!" he yelled at the monsters. Miyako leapt over them, a lasso of red from her spray can wrapping itself around the guard's neck. She spun in the air, lifting him off the ground. As she landed, she swept her arm across her body, hurling the man into the wall. The white plaster cracked under his weight.

One of the men lunged at the taller of the creatures with a small knife. *Grr*. The creature grabbed the man's arm and snapped it like a twig. "Gahhhh!" screamed the man, falling to the ground. Miyako shot another strand of red, grabbing one man by the arm and throwing him into another, larger man. They toppled sideways. A guard further back reached for a holstered gun and pointed it at Miyako's head, but he was too slow. She

216

wrapped her red lasso around his arm and twisted it just in time. The bullet missed her head and lodged itself into that of a nearby guard. Blood spattered the wall as his body fell to the ground.

"Holy shit!" yelled the gunman, frantically. Miyako sprayed a long line on the wall as she ran and then, flicking her wrist, sent it flying at the set of fallen guards. It wrapped around them like a snake and constricted. The gunman shot at her with wild abandon, no regard for anyone else he might hit. One bullet went through one of her creatures as it snapped the necks of the two tangled men. Another hit the leg of a guard who was wrestling with the taller creature. The man fell to the floor, screaming in agony as the creature took its opening and, with a loud grunt, head-butted the man, crushing his skull.

Miyako ran up the wall, spraying a thin red line on it as the gunfire continued to pelt around her. As she lunged towards the man, the red line burst from the wall. She flipped over the man's head as the paint sped towards, and then directly through, his neck. Miyako landed gracefully in a crouched position, as his decapitated head hit the floor beside her. His body fell limply next to it.

She turned to see the blood-soaked corridor behind her. The smaller of the creatures slumped to the floor, the bullet hole creating a tear which would soon consume it. The larger one, however, ambled up beside her, ready for another round.

"Let's get this guy and get the hell out of here," she said.

Grr, the creature responded in agreement.

They found the door with Vicky's name on it. Miyako motioned to the creature with a nod of her head. The creature raised its fist and punched. The door buckled under the force and fell to the ground in front of them. Miyako stood guard as it entered the room and glared at Adam, who was still hanging from the bar on the ceiling. He looked euphoric and smiled from ear to ear as though he had been given a very strong drug.

"Hey there," said Adam to the paper beast. "I don't think you're supposed to be here." The creature stepped over to Adam and placed a fist over Adam's mouth, but the hand was large enough that it covered his entire face. "MMM! Mmmhmmm!" Alarmed, Adam tried to scream and wriggle from inside the monster's hold. The creature raised up its other hand and with a snap of its fingers, broke the handcuffs. Adam's body fell limp. The creature scooped him up into its arms.

"Time to go," said Miyako, entering the room to check the progress. The creature was propping Adam over its shoulder. Miyako shook her head at the image of the paper beast walking around with a nearly naked man on it. "That's gonna raise an alarm," she said, thinking out loud. She scrambled to the dresser, flinging drawers open haphazardly, and found a folded up white blanket. She threw it around Adam's body, covering him as much as she could. "Good enough." She turned to her minion. "Hurry. We have to be out of the building by the time she realizes he's missing."

They took off back the way they came, careful to avoid the bloodied corpses on the floor.

*   *   *

CRASH! Eva was sent flying through a thick black wall and the light around her suddenly changed. A quick look as she rolled along the floor revealed that she was now on the stage. Vicky's army stood at attention below. Diego crashed through the wall, his mass breaking down more of the bricks. Eva jumped out of the way just in time to avoid another huge fireball. She waved her staff and several beams of white light burst up from the floor. Within seconds, a small army of gun-slinging Day of the Dead skeletons were hurling themselves at Diego, stabbing at his body and pelting him with little silver revolvers.

"*Graaaaa!*" he roared. Eva surged upwards, with the help of a burst of light from her staff, to a viewing box to the right of the stage. Diego spun wildly, shaking off the little skeletons, and then shot another fireball at her. The railing supporting her weight disintegrated, and she lunged into the air once more. A purple cloud of smoke appeared beneath her and, as she landed on it, became her broom. She rocketed over the crowd below.

"Stop running and fight me!" bellowed Diego.

Eva turned her broom to face him, her staff firmly at her side. "This has to stop, Diego. You've killed most of the witches in the city. And for what? For her? You think she's your friend? You think this is a big party that you're just going to wake up from and laugh off? She doesn't give a shit about you. Witches don't care who they hurt as long as they get stronger." That was when Eva saw it. It was faint, but she could just barely make out little purple lines pulsating along his massive, scaly body. "She's controlling you, isn't she?"

"SHUT UP!!!" Diego screamed, shooting a massive stream of fire. She deflected it, and then another. And another. He was crazed now, firing at her relentlessly. Eva and Diego hadn't always gotten along, but now, for the first time in her life, she was truly afraid that he might actually want to kill her. As she deflected burst after burst, she could feel the fear ripple through her body. She had offended his master. He was angry and unstoppable. She had no idea how to break a mind-altering hex such as this. The only option that remained was kill or be killed and, in her heart, she knew that she could not murder her own brother.

*　　　*　　　*

Gnawing on his own back left foot, sitting on a dumpster, Zot felt a reverberation shake his body. Eva's fear rocked him to his very core. He sat up at attention, his little wings fluttering on cue. He looked around only for a moment to get his bearings and then took off into the air. Faster and faster he went, racing down the street. The world around him blurred as he passed it by.

Kaboom! He broke the sound barrier as he flew overhead. Cars and bikes and food carts around him shook. People ducked as a little tan bullet ripped past them. Ladies skirts flew up and gentlemen's hats went soaring as he passed. The whole of Lower Manhattan shook. He licked his lips as the skin around his mouth and eyes rippled at the force of his speed. He was almost there. Hopefully he would not be too late.

*　　　*　　　*

Eva was growing tired as she deflected each attack back at its maker. She was trying to extinguish the fires before they hit the helpless audience below or brought the entire theater down, but her energy was reaching its end point. Suddenly Diego lunged at her through the flames, grabbing her body with his claws.

221

"Ahhhh!" she cried in pain. He flapped his wings, swerving over the audience and then took her back over the stage. He twisted his huge black mass and, like a wrestler, body-slammed her to the dark wood below. She landed on her back, knocking the wind out of her. "Gah!" Her head was close to the edge of the stage, and she writhed as every muscle in her body begged for reprieve. So, this was how she would die. Not by a witch, who she had avoided her entire life, but by the claws of her own family. There were worse things, she supposed. After all, no one would benefit from her death. Vicky would not become stronger. She would probably even punish Diego for not allowing her to make the kill. This small bit of solace distracted her from the terror that was threatening to consume her.

Diego landed over her, two feet on either side, trapping her like prey. *"Father always said you were the stronger of us."* snarled Diego. *"Now he'll know the truth. Now they'll all know!"* He pulled back his head, a gentle glow emanating from his throat as the fire bubbled up from his stomach. It was almost peaceful in a way. Eva closed her eyes.

CRASH! The doors of the Veranda exploded open, flying off their hinges, as a tan cannonball punched through them. It zoomed at an unrelenting speed forward like a meteor. As Diego hesitated for just a moment, it slammed into his skull. *KABAM!* Diego was flung backwards, ricocheting into the wall they'd entered the auditorium through and taking the drum set with him. The wall shook for a moment and then the bricks began to come loose. They crumbled downwards, covering the hole and Diego's unconscious body with cement and mortar.

As the collapse ebbed, Eva sat up, catching her breath as Zot plopped down in front of her. His wings came to a halt and tucked themselves away. He shook his head, the little lock jangling from his neck. He panted loudly, snorting like a little pig, and licked his nose as his eyes focused on Eva, searching for approval.

"That's a good boy," she sighed and then fell back to the hard wood of the stage. She just needed to lay there for a moment and catch her breath. Hopefully Miyako's end of the deal was faring better. She thought of Adam and how she'd acted impulsively, not even attempting to figure things out. She hadn't even listened to him when he had tried to tell her that he loved her. She'd just walked away. She had hurt the only person who had ever truly cared for her.

She smiled at the thought of imagining getting him back and having a good laugh at the misunderstanding this had all caused.

I thought you cheated on me, she'd say.

But I was being mind controlled, He'd reply. *We're so silly for ever doubting each other.* And then they would kiss, and everything would go back to the way it had been. It was a nice idea, but Eva knew it was probably very unlikely.

She touched her side where Diego had dug his claws into her. She needed time before she'd be ready to look at the damage done but strangely enough, it seemed that the wounds were already starting to heal. She pondered this for just a moment before closing her eyes. Around her, the skeletons made quick work of the fire, padding it out with their sombreros and bandanas. The audience continued to stare straight ahead as if nothing had happened at all.

Chapter Fourteen

Vicky let the warm water and foamy bubbles wash over her as she lay in the bathtub. The aromas of lavender and rosemary wafted through the air, and she found herself more relaxed than she had remembered ever being in recent memory. Things had really been going her way lately, and it wasn't because of luck or by accident. She had orchestrated even the finest details to make things the way they were. She remembered the day she'd realized having more than one Witch Queen was ridiculous. She'd been sitting in her lofted chair amongst the six other women of the Witch Tribunal and realized that she was cooler than all of them combined and that furthermore, they were boring and poorly dressed.

"My fellow Queens," she had announced into a microphone, which she had pulled from the void. "I am leaving you to pursue that which is rightfully mine:

Everything." When the witches had objected, she had shouted, calling them 'Basic bitches,' and then had dramatically dropped the microphone and stormed out. What were they going to do? Witch Queens were under a magical oath which made it impossible for them to kill each other. They couldn't kill her, she couldn't kill them. Sure, they had sent their bounty hunters and lackeys, but she had annihilated them one at a time, making herself stronger in the process. It was a standoff, and she was winning. Witches really only needed one ruler, and it should be whomever among them was the strongest.

So why not her?

"You're so special, Victoria," her mother would always say. Sure, Vicky had made her say it using the incredibly potent mind-nudging tunes from her guitar. But still, it felt so nice to hear. She rolled the bubbles around in her hands and smiled at the memory. Now she had a new play thing who would lead her right to the witch everyone called the strongest. That is, of course, until Vicky came along. Diego would be unhappy obviously, but chances were he wouldn't live to see Vicky kill his sister. She had special plans for the little wizard after all. He'd played his part well, but everyone had to die sometime.

At long last, Vicky stood, grabbing a fluffy towel and wrapping it around her impossibly toned, body. She wrapped another towel around her hair and then admired herself in the mirror. She had never looked more beautiful. All of the witch essence she'd absorbed gave her the most youthful skin of her life. Everything was coming up Vicky these days. She headed back into the adjoining room to reward herself by playing with her new pet.

"Now," she started, "where were we?" In the main room, she found that there was no one to hear her. It was completely empty. The little handcuffs were snapped clean in two. This was not the work of the mortal man. A witch had been here. Vicky sighed heavily, annoyed. "Oh dear. Now I'm angry."

* * *

Miyako pushed through the concert hall doors outside, running down the steps with her creature and subsequently Adam in tow. She had never moved so fast in her life and knowing Vicky would surely be on their tail was certainly reason enough for it. She could only hope Eva would join them in time to back her up. Besides, it wasn't Miyako's boyfriend that needed saving. She looked back at Adam. His eyes seemed groggy. He looked around from under the blanket as if very disoriented by the entire situation.

"W-where am I?" he managed to grumble. It was as if he was waking up from the world's worst hangover.

"What happened?" He peered down at himself. "Why am I naked?!"

"Calm down, you have underwear on," snapped Miyako. "If you'd been naked, I would have left you there." She smirked at the thought.

"You!" Adam was suddenly becoming hyper aware. The last time he'd seen Miyako, she had been threatening to drop him over the East River. "What is this? Some kind of kidnapping? Eva will find you. She'll kick your ass!"

"Calm down, lover boy," grumbled Miyako. They made their way to an alleyway. She was quickly trying to figure out the best escape route. "She asked me to get you out of there. And you can be thankful I did. At least you're safe." She doubted the truth of that sentiment. "For now," she added.

Her skin began to tingle and there was a loud buzzing in her head. She looked around frantically. A witch was close, but she had no idea of knowing who.

From behind them, long jagged lines of purple snaked themselves along the ground. They were like bloodthirsty animals, having just seen their helpless prey.

SLAM! The arrows exploded from the pavement and hit Miyako without mercy, sending her into a nearby wall. The bricks shook as she hit them, and dirt fell around her. She felt every muscle in her back scream out at her as she slumped to the pavement below.

"Woah!" yelled Adam, suddenly panicking. The paper creature turned to face their assailant, spinning Adam around in the air like a rag-doll. Adam held on for dear life. "Easy boy!" Miyako pushed herself up from the ground as Adam tried to control his panic long enough to get his bearings. "Holy crap!" he exclaimed. "We have to get out of here. I think that singer might be a witch."

"Thanks for the observation," retorted Miyako, rolling her eyes.

"Little witch, little witch," called Vicky. Adam and Miyako looked up to see her, guitar in hand and fully clothed. She approached them slowly from the end of the alley. "You have something that belongs to me."

Adam's skin began to crawl. "Who? Me? Oh, you don't want me." He shook his head vigorously. "I'm scrawny and unemployed. I've got a whole slew of anxiety issues. And think of the kids. Diabetes runs in my family, you know? And cancer. We've got lots of cancer."

"Shut up, Adam," barked Miyako.

"Don't worry," smirked Vicky. "I really only want you for your body."

"Huh," pondered Adam. "I find that oddly comforting."

"I said shut up, Adam," said Miyako, her spray can

materializing in her hand.

Doom. Doom. Doom. Doom. Vicky began to play a low bass line as she continued forward. "Just give me the boy and no one has to get hurt," she smiled.

"You lie about as well as you sing," jabbed Miyako.

"Thank you."

"Not a compliment."

The creature lowered itself, to place Adam's bare feet on the ground. He adjusted the blanket, wrapping it tighter around himself. "Hey," he said urgently, grabbing at the papery arms. "Hey! What's it doing?"

"Adam!" said Miyako, sharply. She stepped between Vicky and Adam, shaking the spray can ominously. "Run."

Vicky drew her hand across the guitar strings as a loud note shook the walls and the ground. *DOOM!*

Adam took off. He had no idea where he was going or how far he needed to go, he just knew that he needed to get away from there and he needed to do it fast. Within seconds, he had rounded the corner and was out of sight.

Miyako stared down Vicky. "You just gave up your only bargaining chip," sighed Vicky. "Such a shame. Now I'll have to kill you."

"Let's go, skank," said Miyako, stretching her neck to the side so that it popped aggressively.

Vicky strummed the strings again, shooting out a

blast of purple as Miyako sprayed her paint can into the air. The red collided against the purple tendrils, and a blinding explosion shook the alleyway. Miyako was thrown backwards again, slamming into a large dumpster.

"Gah!" she cried. Debris and dust flushed towards her. She waved her hand, trying to see through it. She jumped back to her feet and charged forward, painting a line along the wall. "Graaaaaa!" She burst out of the smoke, ready to unleash a flurry of attacks on the Witch Queen, but to her surprise, no one was there. She stopped and looked around, confused and flustered. "Vicky!" she yelled. "Come out and fight me like a woman!" She stood, can at the ready, but there was no response. It had been a diversion. Vicky was gone, well on her way to chasing down Adam. Miyako rolled her eyes. "Oh, fuck!"

*   *   *

Adam ran down the Manhattan streets, everyone's eyes glued to him. Even in a city like New York, a grown man wearing nothing but a white silk blanket is sure to draw some attention. He ran into people as he looked back, trying to make sure no one was on his tail. He saw nothing, yet somehow, somewhere, he could still hear her guitar, softly beating its death ballad.

"Sorry," he exclaimed to a woman as he nearly knocked her down. "'Scuse me!" he shouted after a couple whose handholding had been cut off by Adam barging through the middle of them. "Crazy lady trying to kill me!" He yelled to anyone who might care to listen. No one did.

The green lamps of a nearby subway station beckoned to him. Perhaps underground, he would find safety. If nothing else, there would at least be less of a draft. He ran down the cement steps, his bare feet burning from the harsh ground of the city streets. He was sure they were probably raw and bleeding by now, but he couldn't stop to check. He descended into the station and slammed into a tourist family who looked completely baffled as they grabbed their children and back pockets, protecting their ill-placed wallets. Clearly they thought he meant to rob them.

"So sorry," he pleaded. "Crazy witch. No time to explain." Their blank stares conveyed a sense of cluelessness. "Go NYC WOOO!" he exclaimed. They all smiled and he took off once more. He jumped the turnstile and heard someone yell at him from behind. It didn't matter. The only thing that mattered now was getting away from the psychotic huntress who chased him. He stood at the platform, tapping his foot and looking back and forth for any sign of the L train. The tunnels were black and unforgiving. "Come on. Come on. Come on." He looked around impatiently.

"Ahhhhhh!" He turned to see a woman screaming as she fell down the stairs. The purple tendrils snaked themselves down the steps, their arrowed heads flicking side to side as they searched for his scent.

"Seriously, MTA," he sighed, hoping any train conductor or personnel might be within earshot. "There is just never a train when you need one." The tendrils shot past the turnstiles, throwing several pedestrians out of the way. Adam turned, running down the platform as far as it would take him. The arrows were hot on his trail now. He looked around, desperately searching for a second exit but found none. "Where now?!" he cried to the heavens.

Even before he moved to New York City, he had heard horror stories of people jumping in front of trains, being electrocuted by the tracks, or running into some terrifying underground crocodile. Every rule-following, good citizen part of Adam begged him not to do what he did next, and for the first time in his entire life, he ignored the inferior-laced, anxiety-ridden, insecure voice in his head. He jumped down to the tracks below.

With a loud splash, he hit a murky cold water puddle. There was no way that it was sanitary or good for the exposed wounds covering his aching feet, but it felt so refreshing. He let it soak in for just a moment before speeding off down the dark tunnel. The tendrils were crawling onto the tracks and he could just barely make out the distant faint hum of the electric guitar somewhere behind him. *Doom. Doom. Doom.*

He let out a scream at the top of his lungs. He hoped for someone, anyone, to hear. The blanket kept wrapping itself around his feet, slowing him down. No matter how embarrassing it might be, he had to give it up. Life was far more important than being seen in your underwear, he decided. He let the blanket go and it flew down the tracks, picked up by the stale air of the tunnels behind him.

As Adam's death approached, he saw the past month flash before him. He saw the first message he ever sent Eva Grey on 'Heart Heart Hug.' Hell, he saw the first time he had the less-than-brilliant idea to sign up for the dating website that kept popping up in ads all over his internet browser as if to say, 'Hello, we are aware of your loneliness. Click here to be less of a living disaster.' And he had taken the bait.

He saw their first evening together in all his drunken glory. He saw the moment he could have walked away. The moment when she flat out told him that she was a witch and that she was dangerous to be with. He saw their first kiss, felt their lips press together. He saw the moment he told her he loved her, and then he saw her for the last time as she disappeared into the crowd.

The bittersweet image then shifted, becoming the life he imagined for them. He saw the beautiful house with the vegetable garden out back and the quaint attic where they would store their memories. He saw the wedding and the family. He saw their kids playing in their room. And now, as the visions stopped, he realized for the first time, that it had all been a fantasy. He had dreamed their relationship into existence. Of course she had not said that she loved him. How could she? Even if it didn't mean her dying, they'd only been dating for a month. He had lost himself to her, forgotten that people aren't a certain way just because he imagined them to be. He finally understood that none of it was real, and it hadn't been from the start.

Adam never loved Eva Grey for who she *really* was. He loved her for the pretend person he saw in his head when he looked at her. Now he would die for his error. Lights ahead barreled down on him as the L train at long last made its untimely appearance. He had seen this all before. He thought back to an evening stroll when he'd looked into the orb on Eva's staff and had seen himself on these very tracks. Even her weapon had tried to warn him that their relationship would destroy him. Now, in his final breaths, he knew the truth. He had believed in a make-believe world, in an imaginary wife in an imaginary house. Worst of all, against everything she told him, he had believed in a love story for witches.

With the tendrils behind him, and the train ahead bearing down on him, its horn honking madly, he closed his eyes and waited for the end.

*   *   *

Say what you will about witches, Jasmine thought. *Say they are Satan's minions. Say they are pure evil. Say that they will bring only chaos and death to this world. But do not say it about me.* Jasmine grabbed Adam around his waist and hefted him onto an enormous paper airplane as it flew, dodging the train and the tendrils just as they converged on each other. She pulled up on the paper, causing it to veer through the dank tunnel air and into the opposing track.

She had awoken on a bench on the subway platform, to the sound of a man screaming for his life. All of her magic filled life as a witch, she was told that witches were meant to kill. Yet never once had she performed this act. She'd simply avoided the whole mess. Miyako had always taken the hits and protected them at all costs, even if that meant bloodying her hands. At the end of the day, she did not want power or prestige. She simply wanted to live and be happy living. It was because of her desire for peace that she had known the instant she had seen Adam's dire predicament, that she could not allow anyone, mortal or witch, to die a merciless death. Besides, killing a human violated the Witch Pact of 1893 in more ways than one, and she would not stand idly by and watch it happen. She had quickly pulled an enormous paper plane from her bag and jumped aboard, her bag of folded cranes in tow. She had nearly missed him, yet here he sat. Adam gripped the paper firmly in front of her as they zipped in and out of the iron ballasts of the tunnel.

"I got ya!" she celebrated.

Adam clutched a hand to his bare chest, taking deep gasping breaths as tears poured unabashedly down his cheeks. "I'm alive," he said. "I'm alive!" this time yelling it. He laughed and cried all at once, taking in the pure joy that was being here and not crushed under a subway train.

"Didn't your mother ever tell you not to play on train tracks?" Jasmine chuckled.

"All the time, actually," Adam yelled back over the sound of the air whipping past them. "And for the record, I wasn't playing. I was running."

"From who?" Just as she said it, the purple snakes burst from behind, just missing them as they crashed into one of the metal pillars holding the tunnel together. Soot fell from above as Jasmine twisted in and out of the pillars, trying to avoid another attack. "Hold on!" she ordered, the paper plane flipping upside down as they dodged a third explosion. "There might be some turbulence!"

"Ya think?!" Adam snapped back.

"I've gotta get her off our tail," said Jasmine. She turned around backwards on the paper plane as it continued to rush down the tunnel.

"Are you insane? Who's gonna steer?" shouted Adam who, having just avoided death, was not keen on entertaining it again so soon.

"It's fine." She pulled open her bag and with a wave of her hand, pulled out a large cluster of cranes. They floated majestically through the air, as if part of a flock. Another attack came as several tendrils shot straight for them. The cranes launched themselves, bursting into flames. They careened towards the tendrils and exploded on contact.

"Problem!" Adam panicked.

Jasmine turned forward to see two trains barreling towards them. She grabbed onto the paper airplane and turned it harshly to the side as Adam held on for dear life. They shot between the trains, which flew by at such force that Adam's muscles shook. They soared out the back end of the trains to find light ahead. Another subway platform was coming up.

"Alright," shouted Jasmine. "Let's get the hell out of this death trap." She turned the plane towards the platform. They flew over the heads of the late-night crowd, waiting for the next train to take them home.

They sped through a door marked 'Emergency Exit Only.' They traveled up the stairs and emerged into the night air, zooming over the city street.

Adam let out a sigh of relief. "I could go for a seatbelt," he exclaimed.

"Wuss," smirked Jasmine.

"Just a suggestion."

Doom! Doom! Doom! DOOM! The haunting melody of the guitar loomed behind them once more. "Oh, come on!" yelled Adam. "Can't we catch a break? JUST ONE?!"

Jasmine bowed her head and sighed. There was no going back. For the first time in her life, she would not be able to walk away. She had to fight. They flew up and over a nearby building. "Sorry guy, this is the last stop." She grabbed him by his arm, ready to escort him off the plane.

"Wait!" he yelled, but it was too late. She tipped the plane and dropped him roughly onto a rooftop below. He rolled to a stop as she continued onwards, rising higher and higher into the air. She turned to see Vicky in hot pursuit.

*　　　*　　　*

Eva and Miyako flew side by side, surveying the city below. Eva had run out of the Veranda to the sight of a confused Miyako. They had taken up the search, trying to find any sign of Vicky and Adam.

"You feel anything?" asked Eva, squinting her eyes to try and make out the dorky face she had come to know so well.

"Nothing," said Miyako. In her head, she was berating herself for allowing Vicky to get away so easily.

"You should have gone after them the second she disappeared," said Eva, anger in her voice.

"You should have finished up with your brother sooner," snapped Miyako, not needing one more person telling her she'd screwed up. "Don't you dare pin this on me, Eva Grey, this is as much your fault as it is—"

"What is that?" Eva cut her off, pointing ahead of them. A white airplane seemed to be carrying a large, dark-skinned girl straight into the sky. "Is that a witch? I don't think I've ever seen her before."

"Jasmine," sighed Miyako through gritted teeth. She had told Jasmine to stay underground and yet here she was, flying over the city like a maniac, like she wasn't two breaths from death. From the buildings below, another figure emerged. Vicky rode a long glittering crystal broom with both legs to one side. She held her guitar in hand.

"That's her!" yelled Eva. "Vicky's chasing that witch!"

"No," said Miyako under her breath, her heart

stopping, overcome with dread. "No, no, no, no, NO!"
Miyako screamed but Jasmine was too far away to hear.
"Get out of there!!!" Without skipping a beat, Miyako
tightened her grip on her broom and took off, like a bat
out of hell. Eva snapped into gear, launching after her
and realizing that she had never seen any witch move
quite so fast.

*   *   *

"Stop running!" yelled Vicky. "Face me!"

High over the city, Jasmine turned her great paper
airplane to look down at her opponent, who stopped in
the air, glaring at her, tiring of the chase.

Jasmine reached into her bag of cranes and took a
deep breath. "Yes, ma'am," she called down.

Vicky smiled with excitement in her eyes. Her
fingers flew along the guitar strings, playing an
aggressive progression as she zoomed upwards, closing
the gap, on her crystalline broom. *Doom dun doom dun
doom dun DOOM DUN DOOM!!!*

Jasmine pulled the cranes from the bag and
scattered them around her. They swirled through the
air, igniting with blue fire and creating a cyclone of
flame.

The two girls sped towards each other, Vicky with
purple tendrils coming up from below, all the arrows

241

pointing at their target, and Jasmine and her flock of fiery cranes shooting down from above. The sky lit up, electrified. They soared towards each other like two heavenly forces, both of them hellbent on annihilating the other. Jasmine dodged through the arrows as her cranes surrounded her like a shield. Each hit sent cranes exploding into a papery mess of confetti. Vicky played the song even faster as a hundred purple tentacles burst from the guitar, heading straight for Jasmine. Time slowed as they collided.

*   *   *

KRACKABOOM!!!! Adam looked up into the sky from the rooftop. Blue fire and purple smoke exploded from the epicenter of the convergence like the grandest fireworks show the world had ever seen. He shielded his eyes from the beautifully haunting lights as they illuminated the night sky. From above, little bits of half burnt cranes fell all around him in a macabre confetti rain, like the night's stars were falling to Earth. He took slow steady breaths, waiting for his eyes to readjust so that he could see the aftermath.

He searched the sky with squinted eyes. Something was coming down. It seemed to be floating at first but then it picked up speed. His heart sank as he recognized the falling body as Jasmine's. He launched into a sprint to catch her, and just before she slammed into the cement of the rooftop, he grabbed her body. He fell at the impact and they skidded backwards, Adam not releasing his grip on her. He kept his eyes closed tight, fearing the worst, as smoke filled his nostrils and he realized it was coming from her.

Cough! COUGH! His eyes sprang open as her arms twitched. She was beaten, and her body was charred from the explosion but at least she was alive.

"Oh, thank God," he let out a breath of relief.

"Get away from her!" Miyako landed hard on the opposite side of the roof, followed by Eva. He looked up at Eva with a hopeful glance, but she avoided his gaze.

"I just caught her," explained Adam. "She was falling and I—"

"I said GET AWAY!" Miyako aimed her spray can at Adam. He pulled back, laying Jasmine's head gently on the ground. Miyako came to sit with her, propping her up to ease her pain and running her hands along Jasmine's face. Tears dripped from Miyako's eyes. "What were you thinking, Jazz?"

"I couldn't just stand there and watch him die," said Jasmine, smiling. Miyako put Jasmine's hand into her own and held it tightly.

"Are you in pain?" she asked.

"Miyako," started Jasmine. *Cough! Ca-Cough!* Jasmine tried to hold a hand to her mouth but couldn't.

243

"I'm so...sorry." Blood began to trickle from the side of her lips.

Adam let out a breath as he lifted himself from the ground, wiping the dirt from his bare skin. He held his arms with his hands, rubbing them as he tried to warm himself. Eva looked on, shaking her head.

"Come on, baby," said Miyako, squeezing her hand and staring into her eyes. "You're gonna be okay. You're gonna be fine. We just have to get through this. We're survivors, you and me. We can get through all of this shit." For a long moment, no one spoke.

"You have to do it," said Jasmine. The color in her skin was starting to fade and the blood flowing from her mouth was increasing.

"No," said Miyako. She shook her head madly. "I can't."

"What's she talking about?" Adam asked Eva quietly.

"If she dies now," said Eva, loud enough that Miyako could hear, "Vicky gets her soul. She'll become even stronger."

"You have to do it," repeated Jasmine, looking into Miyako's eyes, pleading with her. "You have to kill me. We promised each other."

"I promised to take care of you!" Miyako was shouting now.

Jasmine took Miyako's other hand into her own,

taking short, staggered breaths. "I'm gonna die one way or the other. I've been dying since the day we first met. Since before you taught me to use my power."

"I...can't..." Miyako's head bowed as if it was too much trouble to hold up any more.

Jasmine laid back, accepting her fate, her eyes searching the sky. She turned her face to Eva. "What about you?"

"Me?!" Eva placed a hand on her chest, taking a step back, clearly surprised.

"Someone has to stop her," coughed Jasmine. "You're already strong. I can feel it. But you'll need to be stronger. You'll need all the power you can get."

"But I," Eva started. "Miyako..."

"She's right," said Miyako, lifting her head up but still avoiding Eva's gaze.

"Please," whispered Jasmine. She coughed once more. "Don't let my soul be taken by that bitch."

Eva took a long deep breath and then gave a small nod. She reached her right arm to her side and held out her hand as a purple cloud began to form from thin air.

Adam stepped in front of her, flustered. "What are you doing?"

"Stay out of this, Adam," said Eva, looking past him.

"You can't seriously be thinking about killing this girl," he begged. "She just saved my life." Eva reached out a hand to his shoulder and finally looked into his

245

eyes. A single tear rolled down her cheek.

"I said stay out. This is the witch's way." She sighed, pushing him to the side. "I have no choice." She waved her staff through the air and a small silver revolver appeared. She grabbed it reluctantly and looked down at Jasmine, who gave a weak smile. "Quick and painless."

"Thank...you..." sighed Jasmine. Her eyes moved to Miyako. "The cranes."

"You were so close," sniffed Miyako.

"They were never for me."

"What?" Miyako shook her head. "I don't understand."

"They were for you." Jasmine squeezed Miyako's hand weakly. "My...wish was for you...to be...*cough*...happy." Jasmine's voice shook. "Don't...let me have made...all those birds...for nothing." Miyako tightened her grip on Jasmine.

Jasmine turned to Eva and gave a small nod, before turning back to look at Miyako's face. Her perfect face. The last face she would ever see.

"Be at peace," said Eva, closing her eyes.

BANG!

*   *   *

Vicky stood on a little patch of grass in Central Park,

popping her shoulder back into its socket. She wiped away the dust and debris from her clothes and then her guitar. In the distance, she could see the crowd from her concert coming towards her across the green fields.

Rumble, the ground shook beneath her in anticipation. Vicky smiled as she massaged her jaw.

"Do you hear that, my darling?" She asked the creature beneath her. "That is the sound of the first gunshot of war." She held out her arms to the park around her and took it all in. "This is where I make my stand. This is where I become the most powerful witch who has ever lived. First New York City and then, the world."

She leaned down and pet the ground as if it were a dog who had just performed a trick. "One way or another, it ends tonight."

*   *   *

Miyako continued to weep over Jasmine's body behind them. The softly glowing wisp of Jasmine's soul entered Eva's mouth and she breathed it in reluctantly.

"You have to leave here, Adam," said Eva, looking out across the city to the park beyond. She could feel Vicky's presence.

"We can leave," said Adam, his voice shaking with fear. "We can run away."

247

"She'll never stop." Eva's voice sounded cold, lifeless. "If I don't end her, the killing will just keep going and going. I couldn't leave knowing I allowed that to happen." Eva turned to Adam. "This is it for us, Adam. It's been fun, but we're done. I'm a witch and this is my destiny. You can't have any part of it." She stared at him with cold eyes. "Go."

"Eva, please, I understand now. I was selfish." He shook as the wind hit his bare body. "I pushed you too far, too fast. Please, we can start over. We can be—"

"I SAID GO!" she yelled, and Adam fell silent. Slowly, he pulled away and with one last look to her, he turned and headed for the fire escape.

Eva turned back to the park and gritted her teeth. "One way or another," she sighed. "This ends tonight."

Chapter Fifteen

Adam's life was filled with perfection. Perfectly folded clothes. A perfectly made bed. Perfectly tidy counter tops. Everything had a place. Everything was always clean. Everything was always organized. He color-coded and alphabetized and put things in numerical order. Maybe that was why he had been too blind to see it at first. He had tried to make his relationship with Eva Grey just as perfect as everything else, but it wasn't. It shouldn't have been. Relationships are the very epitome of messy, taking two people's independent lives and forcefully shoving them together. Adam had realized all of this too late. He sat, alone, not even two hours after she had told him to leave and never come back. She'd told him to forget about her, which was exactly why she was the only thing he could think about.

He tried to go home and clean to clear his mind, but for the first time in his life, this strategy of denial failed.

He showered and got dressed, a polo shirt and jeans, hoping that his normal routine would help. It didn't. Finally, after an hour and a half of counting minutes, hating himself and wishing the train had hit him so that he hadn't lived to see Jasmine's death, he put on a sweater and headed out. He wandered the streets near his apartment until he found the most arguably poetic spot to lose himself for the night: The little bar in the village where only a month ago it all began. He had raised a glass with his best friend Diego to celebrate the start of his new life. He was so sure it was going to be amazing. He sipped at a beer, wearily staring off into space. In only a month, he had become one of those guys who sits at a bar and realizes his whole life has passed him by.

"If this isn't some sort of irony, I don't know what is." The voice was so familiar that Adam didn't even need to look up to see who was speaking to him. He turned his head, gritting his teeth. Diego took a seat next to him. "Never in a million years would I have thought that I'd run into you here, and of all nights."

"Take a seat, Diego. I want to tell you a story," said Adam, his voice just loud enough that only the two of them could hear.

"Oh, good," said Diego sarcastically. "Is it about how you fucked my sister?"

"No," replied Adam. "This one's all about you and

me." Adam took a long drink from his glass and then began. "Once upon a time, I was so insecure and scared that when a guy a year ahead of me offered to show me the ropes, I latched on, never questioning whether or not he was a good guy or not. I followed this guy everywhere. I was weak. I needed to be him."

"It wasn't all bad," said Diego. For the first time, in a long time, he felt a tug of regret in his chest, as if his body was trying to kickstart his heart into feeling again.

"No, it wasn't. You're right. But sooner or later, I had to learn. That guy, I let him humiliate me and push me when I didn't want to be pushed. I let him use me to get himself laid by other guys. I let him succeed when I should have taken a chance and done something with my life. I didn't want to be him anymore. Because at the end of the day, *he* was weak."

"Jesus, Adam you're drunk." He grabbed Adam's arm, but Adam tugged it away.

"Don't touch me," sneered Adam.

"You were never supposed to get involved in this." Diego shook his head. "Your life can still go on. You can go back to folding and dusting and over analyzing. You can go back to daydreaming and looking for a job. You can escape. I'm sure somewhere out there is someone you're meant to be with. Just admit that you fell for the wrong girl this time."

Adam suddenly looked up, a glint in his eye. "'The

wrong girl? There's no such thing, Diego. Hell, there isn't even a right girl. I used to think we found the perfect person and had the perfect life, but life is messy, and you can barely predict tomorrow, let alone forever.

"I used to believe Eva was perfect for me and that we'd spend the rest of our lives together, but that's a bunch of horse shit. She is so incredibly not-perfect for me. I wasn't *meant* to be with her. I chose to be with her. She gave me the option to run away and I stayed. I don't think I really need forever anymore. I'd be happy just to have her in my life. You know, I could get hit by a train tomorrow, but for once I hope I don't. All we really have...is today."

Adam sat up, as if his head was filling with something he hadn't seen before. He looked at Diego and smiled. "Oh my God, you're obsessed with your sister."

"What the hell are you talking about?"

"You want to be her. You worshiped her and put her on a pedestal. I'm guessing everybody always liked her more than you. Boys, your parents, everyone. That's what this is all about, isn't it? It's the reason you followed Vicky so willingly, and the reason she's got such a tight hold on you. She's feeding off your jealousy and your little boy rage."

"Shut up, Adam," snapped Diego. He could feel the blood rushing through his veins.

"All you really wanted was to be liked as much as your sister." Adam grabbed Diego's shoulder and then leaned in, whispering into his ear. "But you're not her. You're weak, Diego, and now, everyone knows it. Even the guy who used to worship you. You got Vicky to fight her because you know, deep down, that you can't beat either of them." Adam leaned back into his chair. "So? Am I right?"

Suddenly, purple lines shot across Diego's face. His eyes changed from pupils to slits like those of a lizard. He grabbed Adam by his hair. Diego pulled him out of his chair and slammed him onto the long bar. Everyone stopped and turned to watch as Diego dragged Adam's body along the bar, sending glasses and liquor flying everywhere. Diego was picking up speed, not feeling Adam's weight, as dragon blood coursed through his arms. Diego hurled him forward and with a loud crash, Adam smashed through a large window at the end of the bar.

Glass fell around him as he floated through the air, falling towards the Earth from the window. He reached out for something to grab onto, but it was no use. He slammed on his back, hitting the street, and felt all the air vacate his lungs.

Diego jumped down to the street, landing on all fours. He moved over to Adam and sat on top of him, grabbing him by the collar. "Now listen to me, you pathetic little weasel!" he yelled at Adam. He raised a fist, ready to crush Adam's glasses and nose.

Adam suddenly noticed that he'd somehow managed to still have a beer glass tightly grasped in his hand. He squeezed it and swung, breaking the mug in half over Diego's head. Diego dropped onto his side, landing on the ground right next to Adam. Adam stared into Diego's eyes. His face softened, and the purple lines disappeared. He looked at Adam with guilt and unease.

"Adam," he said, his breath short. "I can't stop it now. Please forgive me." His bottom lip quivered. "I tried to break free but she's too strong. She's going to kill all the witches. I never wanted to hurt you. I never wanted to hurt Eva. She twisted me until I couldn't tell the difference between what she wanted and what I—" The purple lines returned to his face and he grabbed his head, screaming. "AHHHHHH!" He writhed on the ground and then, like a puppet on a string, his body stood itself up.

The time has come. Diego could hear her voice thundering in his head. It throbbed as he tried to fight her out until at last he gave in. His eyes became cold again as his hands fell to his side. His face hardened and in one quick movement, he turned, transformed into a dragon and took off into the sky.

Adam laid on the ground, catching his breath. He lifted his head, distinctly aware of the crowd gathered at the shattered window above, staring at him. Pain caught up to his body. He forced every muscle to stand up straight. He had to get to Central Park. Despite everything. Every spell, every high-speed witch chase, every warning, he had to get to her.

Maybe he had fallen in love with the wrong girl, or maybe she had replied to a message from the wrong guy. None of it mattered now. What mattered was that a simple beer glass had broken Vicky's spell, if even for a moment. If that was possible, then maybe she wasn't as strong as everyone thought. He had no idea what that meant, but he knew that Eva Grey was the girl who was about to sacrifice herself to save the world.

And he was the man who loved her.

*   *   *

Twilight hung over the crowded tombstones of the Queens Cemetery. In the stillness of the night, no one had seen a sullen Miyako flying in on her broom with the body of her deceased lover. She found a quiet spot at the top of a hill and set three paper creatures to digging in the soil with long paper shovels, made solid by the power of her red paint. Miyako took up a shovel and stood side by side with her minions, digging the sloppy grave. She found it almost therapeutic. When she was digging, she could focus on just that, and not have to feel the feelings that were threatening to crush her.

When the hole was done, the creatures lifted Jasmine and placed her in the ground. Miyako shed a few more tears as she sat a crane on Jasmine's chest. She then touched a finger to her lips, kissed it gently and then placed it onto Jasmine's lips. Her skin was ice cold to the touch.

"Goodbye, Jazz," she whispered. She jumped out of the hole and waved at the creatures to start the arduous process of refilling the hole. This part, she could not be a part of. Miyako sat by a tree as her creatures buried her best friend and thought about how the evening had played out. She had gone into it ready to be the ultimate hero but in the end, it was she who had allowed Vicky to escape. In the end, Jasmine had saved a total stranger and Eva had taken mercy on Jasmine, even though the witch's way was to be as cruel as possible. Why was that? she wondered. Was it simply the way it had always been? Was that a good enough reason to let things continue on in a desperate, murderous rampage, year after year, decade after decade? Was a witch's only purpose in this life to die? Even now, Eva Grey was marching towards death and here she was, miles away. She looked back to see the creatures putting the final bits of earth back on the grave.

There would be time to honor Jasmine. There would be time to give her the proper good-bye. But now was not that time. Miyako grabbed a large rock from beside the tree and lugged it over to the dirt mound. She placed it on top, marking the grave, so she could easily return. She waved a hand, commanding the monsters to tear themselves apart. She grabbed the bag of cranes, what was left of them anyway, and sprayed a red mist through the air, summoning her broom. She climbed aboard and headed for the city.

*   *   *

The concert audience gathered in a wide circle around Vicky, forming a giant protective barrier between her and anyone stupid enough to pry. Beneath her was a small mound of lush grass. It lifted and fell as the creature below took long, restless breaths, ready to enter the realm of the living. Diego dropped from above and hit the ground, transforming back to a human. He walked to Vicky and opened his arms. They embraced.

"Your day of victory is finally here, my Queen," he said, smiling grandly, proud that he had been part of such a momentous occasion.

"Yes, darling. I've waited so long for this, I can hardly contain my excitement." She beamed with joy.

Diego turned and looked out over the park, waving a hand at the crowd of people who had gathered. "Your fans are all here, and the golem is waking."

"Yes," said Vicky, taking slow steps to move up behind him. "It's all come together quite nicely, I must say." She moved directly behind Diego so that he could feel her breath on his neck. "There's just one thing left to do."

"Guh!" Diego's body seized with shock. His eyes slowly moved down to the origin, where he saw that a long, jagged black blade was protruding from his abdomen. Blood trickled through, staining his shirt and pants a dark red. "Why? I did...everything...you asked."

Vicky smiled, twisting the knife so that the blood flowed faster, pouring out onto the ground. "You did well, Diego. But I'm afraid the blood of my most loyal subject is needed to complete the summoning ritual. You might even call it the secret ingredient. I told you from the start, love, sacrifices must be made." She ripped the knife from his stomach and let it drop to the ground. The grass and soil soaked up the blood like a sponge.

Diego fell to his knees. Vicky rounded to face him, smiling as she peered into his eyes. Life was leaving him, his skin was losing its color and turning a dull grey. Blood dripped from his nose as he grabbed at his stomach, shaking with pain. "You..." he started and made one final push to look her in the eye, "You...cunt." His body fell limp to the ground, as the last of his life left his body.

"What can I say, darling?" she asked, shrugging and turning to her audience. "I just really love killing." She held her hands out to the crowd, who cheered for her. Her eyes closed basking in her own glory. The ground shook with impatience below her. She waved her hand through the air, and from a glittery cloud, she pulled a silver crown. She smiled, seeing it in her hand. "Hello, old friend." She placed it upon her head and then, with another wave, conjured her guitar. She stretched her fingers, cracking her knuckles, and then began to play. A song fit for victory. A song fit for a Queen.

* * *

Eva stood at the edge of the park, looking into its long expanse as she tried to control her breathing. Zot hovered respectfully beside her. She watched as the horde of concert goers congregated on the field, creating a massive circle around what she could only imagine was Vicky.

"Way to be subtle," she said under her breath. Zot licked his nose. The ground beneath her began to quake. She took a step, looking around for its source. Across from her, she could see the large Belvedere Castle, looming over the park like a stoic statue keeping watch. It had great stone walls and a tall tower with little windows. There was a little pavilion at the far side with a cobblestone path leading up to it from the park. The castle groaned as the ground twisted beneath it. "What the hell?"

There was a sudden lurch from the ground that sent Eva to one knee. The castle twisted itself from the earth and pulled, bringing with it roots and soil. It lifted high into the air like a space ship awakening after years of lying dormant. It hovered there for a second and then, as if weightless, twisted through the air on its way to the center of the park and Vicky.

Ding-a-ding ding. Da-ding-a-ding ding. The melody floated through the air as Vicky played. From all around the park, bricks, fountains, trees and statues flew towards her. *Ding-a-ding. Ding. Ding-a-ding.* Eva took off at a run, heading for the crowd-circle. She reached her hand to the air beside her and pulled her staff from a purple cloud.

Krackoom! The ground shuddered, and she fell forward, trying to stay on her feet. The hill ahead of her lifted, still attached to the ground, like a snake unraveling itself. The castle broke itself apart and then shifted, affixing itself to the top of a raising mound of grass. The castle tower spun upside down, settling in the center of the mound like a long snout. The pavilion and the barracks went to either side of the creature's face, like large eyebrows. The glass of the windows formed underneath them to create large eyes. A harsh yellow light emitted from them. The lower part of the mound broke open into a gaping mouth.

Eva stared upwards, finally understanding just what Vicky had planned. The Queen had been gaining power not so that she could take on the world of witches as a solo act, but so that she was strong enough to call in reinforcements. Somehow, she had managed to get her hands on an ancient, forbidden magic and had placed the soul of an old god into that of a dormant golem, making the creature come back to life after thousands of years. Eva had read about the spell in her search to free Zot, but never actually saw it performed. It was incredibly dangerous to perform an act of this magnitude without the magic to restrain such a beast.

Another mound of dirt and grass raised into the air, creating a huge arm. Parts of the mud and grass split apart to create fingers as the arm came crashing down to the ground. The earth shuddered again under the weight of the giant. Another arm formed. The great Obelisk, a tower shaped in the form of an ancient Egyptian spire, spun through the air and attached to the second arm, giving it the threatening appearance of a dagger. Two more legs grew from the creature's rear end, helping it to lift even farther from the ground.

Graaaaaa! It let out a roar as it stood at its full height, tall enough to threaten the shorter buildings in the city. Its glowing eyes, grassy back and mane of flora made it look something like a stone lion with the face of a barn owl. It stood on all fours, with a long tail made up of horses and zebras and other creatures from the nearby carousel whipping around behind it. It took a step forward, shaking the entire park. It was the most terrifying monster Eva had seen in her entire life. She held onto her staff tightly.

Doom! Doom! DOOM! The guitar echoed as the ritual completed itself. Eva could not believe her eyes, but she held strong, preparing to move forward. She waved her staff through the air. A bright white rune appeared on the ground beneath her. It was time to put some of the new power she had acquired over the previous weeks to work. All around her, little spots of light sprung from the ground. Little sombrero wearing, pistol swinging, chattering, 'Day of the Dead' skeletons burst forth from them, gathering around her as she twirled the staff in the air. Soon she had amassed an army of her own.

The crowd turned their attention to Eva as Vicky rose into the air, guitar in hand, hovering in front of her golem. She cackled with laughter.

"Eva Grey!" she spat. "I promised your brother I would not harm you for as long as he lived." She shrugged her shoulders. "Sadly, his time came to an end."

Eva's heart heaved. Though she'd never had the

best relationship with her brother who *had* attempted to kill her, the news of his death still took something from inside of her.

She was thankful she had sent Adam away. Now there was no one else for Vicky to use against her. It was just the two of them. Woman to woman. Witch to witch.

"Your death will prove a wonderful coronation gift for my new position!" yelled Vicky.

"And what position is that?" pondered Eva.

"Goddess of Witches," Vicky smirked. "Duh!"

"Yeah," smiled Eva. "That's just not gonna work out for you." Eva spun her staff through the air. Her little skeletal army loaded their six shooters. "This ends here and now."

"Oh, darling," said Vicky. "I could not agree more."

Eva launched forward, pointing her staff upwards. "NOW!" she screamed. A hundred little guns went off as her army crashed into Vicky's fans. Cries rang out into the night sky, and the golem roared once more signaling the start of the battle for all witch kind.

Chapter Sixteen

Adam ran as fast as his human legs could carry him. No paper planes, no jet fueled staves, just his own two feet. He cut through Washington Square Park and then headed up the side streets, avoiding Broadway at all costs, not wanting to get stuck in the crowd. He went past Union Square and Herald Square, Bryant Park and Chelsea. He cut through Hell's Kitchen and then around Times Square. Before long, he reached 59th Street and the southern-most end of Central Park. He was sweating and exhausted, but the adrenaline had carried him there, never stopping to take a taxi. He certainly had no future plans of going back into the subway.

He looked out over the park and his jaw dropped, wiping the sweat from his brow. A huge creature made of dark green grass, dirt, rock and every statue in Central Park, was towering over a crowd of people. Screams echoed from the park, cutting through the sirens and the roar of the city around it. He looked around, noticing several people walking by as if nothing was out of the ordinary. It certainly wasn't how Adam imagined people would react when faced with the end of the world.

"Run!" he yelled to them, but they simply ignored him, writing him off as another crazed street dweller. "Can't you see, there's a witch war happening? It's right there! Don't any of you care about living?"

"They can't see it," came a voice from behind him. He turned to see Miyako walk out of the shadows. Her eyes were red and puffy, and she looked exhausted. "Mortals can't see the affairs of the magic world. Sometimes not even when they're staring right at them."

"But, I see them," said Adam angrily. "I can see it all. Why can't they?"

"She allowed you to. That night when she showed you her staff, she invited you to look into our world and, whether you knew it or not, you accepted her invitation." Miyako rounded on Adam. "I was watching you two from a rooftop nearby. My plan was to kill Eva that night. When I saw her show you, I thought you were special. But you're just a normal nobody, aren't you? Why on earth would someone like you get involved with a witch?"

"I was just naive," sighed Adam. "I didn't know any better."

"Hm, and here I thought you were incapable of

saying anything without snark or sarcasm," Miyako scoffed. "Guess there's something more to you after all."

"Yeah, well, we've all got our defense mechanisms. Mine are just more subtle and don't involve painting people to death." Adam waved a hand goodbye at Miyako and then turned towards the park. "Now, if you don't mind, I really have to—"

"Where do you think you're going?" Miyako grabbed his arm. He pulled it away from her.

"I have to help her," he snapped.

"Just because you can see our world doesn't mean you're equipped to handle it," she said. "You're gonna get yourself killed."

"Then help me!" Adam glared at Miyako with an intensity that shook her and made her feel self-conscious. "How can you just sit back and watch? If I were you, I'd already be in the fight."

"I don't have anything left to fight *for,*" snarled Miyako.

"That girl," said Adam, pointing to the rooftops behind them, "died so that Eva could protect you and your kind." Adam shook his head. "Fight for her." Miyako looked away, ashamed. "Or would you really have let her die for nothing? Would you really let Eva lose this fight, knowing you could have helped?"

Miyako thought for a long moment. She had been fighting all her life. She'd fought to survive, and to protect Jasmine and herself, and now all of that seemed to have been for nothing. Yet, she had returned to the city. Something inside her knew that she was meant to be here. Without Jasmine to protect, she was lost, scared even. Suddenly her mortality seemed very real and present. She thought about Jasmine and everything they'd been through. She thought about Jasmine's final wish and how, if Vicky were to rule the world, that wish would only be a fantasy amidst a short life of terror. She clenched her fists and turned back to Adam.

"Come on."

*   *   *

Eva lunged into the air, swinging her staff as Vicky shot out a barrage of purple arrowed tendrils. Eva summoned a group of laughing skulls engulfed in purple smoke, which intercepted the tendrils and exploded on contact. Eva flew through the smoke and fire of the collision.

"You've grown stronger!" cackled Vicky from above. "Tell me how it felt, Eva. Killing all those girls. Did it feel good? Could you taste their souls?"

"None of them tasted as good as yours will," taunted Eva. The golem took a swipe at her. She evaded it and then used the grassy patch on the top of its foot to lunge even higher. She pulled back her staff and then, with all the force in her body, swung it at Vicky.

CLANG!!! Vicky met the staff with her guitar, which she now held like a heavy metal axe. They toppled to the head of the golem, each of them on either side of the long tower that made its nose. Its glowing eyes pulsed with rage as the two girls jumped to their feet and lunged at each other once more.

Below them, the war between the punk rock fans and the skeletons could be heard, as little pistols went off and the crowd threw themselves selflessly into the fray. Zot led the charge, head-butting the fans and helping the skeletons to their feet when they fell. At Eva's command, the skeletons took a non-lethal approach towards the mindless humans, lassoing them, hog-tying them and then carrying them to the side-lines of the battle.

Eva and Vicky swung back and forth at each other, twisting their weapons through the air like warriors on an ancient battlefield, fighting with metal on metal. Sword to axe. Their weapons slammed into each other, the two girls gritting their teeth and snarling.

"I'm still going to get your little boyfriend, you know," smiled Vicky. "I know he got away, but I really am the cat to his mouse. Eventually I will catch him, and then I'll make all his wildest dreams come true. I'll do things to him he always wanted but was too afraid to ask you. I'll make him feel so good, the words Eva Grey will no longer exist. And when I'm done, I'll cut him up and feed him to my new friend here."

"NO!" Eva shoved Vicky back with more strength than she'd ever felt before. The thought of Adam in pain seemed to fuel her rage. In fact, thinking of him made her feel even stronger. It was a sensation she couldn't quite explain. She had felt it the night she'd fought Zyla and now the same power coursed through her veins.

She jumped into the air, ready to take her opening and bash in Vicky's skull with her staff. But the golem shifted its weight, letting out a loud roar. Eva missed her landing and started to topple down the behemoth. She tried to grab a hold of one of the roots along its arms, but the creature shook her off, sending her to the ground. She waved her staff and a dozen skeletons jumped beneath her to slow her fall. Above her, the monster opened its mouth, a blue glow bellowing from deep within it. She dove out of the way, just before a massive jet of cerulean flame engulfed part of the battlefield. Vicky cackled in delight as several concert goers started screaming, their skin on fire. Zot flew through the crowd hacking up large chunks of saliva in order to extinguish as many of the human bonfires as he could.

Eva pulled herself behind a small bridge, catching her breath and realizing that even now, she was not strong enough to defeat Vicky Davis, the Witch Queen.

*   *   *

Miyako worked quickly. In one hand she carried a large duffel bag, which Adam recognized as Jasmine's. In the other, she held a small briefcase. They approached a long brick wall, the side of a huge hotel bordering the park on the opposite side of the street. Miyako shoved the briefcase into Adam's hands. "Take this," she ordered. "Put them up along this wall. All of them."

Adam opened the briefcase and looked in to see a whole stack of paper creatures of various sizes. They were all folded up neatly and only slightly resembled the hulking beast which had carried him away from Vicky's capture. "How do you expect me to glue them all to the wall?"

Miyako looked at him, rolling her eyes. "Seriously?"

"Right," sighed Adam. "Magic paper doesn't need glue."

He turned and ran to the wall. One by one, he unfolded the creatures and stuck them to the wall, where they stayed with no added glue or adhesive. There were tall ones and short ones, fat ones and thin ones. It looked like a lineup of animals from a children's book. Before long, he had a good system in place, picking up speed as he unfolded the paper army.

Miyako jumped on top of a car parked at the curb and dropped the duffel bag in front of her. She held a hand out over it. The zipper pulled itself back, revealing the horde of nearly six hundred cranes, all that had not been destroyed by the fight with Vicky. She started to move her arms gracefully through the air in a pattern. The wind around her picked up and whipped through her hands. She could feel Jasmine's breath on the back of her neck, her hand around her waist. Miyako let a soft smile grow on her face. Being near the cranes made her feel closer to Jasmine, who was now so very far away.

It was only a single crane at first, but one by one the cranes slowly began to lift out of the bag and enter the swirling wind around Miyako. Soon the entire bag's worth of cranes were aloft and soaring around Miyako. She focused all her energy on keeping the cranes in the air and keeping the ritual going as she pulled out her spray can. With a strong wave of her arm, she pulled the can through the air, shooting red paint onto the cranes as they sped in front of her. The cranes turned from white to the harsh red of the paint. Miyako smiled, reminded of Jasmine's bright red hair, which had always made her seem so cool and different.

With every crane now painted and fully under her control, she turned her body once more and pointed her arms straight ahead at the park. The cranes took off in a flurry of beating red wings, like a bloody murder of crows.

"Hold on, Eva," she said, under her breath. "We're

on our way."

*   *   *

A hand grabbed Eva from behind the bridge and dragged her out into the open. "No!" she screamed. Soon several more punk rocker hands were dragging her back to the battle, back to Vicky. She swung her staff, beating them off. "Stay back!" she yelled, but this only cajoled more of them to attack her. Every swing or magic skull she sent threw one or two back but attracted four or more. It was like a zombie horde, drawn by any commotion or resistance. Even Zot was being overwhelmed by a small crowd of particularly trashy girls.

"That's right, my adoring fans," called Vicky from atop the golem. "Kill her!" The horde turned and charged at Eva. The skeletons jumped at the crowd, but their numbers were dwindling. The crowd was literally on top of her as she scrambled to keep them off. Her vision of the moon above lessened until there was only darkness. Eva looked up to see flickers of red pass across her line of sight, a flock of birds heading straight for her.

"Now what?" she asked, feeling her body start to tire from fighting off the constant attacks. The cranes sped down, broke through the crowd and then, like a force field, began to encircle her. A punk rocker got too close and several of the cranes broke from the flock, pecking at him savagely like a group of angry bees, causing him to fall to the ground, stunned.

"AHHH!" the man screamed. As soon as they were done with one, the cranes jumped to another attacker and then another. They had formed an offensive shield which retaliated against whoever was currently trying to kill her. Eva smiled.

"Thanks, Miyako," she said, looking out over the field. She turned and focused what was left of her power on the golem.

Graaaaaa! The golem looked into the sky and with a deep breath, shot out an enormous stream of blue fire. Eva looked up at it, marveling at how, under different circumstances, one could have found it very beautiful. High in the air, the fire split apart into much smaller pieces and turned downwards. Eva gasped in horror as fire rained from the heavens, exploding on the ground and killing skeletons and punk rockers alike. It was indiscriminate in its merciless murder, and the explosive fire was coming straight for her. She'd done what she could, but the innocent lives of the mortals were beyond saving now. She turned to run for cover.

*   *   *

Miyako's eyes went wide as fire began to pour down

across the field, like a torrential downpour of meteors. "We're out of time, Adam," she said, turning back to him. Behind her, the wall was now covered with every black and white monster she had ever painted throughout her life. It was a small militia, but it would have to do. She pulled one last large piece of crumpled paper from her pocket and threw it onto the pavement of the street where it unfolded into a huge black and white beast. She sprayed little dots of red down the spine of the beast. She went to the wall, spinning her spray can in her hand and then began to walk along the wall, spraying a red line across each creature as she passed them.

At the end of the lineup, she turned to Adam, who stood at the center of the wall admiring their work. "You ready?"

"As I'll ever be," he responded.

Clink. Miyako banged the bottom of the can onto the brick wall. One by one, the creatures stepped out into the third dimension, growling and grunting like bears awaking from hibernation. Before long, the entire paper militia was alive and at attention. Miyako ran to the paper beast on the ground and with a wave of the can, a large cat-like beast leaped out of the cement. It was enormous, standing as tall as a small elephant. It was white with black stripes like a white tiger, but instead of slender and sleek like a cat ought to be, it was hulking and massive. Adam imagined this was what the offspring of a tiger and a gorilla might look like. Miyako pulled herself atop the gorilla-cat and then rounded on Adam.

"You know, I usually get car sick so maybe I should just hang down here with these—" Adam started, but she had already grabbed his arm, pulling him up and placing him behind her. She turned to the park with the army marching up behind her. "Is this the part where you give the troops a rousing speech before charging into battle?"

Miyako raised an eyebrow. "They're made of paper."

"Fair enough."

"Hi-yah!" she yelled, kicking at the large cat-beast. It took off at a fast gallop, the ground beneath its feet shuddering. They rode out into the field as hellfire fell from the heavens and the golem continued to stomp across the park. The remaining skeletons and punk rockers scuffled, following their masters' bidding. Behind them, the paper army was running into the fray. It was refreshing, Adam thought, that he no longer felt like a pathetic, out of work, down on his luck graphic designer with no hope and no prospects. Tonight, he felt like a warrior.

*　　　*　　　*

Eva was doing her best to hold off the horde, and

the cranes were doing their part, but she hadn't been able to get back to Vicky and could feel herself growing more tired. Every swing hurt in her arms and her back. Every spell pushed her limits and made her chest hurt. Her breaths grew shorter. Every extra skeleton she raised threatened to make her nose bleed. She wasn't sure how much longer she could sustain this pace, with no end in sight.

"Enough games!" shouted Vicky from above. "This girl is the only thing standing between me and ruling this pitiful city!" Eva looked up, gasping for every breath she could take. Her eyes fixed on Vicky's as Vicky towered over her. Vicky leapt from the back of the creature and slowly lowered herself until she was hovering just in front of its gargantuan muddy mouth. A giddy hatred flashed across her face and she cackled as her hair flew everywhere in the wind. She strummed her guitar. "FINISH HER!"

*   *   *

The army of paper monsters came over a small hill and charged the enemy, crashing into the punk rockers and pushing them back. The crowd ambled around, confused by the new attacker pummeling them to the ground, leaving them fair game for the skeletons to tie them up. Miyako aimed the cat into a large group of people, barreling through them like a freight train. She laughed as the crowd members toppled like bowling pins. The cat-beast seemed to equally enjoy being used as a human bulldozer.

"That should even the odds," she said proudly.

Adam looked out through the chaos for a sign of Eva. "Where is she?" he yelled to Miyako, his eyes darting from one cluster of fighting to another. "You don't think—"

"There!" Miyako called out, pointing to what was left the little cluster of cranes. The rockers threw themselves maniacally at the cranes who tried desperately to protect their cargo. Every attack resulted in a few more ripped cranes and as they fell, Adam could just make out Eva behind them. She was hunched over, blood trickling from little cuts all along her arms and face. She looked exhausted. She swung the staff, deflecting attacks as best as she could, but it looked heavy and cumbersome in her hands, as if it were an effort just to hold it up. At this rate, she would fall before she got a second shot at Vicky.

Horror filled Adam's face as a large shadow engulfed Eva. Looking up, he saw the golem raising a massive foot over her, positioning himself perfectly to stomp her into the ground.

"Oh no..." he whispered under his breath. Acting on impulse and adrenaline alone, he jumped from the cat beast. Miyako tried to grab him, to hold him back, but she was too late. He fell to the ground rolling and took off into the fray, towards Eva.

"Adam!" Miyako yelled after him, but she too was now looking at the massive foot, lifting higher and higher over Eva's head. Miyako waved her hands through the air, signaling to the cranes. She saw Adam's head bob out of sight as he disappeared into the fighting below. She swung her arms upwards, commanding a large portion of the cranes to the sky. They slammed into the foot just as it started to descend and for a moment, it hung there.

Miyako's arms were outstretched, the full weight of the golem bearing down on the cranes as she tried desperately to keep its foot in the air. Sweat dripped down her face and she gritted her teeth. She could feel pain building in her arms, could sense the little cranes crippling under the goliath pressure of the golem's weight. She let out a shout as she gave the cranes one last psychic push before feeling the last of them crumble, the golem's foot breaking through.

*   *   *

Eva could barely stand. She could barely breathe and to make matters worse, the world around her seemed to be growing darker. The cranes had left her, and the enemy was everywhere. Zot was distracted, head-butting a group of increasingly hateful punk rockers. Time slowed as she looked up to see the large foot of the golem coming down on her. It was almost peaceful. She saw the vines, grass and roots of the foot as it blocked out all light above her. There was nowhere to run. Even if there was, she didn't have the energy to move. She'd given it her all. She closed her eyes, ready for the end.

"EVA!" A shove came from behind, pushing her out of the path of the golem. Her body flew limply and then rolled along the ground. Dirt crammed into her mouth as she skidded to a stop in a rough patch of dry grass.

BOOM! The foot slammed into the ground, knocking every paper creature, punk rocker and skeleton off their feet. She looked up, blinking her eyes, trying to make out what had happened. How was it possible that she was still alive? The golem raised its leg once more and there, lying in the footprint of the behemoth, was Adam's lifeless body. He had pushed her out of harm's way at the last minute, taking the hit. She'd told him to leave. She'd begged him. Yet here he was, and he had given his life, worth so much more than her own.

"No..." she coughed out the mud in her mouth and pushed herself up from the dirt. "Please...no..." She lifted herself onto all fours and began to half-crawl, half-limp towards Adam's body. She already knew he was gone but refused to accept it. Tears began to stream down her face. She felt the pain of everything important in her life ceasing to be all at once

"AH HAHAHAHAHA!!!" Above her, Vicky laughed maniacally with abandon.

"No no no no no," Eva wept, crumpled over Adam. She placed her hands on his shoulders and shook him. Her face was red, and she could barely see through the tears pouring from her eyes.

Miyako rode up on her mighty cat-stead, taking a deep breath and holding it until she dismounted. She looked down, taking in the whole scene. Eva shook Adam's body relentlessly. The two of them were perfectly framed by the indentation the golem had left in its wake. "Dammit, Adam," she said, shaking her head in disbelief.

"Come on, Adam," said Eva. "Please. Open your eyes." She could taste the salt of her tears in her mouth. "COME ON!" she yelled.

She slumped over his body, putting her face up next to his, their skin touching. He was getting colder by the second. Surely Vicky was readying a final blow for her, but she didn't care. None of that mattered anymore.

"Eva..." said Miyako from the side of the footprint. "He's gone."

Eva couldn't hear her. She couldn't hear anything. She was listening for a breath or a heartbeat. Any sign that Adam was still in there, somewhere. "You can't be gone, Adam. I can't lose you. Not yet. Not now." She pulled back and looked into his still eyes as they stared back at her, unseeing. "Adam," she whispered. Her tears dripped down onto his face, offering nothing in return. Adam remained silent. He had already said everything he needed to say. Now it was her turn. "Adam...I love you."

Chapter Seventeen

"If it's to be a fair wager, there ought to be rules."

"Then you mean for us to go through with this?"

"Why wouldn't we? I've lived for millions of years and watched the humans squabble this way and that. It was entertaining enough for a time. But just think of what they will do with something like this."

"You mean, magic?"

"Of course! You think they're fun to watch now, just wait until they get their hands on this."

"What are the rules then? I can really only think of one."

"Oh? Do tell."

"No love. You have your chosen and I have mine, but they can't fall in love with you or I."

"Well, that's no fun at all. Why take something so potent out of the equation?"

"Because its cheap and I'd rather this be a real test

of which among us has the stronger will, not just a race to make them fall in love with us. Besides, you're so crafty and smooth-tongued, it wouldn't be a fair battle. I, for one, wouldn't have any part in a one-sided duel.

"Very well. We each grant magic to one human. I'll have mine and you'll have yours and they can't fall in love with us. Otherwise, we must forfeit, and the game is over."

"Agreed."

In the darkness, Adam could hear only the voices. He just barely understood that he was in fact himself and that this place was in fact here. Around him, he could see a soft blue light and a harsh red light, and they seemed to speak to each other in an ancient language, yet in his head he understood every word. They were making a deal of some kind, a wager, a bet. The red light made him feel uneasy, as though he were having a dream where he showed up to school to find out that he was in only his underwear. The blue light, however, was warm and reassuring. It felt strong and sure. When it spoke, he believed anything was possible.

"That's how it began." A voice came from behind him. The voice spoke in French, yet again, he seemed to understand completely. "Two spirits, two angels, two powers, whatever you want to call them. They made a wager for all of humanity through all of time. The fire spirit went off and found a young boy in ancient Egypt, named Imhotep, starting the line of Wizardry, though it would not come to be called that for some time. The other, the air spirit, he found me."

"Who are you?" asked Adam. His voice sounded distant in his head and he realized he didn't have to move his mouth to speak the words. He wasn't even sure he had a mouth.

"My name is Joan."

The world around him shifted like a dream and he found himself in a garden. A young girl of about twelve walked through the flowers and perfectly trimmed hedges. She had fair skin but a rougher look in her eyes, like she was ready for a fight. In a way, she seemed more similar to boys of her age, with strong shoulders and a chiseled chin. She had long, mousy brown hair that was braided with flowers in parts and she wore a light blue dress that didn't quite seem to fit her boyish face. As Adam watched, the blue light appeared above her. She pulled back, surprised by its appearance. Its surface ebbed with a pulsating light. Adam could see that it comforted her. She moved to it, like a moth to a flame.

"Joan, be not afraid. I have come to show you the truth. I have come with a gift and a prophecy of things to come. You will change the fate of this country. Your name will be sung throughout all of history from this moment forward."

"I don't understand," said the young Joan. The light

of the blue essence flickered in her eyes.

"You will in time." Suddenly a long, glistening sword appeared in front of her. She jumped back once more. "This gift I give to you. To it, your power will be tied. You can summon it at will, but always swing it with justice in mind. Be careful not to reveal it until the time is right. To lose this gift would be disastrous. Do you understand me?"

She nodded her head. She grabbed the sword. As large as it was, it seemed light in her hands. In a puff of silver smoke, it disappeared, and the blue essence softened.

"Now, I shall tell you of how you will change this world."

The landscape shifted again, and Adam watched as Joan became a young woman. He watched her fight and surpass men who thought themselves stronger than she and slowly, she gained support in a conquest to be by the King's side. All the while, he saw the blue essence counseling her, telling her where to go and what to say to gain the trust of those around her. She inspired followers and grew from a young girl, using hand-me-down armor, to a religious crusader. Everywhere she went, every battle she fought, she was seen as a holy warrior, exacting the justice of God over her opponents. Around her, Adam saw anger begin to fester, and an increasing number of those who refused to believe her, even when she did exactly what her master asked of her. She ignored these naysayers and pulled the French through to victory. Every swing of her sword decimated the opposition.

The world around Adam solidified, and he saw Joan in a small room with a wicker bed and a little fireplace. The blue essence appeared before her and she ran to it with gleeful pride, as though her husband had just come home from a long day's work.

"My lord!" she cried. She looked not unlike her male counterparts now, her hair cut short and her body toned like that of a fine young warrior. "It's been so long since I've seen you. Longer than usual."

"Joan of Arc," said the spirit. "You have done well in this war and your success is proving that loyalty and purity are the greatest embodiment of magic." It paused. "I am proud of you."

"I'm glad to hear it. I too have something to say." She blushed and softened her poise, resembling her younger effeminate self. "All these years you have guided me, but I don't know your name or even what you look like. Won't you please show yourself to me?"

"Those things, my name, my appearance, they are unimportant to you and to your purpose." The blue spirit was firm in its decision.

"But my lord," she said shyly. "I must know the name of my love."

The spirit flickered. "No."

"I said," she swallowed. "I love you."

Without warning, light suddenly spilled forth from her body in all directions as if something had been triggered within her. Adam knew what he expected to see. If this girl was a witch, he was about to witness her lose her powers, but this is not what seemed to be happening. She rose into the air, the glow increasing. Adam felt a surge of energy, not the diminishing of it. It was as if she were growing exponentially stronger by the second.

"No," said the spirit. "NO!" A long white hand reached from the blue spirit and grabbed her chest.

"AHHHHHH!" she cried. Adam watched as the light was ripped from her, sucked out by the force of the being. It absorbed the light, Joan's face draining of color. She looked horrified as her body fell from the air and crumpled to the floor in front of the fire place. The fire went out.

"You have lost me EVERYTHING!" The spirit was filled with rage. "I expected *him* to use love to win this wager, but instead you have made me into a cheater. I promised you would never die on one condition, that you would never love, and you have failed."

"I was so young," she panted from the floor, crying into the wood boards beneath her. "Surely you did not expect that could last. To find love is to feel alive.

Without it, I surely would rather be dead."

"That," said the spirit, "can be arranged." With that, it vanished, leaving her alone on the floor.

"I really was just a child," came the voice from behind Adam once more. He continued to watch this poor girl, abandoned by the only friend she had ever known. "So naive. How could I have known that it was not my love which had left me powerless, but the will of a god who was more concerned with a wager than the fate of all humanity. So badly did he not want to be seen as his more devious brother that he left me, like a piece of garbage on the street. Little did he know that once magic had touched this world, it would only grow and thrive and expand. Nothing so powerful can be contained."

Adam watched as Joan rode to battle once more and was pulled from her horse, captured by a lone archer. Without her magic, her spirit, she was weak, unable to fight back. She surrendered willingly. He watched her rot away in a cramped and filthy prison cell as she awaited her persecution. She spoke the truth in her trial and talked of how the spirit had asked her to fight for God and how she had done exactly what was asked of her. She spoke of how she was unworthy of his love. In the moments before they finally came to collect her, he saw her write a letter to anyone else who might find themselves with the gift of a god and the promise of eternal life.

"*Let it be known,*" she wrote, "*that I have seen love and it is a vile contemptuous thing. It has left me forsaken and powerless. Beware my sisters, for she whomsoever loves, will surely perish.*"

Shortly after, she was taken away and burned alive in front of a crowd of people, her hands tied behind her at the stake. As the fire consumed her, Adam saw the last images of the letter being found by a young girl and then passed down year after year, century after century. Then, everything went black.

"How could I have known?" Joan spoke to him through the darkness. "How could I have understood then that my belief in the evil of love would create the world you now live in?"

A girl appeared before him, glowing a golden color. She wore peasant's clothes and held a long scepter in her hand. She smiled back at him. "If to love another is so evil and takes your power, then the only thing left to live for is to hate each other," echoed Joan's voice. Suddenly, other girls began to appear, each holding a different item in their hands. A mirror, a lute, a staff, a wand. Girl after girl, witch after witch, they appeared before him. "The spirit thought to control the witches by tying their life to their power, embodied in their chosen weapon. Our powers become untethered as soon as our life ends, thus leaving only our souls, which we quickly learned could be consumed. The death and fighting came easily to the witches as they discovered a means to become even greater. War after war ensued as the witches sought glory, never understanding, that the key to the greatest magical gifts of all was love." Joan reappeared before him looking as she did on the way to her death and gazed at him with kindness in her eyes.

Suddenly, thousands of witches sprang into view. It was breathtaking, and Adam spun in awe. He saw golden witches from days past, for miles and miles in every direction. Soon, every witch who had ever lived, and died, stood before him. "Despite our ancestors' missteps," came a voice to his side, "there is hope." Adam turned to see a young girl with green highlights in her hair and a pair of long combs in her hands step up to him. "She needs you," said Lexie.

"Eva can't break the cycle and change the course of this world alone." Another witch, with a long boomerang, stepped to his other side. "She needs you," pleaded Stephanie.

"We are sisters. Help us stop hurting each other." A very young girl holding a large metal scythe appeared behind him. He spun to look at Zyla. "We need you."

"Don't let me have died for nothing." From the crowd, Jasmine stepped out, holding a single paper crane. She smiled at Adam and placed the crane in his hand. "Eva needs you." He looked down at the crane and watched its wings flutter for a moment and then take off, soaring over the souls of witches. A tear rolled down his face.

"You don't understand," stuttered Adam. "People died because I couldn't just let her go. Maybe...maybe I'm supposed to be here."

"If you stay, the cycle will only continue," said Joan, placing a hand on his shoulder. "You have a chance to change everything."

"What makes you so sure?" asked Adam.

Joan thought and then smiled. "I once said that to never love, was to never die, but I was wrong. To never love, is to never *live*. I believe that there is more than the senseless killing and the hatred that every witch here felt their entire lives. I believe that alone we are strong, but together we can be invincible. I believe that love is the key to everything our power has to offer and most importantly," she touched Adam's chest, feeling for his heart, "I believe that even witches, cruel as they are, deserve to be loved."

"I believe," came a voice from the crowd. "I believe," said another. "I believe." Voice after voice called to him from the crowd until, soon, a cacophony of voices sang to him from every direction.

Jasmine smiled at him, no longer in pain, no longer dying on a rooftop. "I believe," she said.

Joan extended a hand to him and over the cries of the witches she asked, "So Adam, what say you?"

He thought for a long moment. He thought about Eva's smile. The way she laughed and the way she cried. He thought about her at her happiest and when she was in the most pain. He thought about her out there somewhere fighting Vicky, a battle she could not win alone. Finally, he spoke. "I believe in a love story for witches."

*　　　*　　　*

"I love you."

Light shot out of Eva's mouth, eyes and hands. It exploded across the battlefield, knocking everything around her to the ground. Miyako put a hand in front of her eyes to shield them as she fell backwards. Eva's body floated into the air, peaceful and serene. The shockwave rocked across the battlefield, ending any remaining squabbles. The combatants were eclipsed by the radiant light that now sparkled at the epicenter of everything.

"Oh, come on," cried Vicky, rolling her eyes. The whole affair of killing Eva Grey was taking far too long for her liking. "What now?"

Eva's body slowly lowered and as her feet touched the soft ground, her eyes returned to normal and the light dimmed. She could feel everything, sense everyone. It was as if pure power was pumping through her veins. She could feel the heartbeats of the crowd around her.

She could hear the low grunting of the paper creatures. Every little chatter of the skeletons' teeth echoed in her brain. Somehow, she walked right up to the threshold that no witch dared cross, and not only had she not lost everything, she felt a power unlike anything she'd ever imagined before. Everything was clear in her mind. She felt no fear or hesitation. She knew exactly what she had to do and how to do it. Most importantly, she knew she was capable of any and everything. All of Eva's wounds healed. She was re-energized, as though she had just woken up and was full of energy. She looked up, staff in hand, and smiled at Vicky.

"Eva?" said Miyako, afraid to make any sudden movements. She had never seen a witch confess her love for someone before, but she was pretty sure this is not how she imagined what losing all one's powers would look like. "You okay?"

She certainly looked okay. Better than okay. To Miyako, Eva seemed renewed as though she just showed up to the battle and everything before had been wiped away.

Vicky's smile faded as she looked down at Eva's fearless expression. "Kill. Her!" said Vicky. "Kill her now!" The golem rose up behind Vicky and raised its obelisk hand, ready to impale Eva.

"Zelerot! Come to me!" commanded Eva. From behind her, Zot appeared, his little wings flapping. She pointed her staff at the lock around his neck and a beam of white light shot out, slamming into the lock and destroying it, sending little metal shards spraying in all directions. What once had been an impossible task of breaking a demonic seal, now seemed as easy to her as snapping a twig in half. Suddenly, he was no longer the little pug. His body grew, expanding at an exponential rate. His fur disappeared and was replaced by a smooth black surface. His wings grew to a huge expanse of leather and claws. His neck thickened and grew in length and his squashed-up face became a large toothy maw with jet black eyes. Where once stood an adorable pug dog, now stood an enormous black demon, on all fours, as tall as the golem and with a huge wing span. As the golem attacked, Zelerot grabbed its arm and with a quick twist, snapped the entire thing off.

"Graaawwweerrr!" The golem roared in displeasure. Vicky looked like she was going to have a panic attack. Zelerot shoved the golem back, shifting its weight towards its hind-quarters. It was unable to keep its balance with only one arm left. Vicky hovered out in front of it. She held her guitar, fuming with hatred.

"No!" she growled, playing her guitar furiously. She shot a barrage of purple jets of light at Eva, but they all deflected off of her as though she was surrounded by a magic-proof barrier. "No! No! NO!"

Eva lifted her staff and pointed the orb, now filled

with a white glow rather than purple, directly at Vicky. Light began to permeate from it, growing in brightness as though it was building up energy.

"It can't end like this!" cried Vicky. "I've been fighting for this moment all my life. I've killed *hundreds* of witches!" As the light grew, the strings on Vicky's guitar began to snap, twanging as they gave out. "What did you ever do to deserve such power? Huh? Nothing! All you did was LOVE SOMEONE!" Vicky's face was red, and she looked like a petulant child as she whined and moaned, suspended in midair in front of the teetering golem. "It's so drab! It's so been there, done that!" She screamed the way a little girl does when she doesn't get the doll she wanted on Christmas. "IT'S NOT FAIR!!!"

"Hey, Vicky!" called Eva from below as the orb blasted forth bright white light. Vicky looked down at her in horror. "Go to hell, bitch."

KRACKABOOM!!! The light exploded from the orb, shooting up through Vicky, engulfing her and then through the golem behind her, bursting out the back of the creature and destroying it from the inside out.

"AIIIIEEEEEEEEE!!!!" screamed Vicky as her body disintegrated in the light. Zelerot gave the golem one last massive shove. The golem fell backwards and erupted, the mud, grass and statues of the whole beastly thing flinging themselves across the park.

Finally, the light subsided, and Eva lowered her

staff, looking around at what was left of the battlefield. All around her, paper cut-outs and skeletons worked to stand up and put themselves back together. Vicky's followers were dazed and confused as their senses returned. They looked around, scared as they tried to figure out how they'd gotten there. She turned to Miyako who stood next to her great cat-beast.

"It's done," said Eva. Miyako nodded in agreement. Zelerot shrunk, his large muscly limbs once again becoming scraggly and furry until he was a tiny pug once more. He panted, his mouth wide open, making little snorting noises as he scooted his butt along the ground, trying to tame the anxiety of being so large and powerful. Apparently, he had found comfort in his smaller, less demonic form and now preferred it.

Eva ran to Adam's body. She fell to her knees next to him, grabbing his cold hand and became choked up. It was painful to even look at him. She took a deep breath, gathering herself enough to speak. "I'm so sorry, Adam."

"Iloyoto..." the voice was so faint, had she not been right beside him, she would have missed it. Adam's fingers twitched ever so slightly.

"Adam?!" Eva's face lit up with shock. She knelt over him on all fours. "D-did you say something?" She leaned in to listen as his eyes peaked open. He looked up at her through the haze and smiled, or at least he moved his mouth in an attempt to smile. "Adam..." Adam tried to speak but his mouth was dry, and no words came out. He swallowed down a mound of dirt and blood in his mouth. Every muscle in his body hurt, but he was relieved to *feel* those muscles at all. "Adam," she said. "It's okay. Don't talk. Save your energy."

Adam finally managed a weak smile as he looked up into her teary eyes. "I love you too."

Eva began to cry, wiping his muddied hair from his face as she rested her forehead on his. "How did you...how are you alive? I saw you...ya know..."

"Well," started Adam, pulling his stiff arm up to grab hers as she held him tightly. "It wouldn't be...a very good love story...if I died."

Rain started to pour, cleansing the bloodied earth. The paper army shredded themselves. The skeletons returned to the ground, and the punk rockers returned home. In the morning they would wake up, not remembering any of it and feeling as though they had the worst hangover of their lives. Those who had not survived the battle, which thanks to the efforts of the skeletons and cranes were minimal, would be found by the police. Their deaths would be calculated as a mass suicide in honor of some rock goddess that no one would be able to reach for comment.

Miyako smiled as she watched Adam and Eva kiss. She jumped back atop the cat-beast, spurring it on with a kick of her feet, and rode away. Adam and Eva were left alone to hold each other, which they did happily until the sun rose.

Chapter Eighteen

Two Months Later

A soft breeze blew through the air over the Queen's Cemetery, breaking down some of the summer humidity that had overtaken the city. Birds chirped all around and the grass swayed here and there. Miyako sat in front of a large marble tombstone she had made. Jasmine's name had been crudely chiseled into the rock along with an epitaph: *Sacrificed herself to save the love of a stranger. I'll miss you, my crane.* She truly had been something special. The patch of dirt where she had been buried was now covered with lush grass and flowers. Part of this was due to the frequent rain, but the red roses that grew all around it were a special touch from Miyako.

Miyako pulled a perfectly square piece of paper from a knapsack beside her and started folding. She ran her fingers along each fold and crease, with the same care and reverence as if she were touching Jasmine. Fold, flatten, turn, repeat. Fold, flatten, turn, repeat.

The paper transformed. Finally, she adjusted the head, as if touching Jasmine's face and then folded out two wings, like Jasmine's arms opening to embrace Miyako one last time. Miyako's eyes closed, feeling Jasmine's arms around her. She wanted to never let go. She opened her eyes to see a perfect crane, turning it to see it from all angles. Beautiful. Perfect. She rolled forward on her knees, placing one hand in the grass. She sat the crane atop the tombstone.

"One thousand," she said. She then placed two fingers to her lips, kissing them. She touched her fingers to the stone and smiled. "No more pain." She stood, throwing a bag over her shoulder. She backed away slowly, still watching the tombstone. As she did, a ring of nine-hundred and ninety-nine cranes encircling the grave came into view.

Miyako had spent the months since Jasmine's death completing them and had saved the last to make with Jasmine watching over her, checking for mistakes. Now that a thousand had been finished, she knew the cranes could not bring a soul back to the living. That one wish would not be granted. But maybe Miyako's secondary wish would. She smiled and looked at the crane on the tombstone, wondering if, somewhere out there, Jasmine could hear her. *I wish you could forgive me.* She stood, holding her breath, awaiting a reply. As she exhaled a gust of wind picked up around her. Her hair blew in the wind.

A wisp of hair, like a gentle touch, caressed her cheek.   The cranes picked up from their circle and started spinning through the air, as if being guided by an invisible cyclone.   Higher and higher they rose.   As Miyako watched them, she laughed with abandon. Tears rolled down her face and into her smile.   The cranes vanished into the clouds above. All but one. The final crane stood guard atop the tombstone, protecting Jasmine even in death.   Miyako nodded to the little crane and then turned, walking down the hill.

*   *   *

At the entrance to the graveyard, she saw a familiar face leaning on the gate, playing with her phone with her earbuds firmly planted in her ears. Eva bopped along to the music. Miyako walked up and stood directly in front of her until Eva looked up, smiling and removing the ear buds.

"A little birdie told me I'd find you here," said Eva.

"Really?   And who might that be?" asked Miyako, unamused.

Eva looked confused. "I didn't get his name. Birds are always in such a hurry. So difficult to get them to chat at all. Oh. Did I mention I can talk to animals now? I can even talk to Zot, though he doesn't say much."

"What are you doing here, Grey?" asked Miyako, ready to be rid of this city and this witch.

"I just want to talk." Eva smiled sympathetically.

They walked together down the hill. As they got closer to houses and the upper part of Astoria, the smell of Greek food filled the air, and cabs started to pass them, along with bike riders, and men and women out for a late morning jog.

"I was just saying to Adam," said Eva, "It seems silly for witches to continue the way we have for so long."

"By that, you mean killing the crap out of each other?"

"Right, that. Especially given what we now know. And seeing that I am now technically the strongest witch who's ever lived, it really comes down to me to make the first move when it comes to social change."

"Oh joy," said Miyako, obviously not joyful. "You've decided to be political."

"No, it's not that," sighed Eva. "It's just—" Eva grabbed Miyako's hand, turning the girl to face her. "Look at how strong we all got on our own. We fought to survive, and we adapted, and we became trained killers. We did all that just so we could fight *each other.*"

"What's your point?"

"My point is that we are not the only force of magic out there. There are things ten times worse than Vicky or Diego, and now that we aren't so busy murdering one another, we can finally focus on those things. We can help bring balance to this world. I've heard stories about overgrown yetis in the North, a pack of werewolves that are killing humans down South. There's a friggin' wizard living in this lake in Ireland who shows itself to humans as a water dinosaur, just to amuse himself."

"Sounds like someone prefers the long game when it comes to practical jokes." Miyako smirked to herself.

"My point is that we can finally do something about all of that. The power is in our hands." Eva was filled with conviction as Miyako stared at her.

"What are you asking me, Eva?" pressed Miyako, already knowing the answer. "Are you asking me to be part of the magic police?"

"I'm asking you to join me. Fight by my side. Together, we can be something far stronger than if I tried to do this solo. We can find other witches too. We'd be unstoppable." Eva was excited like a child when they make their first friend.

"What you're proposing," said Miyako firmly, "Is actually insane. Witches don't know the first thing about working together."

"I'm willing to give it a shot if you are." Eva winked. "What's the worst that could happen?"

Miyako thought for a long time. Minutes passed and the wind picked up again as they stared at each other. Several people walked by, giving the two girls awkward glances as they stood unmoving. Finally, Miyako spoke. "I'm not saying yes." Eva's face fell. "But... I'm also not saying no."

"Yes!" Eva jumped on Miyako, hugging her.

"Stop touching me!" Miyako shook Eva off and then shoved her back. Eva smiled, scratching her arm nervously and then reached it out. The two girls shook hands, no longer enemies or rivals, but allies.

*   *   *

Adam sat at his computer slaving away at the final touches of his latest project, a piece that had taken all of his design school talent and put it to the test. He had created a website lovingly entitled *Spellcaster*. It was a dating site specifically for those of the magic world who wanted to connect with others like them, or even those who were interested in someone with a little extra magic. Underneath the header it read: *"Cast your spell today."* It was cheesy, but Adam couldn't think of a good dating site that didn't have a little bit of cheese to it.

Over the past two months he had recovered little by little. After all, mortals don't simply go on their merry way after being trampled by an ancient god in the body of a gigantic golem. The scratches on his face and body were nearly gone, and he was walking with only the slightest limp. He had told the doctors that he was simply hit by a bus, which was far easier to explain. His physical therapy had been difficult and at many times, truly awful, but Eva had been there for every second of it. She celebrated his successes and cheered him on when it got hard. She'd even gotten piss drunk with him when he didn't know how he'd face the next day.

Today he could feel his body getting stronger. He was ready to hit the "Publish" button, making his very first website a reality. He was going to finish earlier than expected and was glad for it, as he and Eva had big plans for the day.

"Hey babe," she said, coming in the door to his apartment. He'd had a key made for her so that she could help him when his body was at its worst but now, her coming and going seemed like the most natural thing in the world. "Working on *Spellcaster*?"

"Yep," he said, looking over the logos and buttons one last time. "How does it look?"

She walked over to Adam. "Let me see."

"Oof," groaned Adam as she sat on his lap, placing her arms around his neck and peering at the screen in front of him.

"This looks amazing," she said, beaming proudly at him. "I'll definitely use it. You won't mind, right?"

"Why would you need a dating site?" whined Adam jealously.

"So, I can meet a cute wizard," she winked at him.

"Obviously."

Adam put a hand on her back and laughed. "You sitting on my lap like this is very distracting."

"Yeah," scoffed Eva playfully. "I don't really care." She gave him a kiss and they held each other tightly, closing their eyes. Eva pulled away, stood and offered a hand to help him to his feet. "Come on, we're gonna be late."

"Oops, almost forgot," said Adam, turning back to his computer. "Just one more thing." He pressed the "Publish" button, sending the site live and within minutes it was worldwide, connecting users and topping several searches that once would have yielded little to no results. In the months to come, it would be heralded in the magic community as the best thing to come along since healing potions.

Adam grabbed his keys and wallet and gave Zot, who was lounging on the sofa, a quick pat on his head and a treat. Zot eyed the treat suspiciously and chose to lick the couch instead, which oddly made his back leg shake uncontrollably. He would need to investigate this further to understand exactly why licking made his leg shake. Zot went to work on this task as Adam took Eva's hand and they headed out the door.

*   *   *

Adam thought about the past year of his life as he looked at Eva, the two of them standing atop what had once been his least favorite mode of transportation, a large cruise ship. They smiled at each other and Adam reflected on the first time she had made him face his mortal fear and how that night had changed his life forever. The ship left dock and set out to the ocean ahead. The sun was getting low over the horizon in front of them, lighting up the water with a series of radiant oranges and lush yellows.

Love certainly was no fairy tale. He knew that for sure. He understood now that all the assumptions and misconceptions he had ever made about Eva had only gotten in the way of him really knowing her for who she was. *If we can just let go of our fears,* he thought, *and stop worrying about what we THINK love should be, we might just get a chance to see love for what it really is.*

The ship sailed further out to sea, into the unknown, and for the first time, Adam felt no fear at what might be out there or what might happen because he knew that with Eva by his side, he could face anything. Love, he realized, was something which made people stronger than they could ever have imagined. It made them capable of things they once thought impossible. Maybe love wasn't for forever. Who could really tell? What mattered was here and now. There were still days Adam felt like jumping in front of a moving vehicle just to avoid whatever scary situation came next, but at least now he had an equally good reason not to.

"I love you," he said to Eva as they held each other, looking out over the water, hanging over the rails at the side of the boat.

"I love you too," she replied. They kissed and then turned to watch the sunset.

Adam closed his eyes and breathed in the warm summer air. *If we can let go,* he thought. *If we can remember that love is one hundred percent unpredictable and out of our control. If we can allow love to make us stronger and stop expecting love to be one way or another and simply let it be just as it is, then maybe, just maybe,*

there might just be a love story

for everyone.

Acknowledgments

First of all, I need to thank two ladies who were kind enough to read this little story when it was still a comic book script, which it was originally intended to be. Carina and Vicky, you two made writing the script such a wonderful experience and your feedback was so unbelievably kind that when I was given the opportunity to turn 'Witches' into a novel, I jumped in feet first. Thank you to Jeff and my mother for reading the book chapter by chapter, month by month as I wrote it. You guys got the roughest, crudest version of the book and your reactions and criticisms were integral to this final piece. Thank you to Carina (again) and Amy for being my test readers and editors, taking the time to really dive in deep when the book was almost done. You two had the difficult task of translating this book from Jaysenese into something legible and you have no idea how much it means to me that you took the time to do it.

I know I already thanked my mother for reading the

book, but I think she would have done that even if I didn't ask. Your support through the last six years of me trying to make it as a writer have meant more than I think you will ever know. There are not many people who can say their mothers come to Star Trek conventions with them to help promote their work, but I am glad to say I am one of those people. You've watched me grow up not only as a human, but as an author and you've been there for me every step of the way. Don't take it too personally when I off parents in my writing. That's just one of those things I do. It's a bad habit.

My Grandmother also deserves some credit. You always check in and, even though you may not quite understand what I'm writing about or how I "come up with all this," you're always ready to tell friends and family about the next big thing I'm working on.

A special thank you is for L.W. Marks who created a beautiful cover for this book, pouring in hours long into the night to make something special. Your work always blows me away and as someone who has been with me from the start of my career, having you be a part of this book is fitting in every way possible.

I have to give my undying gratitude to my partner, Carl. Not only did you support me every step of the way, but you literally went line by line with me in order to ensure the book would be the best it could be. In many ways, this is a story about us. Your constant positivity and encouragement has changed the way I see each day and just like Adam and Eva, I hope we carve a path for ourselves, defying everything and everyone and, in the end, I imagine we will shock them all.

Finally, I have to thank you. For every one of you who ever came to my booth at a convention and told me that my work had affected you. For every one of you who ever read *The Class* or *Jazu*. For every one of you who ever came to a Rabblebytes show or asked me a challenging question while I was on a panel. For every one of you who retweeted and favorited and liked and subscribed and commented. This book is the culmination of everything so far, and there is so much more ahead that I can barely contain my excitement. This book is not for me, it's for you, all of you. From the bottom of my heart, Thank You.

-Jaysen Headley

About the Author

Jaysen Headley was born and raised in Lakewood, Colorado. Eventually, he packed up and headed to New York City where he met his husband, and editor, Carl Li. They now live in Orlando, Florida, with their dog Izzy, where they go to theme parks, eat delicious treats and have tons of fun every day.

Jaysen loves to read books, play board games and blast away at monsters in a good video game. He is also an avid healthy eater unless it comes to cookies. He will forego any diet in the name of a good cookie!

Jaysen is also the author of *A Home for Wizards* and *Longtails: The Storms of Spring*, both of which can be found in store and on Amazon and Kindle.

Now Available

A Home for Wizards

The Exciting Sequel to A Love Story for Witches

Available in Print and E-book Formats

JaysenHeadleyWrits.com

Longtails

The Storms Of Spring

Available in Print and E-book Formats

LongtailsSaga.com

Printed in Great Britain
by Amazon